Damnation
DAY

1 :- Hell's Angel

Val Cornish

Published by

MELROSE BOOKS

An Imprint of Melrose Press Limited
St Thomas Place, Ely
Cambridgeshire
CB7 4GG, UK
www.melrosebooks.com

FIRST EDITION

Cover designed by Jeremy Kay

ISBN 978-1-907040-23-8

Printed and bound in Great Britain by:
CPI Antony Rowe. Chippenham, Wiltshire

MIX
Paper from
responsible sources
FSC
www.fsc.org   FSC® C013604

To Ash and Kaz - as promised, this is for you, kids.

Thanks as ever for helping me 'keep the faith'.

Prologue

No one claimed to have started it. Or to know how it had started. Or if they did, there were few left to hear their explanations – or, in truth, to care. The day after. Or the day after that... or for many days to come.

It took years for the static to die down, before communication could be made between the isolated outposts of survivors. It took years before anyone dare send out even robot probes to find out if it were safe for anyone to emerge from the shelters.

Damnation Day, some called it. Others called it Judgement Day. Most of us called it Hell. Hell on Earth.

Who am I? Allow me to introduce myself. My name is Angelus. That's not the name I was born with, of course, but as I have no one to gainsay me, I call myself what I choose. Why not? The child died that terrible day. The man who emerged was... different. Shaped and formed for the new world, such as it was. Oh brave new world, as someone once said.

What am I? A messenger of sorts. I travel between one settlement and another with messages, trading, surviving as best I can. Sometimes I'm alone, sometimes I'm not – it depends. On who wants to risk the wastes with me. I'm not always welcome, you see: sometimes I bring bad news. The black crow, some call me – and sometimes less flattering things – partly, I admit, because I tend to dress in black. Leather wears well, you see, as well as providing protection against the elements. The storms can be something fierce – mag-storms, twisters, dust storms – we get them all. Rain – sometimes it's even simply water. Often it isn't, and you don't always know until it's too late. Many have scars as evidence of their mistake.

What do I look like? I suppose that may be important to you. To give you a picture of the one who's writing this record, I'm quite tall, slim – most of us are –

my hair is long, straight, blond almost to white, when it's clean; most of the time it's a sort of dusty yellow, I guess. My eyes? My eyes are pale in comparison to many and I guess a little weird, the left one being blue, the right one being green. There.

What else? How old am I? I don't know for sure. Few of us do. I'm not a child, but I'm not old either... around thirty, maybe a little less. Am I handsome? In some lights, perhaps. I've been told so. To call myself so would be vain, wouldn't it? I've been blessed, I've been told, and I won't argue. I'm alive, I'm my own master, and if the world's gone to hell in a handbasket, I get to see more than most people do and I'd rather that than be locked up below ground in a bunker.

So there we are – a brief introduction, as far as it goes.

I'll tell you about my travels, whoever you are, and perhaps you'll follow me. I'd like that. To know what happened to those I left behind.

My name is Angelus. Welcome to my world.

Chapter 1

ike I said, I travel a lot. Not much point in settling in any one place when there's no place to settle that I'd like to call 'home'. Not any more. Mostly, it's pretty routine – I won't say boring, because that wouldn't be true. It's never that. Once in a while something happens that breaks the routine, the dreary days on the road. Such as the day I came across the burnt-out wreckage. Normally, I try not to be too curious – often as not, it's a trap – there are lots of bandits in the wastelands, you see, who prey on unwary travellers – so obviously I had my sawn-off in my hand as I approached. Not a sound except for the wind blowing through the rocks – until I came close. Then I heard it – the soft whimpering. There was the smell of burnt flesh as I approached. I knew the smell, of course – put me right off any thoughts I'd had of searching for anything I could sell (I never claimed to live up to my name, did I? In this world, you take what opportunities come your way…). Cautiously, I took a peek and tried not to gag. The stench was... well, you can probably imagine. If you can't, I'm glad.

It was then I saw him, curled up amongst the carnage. Bright eyes, fevered, a man-child of indeterminate age. "It's okay," I said softly. "I'm not going to hurt you." He kicked out but didn't scream, struggling with what little strength he had, even trying to bite me. I almost dropped him. "You little bastard," I began, but shit, if I'd been through what he probably had, I'd bite me, too. "Stay." I placed him outside without freeing him, as he'd probably try to run if given half a chance, although he wouldn't survive if he got out into the wastes. Besides, I had to go back inside. I'd seen something else, you see.

I turned back to the wreckage and reached inside once more. "You're not going to kick me, too, are you?" I asked cautiously of another body while pulling at what I guessed was a leg and cursing as the torso threatened to slip. There was no answer so I hoped I was safe. "I'll try not to hurt you," I continued, pulling on arms until I had enough free to realise it was female and, like the child, bound at the wrists and ankles. A slave shipment most like, I thought, wrinkling my nose in disgust. As I said, there are some nasty types in the wastes.

I placed her next to the man-child and brushed back my hair.

"Water?" she croaked, and I snapped back to reality.

Running to my vehicle, I grabbed my canteen and my knife. Placing the canteen to her lips, I helped her drink. She wasn't stupid – she drank slowly despite what must have been a raging thirst. I freed her limbs and those of the man-child. She could give him a drink if she wanted to when we were on the road. He was less likely to kick her – I hoped.

He didn't fight me this time, simply watched me with cautious, defiant eyes.

"Thank you," the woman croaked.

"They call me Angelus," I said, "but intros can wait. We need to get the fuck out of here before someone else comes along. I want to put some miles between me and here before nightfall. Can you stand?"

"With help."

I helped her up and into the back of my rig. Then I went back for him. I found him standing silently, watchfully. He wouldn't let me help him in. I figured there was a reason why and that the woman would probably know. Still, I figured it could wait while I put my foot down and drove like the hounds of Hell were after me for as long as I dare.

As I knew these parts, I felt reasonably safe, but I kept my weapons to hand and the fire well hidden. I figured they needed a good meal inside them – well, what passed for one – more than anything.

Both ate greedily, so I figured they hadn't been exactly cared for. The man-child eventually fell asleep and the woman moved a little closer to me.

"He hasn't spoken since they took us," she said. "Someone told me his name is Micah. Mine is Faith."

"Nice name."

"Thanks. And you're – Angelus?"

"That's what they call me. I'm told it means 'messenger', so I guess it'll do."

She held my gaze for a moment and then smiled. "That's cool. Whoever you are, I'm sure glad you came along."

"Where were you taken from?"

"We were in a settlement up by Seven Springs. When they came, we offered trade – anything – our leaders did... but they came with... with guns and fire," her voice caught. "Anyone who could work they took. The rest they…" I waited, but she didn't continue. I didn't figure she needed to. I knew the story well enough. I'd seen enough of it on my journeys.

"How did you end up—?"

"Roast meat?" she offered. "An argument, I think. Something got knocked over – I remember a crash... fire. I remember the smell, the fear..."

"Try to get some rest," I suggested. I'd heard all I needed to right then, and it was going to be a long night. "It's a long way to the nearest outpost and most of it's wasteland."

"I could drive... if you let me. I'm not very good, but if there's nothing to hit…"

I laughed softly. "I can go a long time without sleep." I knew, though, that I might have to consider it if my endurance was pushed. It might prove necessary to trust someone else at the wheel while I catnapped. "You can always have a driving lesson when there's enough light. Okay?"

"Okay." Satisfied, she curled up in a corner and went to sleep, leaving me alone with the night and my gun. Far away, I heard a sound. Howling. Not a wolf, unfortunately… there weren't many wolves any more. At least, not the sort that once wandered the wilds.

Chapter 2

"Where are you from?" she asked as I drove.

"Everywhere and nowhere," I replied, with a quick glance her way. "Somewhere up north, as far as I recall. I don't exactly know, and that's the truth. The first place I remember is a place called Anderson. Don't know whether I came from there or not. I never fit in – too much of the wanderer, I guess." That was about as much as I was willing to tell... about as much as I'd ever told anyone. It was even true, as far as it went. "You still want to learn?"

"Sure."

I pulled over and we exchanged places. "You might want to hold on to something, Micah," I cautioned. He didn't reply, but then I didn't expect him to. He simply held on, his eyes burning into the back of my neck as I leaned over and explained to Faith what did what and what to do with it, very much aware that I'd inadvertently aroused his protective instincts – maybe he even fancied himself in love with Faith.

After a few failed starts and a lot of laughter, we got her moving.

"Where are we going?"

I considered for a long time. "Nearest outpost is Deepstar. I can put you off there, if you like. It's a sizeable place – you should be able to hitch up with someone going somewhere you want to be."

"Can't we stay with you?"

I laughed softly. "I travel light, honey. You'd be safer hitching a ride with one of the convoys, believe me."

"Maybe you'll change your mind. Is there anything I can offer to make you change your mind?"

Micah didn't like that, I noticed. He assumed she meant sex. Maybe she did. I wasn't sure and wasn't going to presume. Not because I didn't want a knife in my back but because I'd something – someone – better suited to my tastes and who happened to be in Deepstar. Her name is Trinity, and I guess you'd probably call her a whore of sorts. She runs the cathouse, and sometimes, when I'm passing, we... play.

I looked forward to reaching Deepstar, and not just because I was in need of a little R&R. I had messages to deliver, goods to trade, and I'd been on the road long enough to be in need of a bath and something that passed for decent food. Pulling in was close – we almost didn't make the curfew – but they know me in Deepstar and they held the gates for me. I waved to a few people who called my name, pulled up in the yard behind the inn and almost fell into the arms of the innkeeper, my friend Boz. I'm tall, but Boz is taller and twice as broad, or so it seems.

"Good to see you, you bastard," he greeted me with a bear hug that made my ribs creak. "Where you bin?"

"Out west," I replied, glancing back. "Picked up a couple of strays on the way that could do with a room and a bath. I'm good for it."

"Know you are. What you got?"

"Stuff you asked for... few boxes of smokes extra. They were on a slaver, Boz. I'll tell you later."

He met my gaze and nodded in understanding. He knew how it went without my saying. Just as they were climbing out, I heard a shriek from behind me and found myself rocking back as Trinity launched herself into my arms, wrapping her legs around my hips and giving me a kiss that almost made me blush.

"Missed me, Angel?" she asked cheekily. "Damn you to hell, you bastard!" I laughed as she struggled to free herself. She had her breasts pressed against my chest and was jiggling nicely... hell; she was never one for undergarments even when they were available, and that was more than evident. "Who're they?"

"Someone I rescued, I guess."

"I look forward to hearing all about it." She pressed her lips to my ear. "Later. You been playing around?"

"No," I replied. "Why? Jealous?"

"No, but I think she is." I guessed she was watching Faith while she bit my ear. "You stink, you know. Come on, let's get you clean."

I couldn't help but grin. "Faith, take Micah and go with Boz. He'll look after you. It's okay – he's a good man."

"Where are you going?"

"With me, honey," said Trinity, slipping her arm almost possessively through mine. "Angel?"

I left Boz perusing his stock, trusting him to take care of Faith and Micah. My hormones were already racing, and I was looking forward to soaking in the large tub Trinity had. Once inside her doors, she turned to me. "So where did you find them?" I told her briefly. "Never seen you as the charitable type. What changed?"

"Nothing. I… it brought back memories, I guess. You had to be there. What was I supposed to do anyway? Leave them?"

"I guess not. Come on; drop 'em while I fill the tub."

I was only too willing to obey and dropped my holdall on the floor. As I began to peel off my clothes, I looked around. A few new things had been added since I'd last been here, perhaps acquisitions from other traders, perhaps offerings from other visitors such as myself. Trinity didn't entertain often, but I was by no means the only one – as far as I knew.

When she came back into the room she was wearing only a shift that clung to her in all the right places. "That's what I like about you, Angel," she told me, slipping her arms around my neck and giving me a kiss. "You don't even try to pretend."

"I couldn't if I tried," I replied. "I'm not that good an actor."

Laughing, she slipped her fingers under the waistband of my battered jeans and pulled gently. I didn't fight, simply allowing myself to be led into the bathroom. The massive old tub was filled with water and bubbles, as I'd anticipated. I hoped she'd join me… sometimes she did. Sometimes she made me wait. Sinking into the water was an almost sensual pleasure, although not as much a pleasure as having her bathe me. She took it slow, taking pleasure in 'torturing' me, but I didn't mind. She was almost as wet as I was by that point, and her slip was clinging to her and hiding absolutely nothing.

"Stand up," she instructed, and I did as she asked, to be enveloped in a soft bath sheet. "Have you lost weight?" she asked, studying me critically as she dried me. "And I don't remember that tattoo." I jumped as she touched my hip. "Or that you're ticklish."

"I'm not. Usually. No, it's new… newish, anyway."

"What is it, a little angel?" She smiled and murmured, "My fallen angel," as she knelt to press her lips to it. "Are you tired, Angel?"

"Not any more," I admitted truthfully as I felt her smile widen. She always called me Angel when we were… playing. I've never asked why. Perhaps it amuses her, I don't know. Perhaps it's something to do with the games we play. Sometimes

I'll bind her wrists and ankles with ribbon and tie her to the bed. Sometimes she'll do the same to me. There's never any pain, but it's not exactly 'angelic' – right? But I wasn't feeling particularly virtuous as she made my body vibrate to her touch. When I fall asleep in her bed I don't dream – I rarely do, or remember if I have – and I slept deeply. It's one of the few places I do sleep. I'm sure that's telling, although of what I don't know and I wonder if I really want to.

By the time I woke up, night had fallen – or what passed for night these days. The sun goes down to be replaced by a fiery sky born of mag-storms, or so I've been told. I'd some friends to see, business to conduct, and I wandered into the inn to seek out Boz. He smiled as I made my way through the crowd and set up a drink before I'd even reached him. "You're a lifesaver," I said, perching on a stool. "Join me?"

He smiled. "Why not? So... what gives with the 'good Samaritan' stuff?"

I chuckled. "Couldn't leave 'em, could I?"

He nodded and looked up from the stock he'd been shifting. "Some of us still care, I guess… so, she wear you out, you lucky bastard?"

I laughed. "Not yet. She tried, though."

His grin widened. "I just bet she did. Uh-oh. Look who just walked in."

I turned my head slowly. His name, as far as I remembered, was Dash. At least that's what he called himself. One of the local toughs, usually accompanied by two heavies called Jake and Timo, or something. With any luck, he'd ignore me, unless he was in the mood to throw his weight around. I'd heard he'd been having a little competition recently, and although I didn't see how his beating up on me was going to help him any, I wasn't about to let it happen. "I won't start it," I told Boz.

"But if he does—"

"I'll sure as hell finish it." I wouldn't have any choice, I admitted to myself.

Sure enough, he wandered over my way, the crowd parting and turning to watch the fun. I nodded pleasantly and sipped my drink. "Dash."

"Angelus. Long time no see," he said in acknowledgement. "I hear you've been bringing some stuff in."

I shrugged. "Favour for a friend."

"I don't like people who do favours. They want something in return."

"I'm just passing through, Dash. I'm no threat to your little empire."

"True," he admitted, "but that's not the reason I want to grind your pretty face in the dirt." He met my eyes and I didn't like what I saw. Okay, so I did a little business, but it really didn't threaten him. So it had to be something else. Trinity, I reasoned. It had to be Trinity. I'll admit she's worth fighting over, but I'm not sure she'd be flattered if I got myself splattered over the floor of the inn! I'd heard a rumour that Dash didn't treat his women very nicely, that he was more than a little rough, and I could well believe it. He had the look. And there was real malice in his eyes, even hatred. "And I'm going to enjoy every second of it."

I sensed Boz moving and raised a hand to forestall him. I didn't want him involved. And although I didn't relish a fight, it wouldn't be the first and it wouldn't be the last. Tossing my coat over the bar, I saw the crowd moving back, anticipating a battle royal. "Keep your goons out of it," I said, smiling coldly.

"Oh don't you worry, you're all mine."

I slammed my foot into his belly and retreated, reminding myself that bar-room brawls don't follow any rules. This wasn't a martial arts contest; it was a full-blown 'knuckles and knees' job. By the time it was over, we were both on our knees and bleeding from the nose and lips. He grinned savagely. "Had enough yet?"

I smiled back. "Why, have you old man?" He didn't like that, I thought. But then, I didn't like being called 'pretty' either. I can't help having a good bone structure – that's an accident of nature. But then, he couldn't help being a prick, could he?

Neither of us took kindly to the pail of water that suddenly cascaded over us. After the shrieks of outrage, we both found ourselves looking up into a pair of blazing green eyes. "Grow up, you dickheads, you immature fucks, you…!" We both blinked at Trinity's language, glancing at each other. We came to a mutual understanding then, in his look of sympathy. He was going to get off lightly, he thought. I was going to get looked after – and in her present mood, she wasn't going to be gentle. "Oh, get up!" I gave a yelp of outrage as she grabbed my hair and yanked, and found myself looking across the room at Faith and Micah, standing in the doorway. I could imagine what I looked like – dripping wet, blood running from my lip. She didn't look pleased, but hell, I didn't want her to regard me as her saviour! I gave a bow to the applause and nodded, once, to Dash. Truce, he agreed, providing I didn't overstay my welcome. But that went without saying, I thought.

"What were you—?" Trinity began, until I dragged her against me. It was her turn for outrage – I was rather wet – but she got her revenge by pressing hard against me and giving me a kiss that drew fresh blood. "I think she's got the hots for you," she murmured, glancing over her shoulder as she drew wolf whistles and cheers of encouragement by running her hand over the bulge in my pants. "But I can't say I blame her. C'mon, lover-boy. We don't want you to catch a chill, do we?"

I didn't think I was going to escape chastisement, however good the cause, and I wasn't wrong. Buttons flew as she ripped at my shirt and it was all I could do to prevent the stud on my pants going the same way. A shirt I'd sacrifice, but not my beloved pants, but it was a close thing. Although it was a relief to get out of damp clothing, it left me vulnerable to her nails and teeth. And I had a feeling I was going to end up in a hell of a lot worse state than Dash had left me in!

I woke up chilled and a little stiff. Easing myself away I realised that the fire had gone out. As I knelt to relight it, I heard her stir and turned to see her looking at me strangely. "Times like this, I'm not sure whether you're an angel or a demon," she said softly, running a hand down my hip. "It's not fair; you don't come around for months; it's your fault if I can't keep my hands off you." I wasn't sure I understood her reasoning, but I guess I wasn't not intended to. "Do I want to know what that was all about?"

"Probably not," I replied, wincing as she ran a finger over my lip.

"Poor baby," she said, following its trail with her tongue. "I love to touch you, you know? Do you mind?"

"No, of course not. What guy can resist a beautiful woman?"

"I'm not beautiful."

"I think you are," I told her truthfully. "Inside and out." I reached out to cup her chin and drew her mouth to mine. If I took it slow, I reasoned, it wouldn't hurt too much. Kissing Trinity's always a pleasure, but she was intent, for some reason, on pushing all my buttons and I wasn't sure what I'd done to deserve it.

"He could have killed you, you stupid son of a bitch," she told me, running her fingers lightly over my skin. "I was kind of tempted myself."

"Right now, I think I'd die happy," I replied as she pulled at my hair, more gently than before, tilting my head back to give her access to my throat, my neck. "It might be best if you leave town for a while," I said softly, as her mouth brushed my throat. "Just in case. Can you do that?"

Trinity grew still. "I might, given a little incentive." I groaned. We'd always kept it light, never serious. I wondered how we would both deal with the intensity on a long-term basis. If it would burn out, or change into something more – if she was proposing what I thought she was. "Maybe you'd like a little company on the road," she offered, threatening to make me lose what senses I'd got left. She wore me out when I came by – the thought of being on the road with her was both pleasing and alarming. "I could keep you warm at night."

"Thoughts of you usually do," I admitted, turning towards the bed. "But right now my butt's freezing."

"I'll soon put that right," she said, rising to her feet. "Or don't you want me to?"

"Keep me warm?"

"Travel with you."

I'd hurt her feelings, I thought. "Honey, it's dangerous..."

"Travelling with you?"

"Keeping me warm. I'm likely to agree to anything."

"Yeah?"

"Yeah."

"Well then, I guess I have to persuade you, don't I?" Her smile was decidedly wicked as she pushed me back onto the tousled bed. "Tell me what you want me to do."

"Let me sleep?"

"Not a chance, mister." She ran her tongue over my belly. "Just lie still. I'm going to drive you out of your mind."

Chapter 3

looked like hell, I thought, looking into the mirror next morning. My lip was still swollen, I'd got a black eye and more than my share of scratches – courtesy of Trinity – and a rather stupid grin on my face, I decided, trying to look serious.

There was a note on the table telling me to help myself to breakfast if I wanted, that she'd gone shopping for one or two essentials – she didn't say what – and that she'd meet me later. So I figured I'd visit the inn, see if I needed to apologise to Boz and pay for any damages. I found him shifting some caskets of bootleg booze, so I figured I'd best give him a hand. He grinned at me but accepted my help, such as it was.

"You in one piece?" he asked.

"Seems like," I replied, tying back my hair. "Where do you want this? In the cellar?"

"Over by the back wall." He flicked his head. "Mind how you go." I'd hit my head on his low beams once or twice in the past but somehow I still managed to forget. Over by the wall, I recognised the crates as bearing the mark of an old friend. Guns, I thought, giving them barely a glance. I didn't ask why they were there; it could be for self-defence, it could be 'favour for favour' – and none of my business. I'd run guns myself on a few occasions, and didn't consider their presence unusual, although what passed for the law around these parts just might. Unlikely, if it was still who I thought it was, as he was a former gunrunner himself. Well, they do say, 'set a thief to catch a thief', don't they? Boz caught my glance, though, and asked, "Need any bullets?"

I considered for a moment. "Guess it wouldn't harm. I'm heading out towards Vesta and that can be a rough run."

Boz nodded in agreement. "That it can. You takin' Trinity along?"

"Her choice. When she knows where I'm bound..." I shrugged. "Don't know if I can stand the pace. I'm getting too old, Boz."

Boz snorted derisively. "Don't talk crap. Sure'll keep you warm at nights, though. Hot blood like you can't turn down good love."

I rolled my eyes and kept my mouth shut. By the time we'd finished shifting barrels, it was coming to life upstairs. He gave me a list for my next run back this way and I made my way down the street to the fletcher. While I've been known to transport guns and use them myself when I have to, if I'm hunting I prefer my bow, because arrows – or rather bolts – are recyclable, although I do tend to lose a few now and then and they don't last forever. Kaz makes bows as well as arrows and bolts, of course, and he was working on a beauty when I walked through his door. He grinned and rose to his feet, clasping my hand and clapping me on the back, as he always did, particularly when I tossed a packet of smokes his way.

"You're an angel," he said, almost ripping the pack in his haste. "Crap I can get anywhere, but you always bring good stuff." I grinned, my eyes scanning his workbench. The usual assortment of tools, a few half-completed knives and shafts. But it was the beauty he had been working on that caught my eye, as he'd known it would. "Go on... you know you want to." He grinned broadly, his shrewd eyes on my face. I was itching to pick it up and he knew it. Kaz didn't often make crossbows, and it was a rare treat. "Want to give her a try?"

Did I? You bet I did. A twin, too, beautifully carved, tooled with silver, perfectly balanced, as you'd expect from a craftsman. He handed me a bolt and made an elaborate gesture towards the back door. Outside was his testing range, with a variety of targets. I slipped off my coat and tossed it over a stool, leaving my arms bare. It was a shoulder piece, so my vest would protect me – I hoped – perhaps it was bravado, I don't know. "Feels good."

"She should." He stood to one side of me so that he could watch both me and the weapon.

She had a beautiful feel to her, I decided, as the bolt struck home. I didn't even notice the ache in my shoulder. "I think she pulls just a fraction to the left," I said, offering it back to him.

"Try it now," he said, returning a moment later and watching with the same keen eye. "Better?"

"Much."

"Good. You'll need a few bolts, I'd imagine." He caught my puzzlement. "Who else would want a weapon like this? I promised, didn't I?"

He had, although I hadn't taken him seriously. I'd staked him when he'd set up shop in Deepstar and we'd had an arrangement ever since: I kept him supplied with smokes and other bits and pieces; he kept me in bolts and occasionally arrows. He'd promised me, back then, that he'd make me something special, and he'd done just that, and refusal would offend. Kaz wasn't one I wanted to offend. "You did indeed. What can I say? Thanks doesn't seem enough."

"It didn't when I had to say it either. Even?"

"Even." I gripped his hand firmly and nodded my gratitude.

He'd made a leather bag for it so I didn't have to walk through the streets with a displayed weapon (which was frowned upon, particularly during daylight hours). It took a while to get back to Trinity's because I ran into a few people along the way, and I found another note saying she'd gone to see Boz, so I put my new acquisition away and hurried after her.

"Trinity here?" I asked Boz as I sat down.

"No, but someone else is." He nodded towards the corner. I turned my head slowly. Crouched over a bowl of stew was Faith with Micah by her side. I thought I'd better go over and say hello at least, which I did – and received the usual glare from Micah for my pains.

"You being looked after?" I asked.

She nodded and swallowed a chunk of bread. "Boz has been most kind."

"Have you made any plans yet?"

"Not yet. I've been trying to find a caravan heading somewhere – safe – but..." She shrugged. It wasn't easy getting passage, not unless you had something to trade or something with which to pay.

"Not the best time of year," I admitted. "Some of the routes are closing, and it's not a major site. How's Micah?"

She glanced at him. "He slept last night, more or less. Didn't wake screaming, at least."

"That's good. It takes time."

"You sound like you know."

"I do." I didn't elaborate and she didn't press.

"So... you going to be around long? I hear you don't linger."

"I don't usually," I admitted. "No, I'm heading south in a day or two... least, that's the plan. I've got a client to see first, and I'm flexible—"

"Damned right you are," chuckled a soft voice at my ear followed by a nip. I'd never thought of Trinity as the jealous type, but the hands sliding over my shoulders seemed to be decidedly possessive. Still, I chuckled and tilted my head back to see her leaning over me. "Missed you."

"Ships that pass in the night," I shrugged in an attempt to keep it light. "Been to see Kaz."

"Ah, that explains it," she grinned, slipping onto my lap, which gave me a less distracting view, given the fact we were in public. Trinity snuggled against me, which puzzled me, as she wasn't usually so demonstrative. Micah was trying not to look at her cleavage. I was tempted to stand up and drop her on her behind. The last thing I wanted was for her to start a catfight, though why she should want to I really didn't know.

Making our excuses as soon as I decently could without appearing rude, I almost dragged her back to her place. "What the hell are you playing at?" I asked, slamming the door. "That was embarrassing!"

Trinity stood, hands on hips, glaring back at me defiantly. "What was I supposed to do? It was almost sickening, watching her making sheep's eyes at you!"

"Making what?"

She swore. "How can you be so blind? You saved her life. She's grateful. She needs to get out of here. Do I need to spell it out?" I must have looked confused, because she laughed, breaking the tension. "For a lecher, you can be naïve at times, lover."

"I just never thought of you as the jealous type, 's'all."

Her brow puckered. "Nor did I." She laughed and slipped her arms around my neck. "Guess we both learned something, huh?"

"Guess so." My hands rested on her waist as she reached up to untie my hair. She preferred my hair loose. "Honey..." I groaned in protest, albeit half-heartedly, as she loosened the tie on her blouse, shaking herself free. Her hair tumbled forward so that her nipples peeped through the curtain of her hair and I felt my mouth go dry. Damn the woman, I thought, fighting laughter. She knew how to push my buttons. "Play fair..."

"Play fair?" she smiled, pulling away from my loose grip. "Okay." My idea of 'play fair' and hers clearly weren't the same, I decided, as she let her skirt fall to the floor. "One of us is overdressed, Angel," she said huskily, her fingers reaching for me. The sight of Trinity naked would heat any normal male's blood, and I was no exception. Her touch was designed to tease, to stir, and I was more than willing to allow her to undress me. Business could wait, I thought vaguely, deciding that it may as well be my turn to 'play'. I watched the smile on her face grow wider as I exerted a little strength, holding her hard against me as we kissed.

I wasn't exactly sure what was going on here, but at that moment I didn't particularly care. I was dimly aware of the cool sheets of her bed at some point, and that the day was unusually hot. I didn't think much after that for a while, until I dragged my eyes open to darkness. When I grew accustomed to the light – or rather lack of it – I realised that the storm shields were down. "Bad one?" I asked.

Trinity, who was drinking something by the light of the candle, replied, "You slept through the siren."

"I guess you wore me out."

"Oh, I think you've a little left in you yet," she laughed, coming back to the bed. Laughing, she trailed the ice-cold bottle over my skin. "I was saying goodbye to an old friend," she said almost conversationally, her tongue following the trail of damp. She probably meant a client, or perhaps the guy who'd set her up in business originally. I'd never asked his name, and she'd never told me... and I'd never been jealous. I wasn't now, although I did wonder if she wanted me to be. "He wished me luck," she said, her nails scraping my belly. "More to the point, he wished *you* luck – that is, if you still want me to come with you when you go."

"Honey, that's your decision," I pointed out, catching my breath as her fingers strayed. "I just thought it might not be a good idea to be around Dash."

"Which means getting out of town," she reasoned. I felt the bed move as her weight shifted. "I know you don't want commitment, but we're good together, aren't we? If you don't want me, say so. I'd rather know." I gritted my teeth as she straddled my hips, holding her. "We can go our separate ways, if you want," she said, some time later, her lips at my ear. "I won't scream or cause a scene. I just wanted you to know you were never a... that when we made love I never pretended."

I understood, of course, what she was saying. That even in the early days, she'd never taken money from me. Oh, I'd brought her things from time to time – luxuries – but I'd never given her money. I'd always treated her as a woman, not as a whore. But I didn't want her gratitude then, and I didn't want it now. If she went with me, it had to be for the right reasons. But whose reasons? Hers may be different from mine, and while I knew hers – or thought I did – I was by no means certain of my own. I could be callous and say it was because when I needed a woman she was as good as any I'd known. Or I could be a little more honest and admit I enjoyed her company, and that it would be nice not to be lonely for a while. I also had a feeling that my conscience would begin to prick and that I'd find myself offering Faith and Micah a lift to my next port of call and she would be useful 'protection'. I didn't want to admit which was nearer the truth.

I'd business to attend to, but that would have to wait until the storm shields went up again, so this was as good a place as any to spend the time.

"Angel."

"Mm?"

"Have I said something wrong?"

I heard uncertainty in her voice and frowned, which of course she couldn't see. "What makes you say that?"

"Because something's... different." I felt her weight shift and a moment later candlelight flickered. She sat on the bed, her knees curled up protectively as she looked at me. "Was it because of Faith? I know we always agreed…"

I shuffled to sit up and she seemed to flinch away, but that could have been the light. "Trinity, nothin's changed. Not as far as I know." I raked back my hair, which was falling over my face. "Okay, I was a little surprised because you never done that before."

"Just because I'm a whore don't mean I don't have feelings," she replied defensively.

"Honey…" This time, there was a definite flinch. I wondered if someone had hurt her in the past. Physical abuse in her profession wasn't unusual, after all. I raised my hands in surrender. "I'm not going to touch you, Trin. I wouldn't. I've never hurt a woman in my life."

She bowed her head onto her knees for a moment. I wanted to reach out: to touch her, to reassure her, but I didn't think it would help.

"I know. I do. But... let me... let me try to... don't say anything. Don't look at me. I can't say this if you..." I was really worried by this point, but I did as she asked. I bowed my head enough to shield my eyes with my hair. "Maybe I'm rushing things, I don't know. Presuming too much. I know we... keep it light... but you gotta know you're not just a mark, that you never were. You were the only guy who ever looked at me and treated me as something other than a piece of meat, you know? I know we always said keep it light, but guess I'm not no different from any other woman." I must have moved because I felt her arm on my shoulder. "No... please. You gotta know how good it feels when you come around. How much I love bein' on your arm, knowin' how much I'm envied."

"What?" I couldn't help it.

She laughed softly and brushed at my hair, running it through her fingers. "You really don't know, do you? Don't know as I should make your head swell, but you don't imagine that it's just kind hearts that brings all those women around when you pass through, do you? You're the hottest thing as comes this way, Angelus." I must have looked sceptical because she laughed, tilted my chin and kissed me lightly. "Try lookin' in the mirror, lover-boy, other than when you're shavin'. You ain't chopped meat, mister."

I ventured to raise my head. She didn't say anything. "Can I say something? Please? Look... for one thing, I'd never hurt you, just so as you know, cos flinching worries me some." I grinned suddenly. "Jealousy, now... guess I should be flattered, huh? Mind you, I'm a guy. S'pose I should be. Specially when it's by you. Case you hadn't noticed, honey, you're pretty hot yourself."

"That's my job. Looking—"

I placed a finger on her lips to silence her. "I mean underneath... the lady the public don't see. You know I ain't fakin', Trin. You know what you do to me." I didn't know what to say; this was getting pretty deep. Just then, the all-clear siren sounded, which gave me the opportunity to take a deep breath. "Look... I got business, then we're out of here, okay? Let's hit the road and see where it takes us. How quick can you pack?"

Trinity looked around her slowly. "I don't have much that I want to take anywhere. The rest can stay, I guess. I'll be ready by the time you get back, 'kay?"

I gave her a nod and slipped from the bed to hunt for my pants. "Sounds good to me," I affirmed, wondering where my boots were. We had matters unresolved, I thought as I dressed, but too much was happening for me to get my head round right there and then. Maybe putting it off wasn't a good idea, but facing it didn't seem so hot right then either. "But don't rush. You know what it's like when we get together."

"Don't I just." She rolled her eyes. "You want I should chase you up if you don't come back?"

I shook my head and grinned. "Won't do my rep much good," I replied. "Still, I don't know; maybe it would." I remembered an occasion that seemed a lifetime ago when I'd been running guns into Deepstar. It had been new then, and very much frontier – weapons had been in demand, and I'd brought some good stuff in. I'd been celebrating, as I recalled, and was more than a little drunk. Then she'd walked in. She'd been with some of her girls, but I'd only had eyes for her. I'd seen her on my last visit; wondered back then if I'd ever be able to afford her. Someone had told me she worked the girls, but sometimes she made exceptions. She'd made one that night for me: taken me back to my room, to my bed, undressed me and taught me not only what she liked but what I liked, too. That had been the first time, and it must have made an impression on her, too, because whenever I came by, I found an invitation.

Chapter 4

"Thought you'd be by," were the words I was greeted with when I finally reached my rendezvous. A drink was placed at my hand automatically. "Business good?"

"Can't complain," I shrugged.

"Guess I wouldn't complain much either with a woman like that to warm my bed," Niko grinned. I've known him longer than I've known Trinity, so I allowed the familiarity. "You look…" The word he used was gutter slang, and he knew full well that if it'd been any other guy but him who'd used it in my presence, I'd have had his balls for breakfast. But I owe Niko a lot. My life, in fact. "You lucky bastard."

I swallowed the fiery liquor in one gulp. "If we've done with my sex life, I hear you got something for me?"

He laughed softly and proceeded to tell me what he had and where he wanted it to go and what he wanted for it when I got there.

"What's my cut? I don't run things for nothing, you know." He named a figure, which sounded good to me. "Okay. Is it ready to go now?"

"Soon as you give the word."

"Fair enough."

Another drink followed, as someone else wandered over for a word with Niko and, through him, with me. I began to regret not having Trinity there to create a diversion or at least a distraction, but it was too late for that. I considered walking away, but that would be out of line, as these were my friends as well as business associates, and a little heavy drinking wouldn't do any harm – or so I thought. I really don't remember loading my rig: I certainly don't remember agreeing to take Faith and Micah along for the ride. When I opened my eyes I gave a groan of pain and sagged back onto the seat of my rig, on which I'd been curled up, closing my eyes tight again. The sky was lurid – red and orange mostly with a flash or two of purple and I felt like throwing up.

"Don't even think it, mister," warned Trinity, as if reading my mind. I'd swear she was finding every rut in the road she possibly could as a form of revenge. "You really tried one on, mister."

My mouth felt like something had curled up and died in it, so I didn't argue. "I need..."

"When you can sit up, you'll find a flask and a couple of pills within reach. Serves you right." I didn't argue. For one thing, my head was threatening to split, so I was pretty sure I'd come off worst.

By the time I'd slept it off, we'd covered a lot of ground. I hadn't realised that Trinity was such a good driver. But then I guess I'd never asked. I guess I'd never asked a lot of things. "You want I should stop so as you can wash up?" she asked when she realised I was awake.

"Where are we?"

"Been on the road about six hours, give or take. Guess I could do with a break." Trinity cast a side-glance my way and smiled. "You look like hell. You try to out-drink Niko again?"

"Yeah. Think I'd learn, wouldn't you?"

"If it's any consolation, he didn't look so good."

I smiled, but even that hurt. When she pulled over I headed back to the small closet, where I poured what water I could spare over my head. As I walked out, dripping, I realised we had company. I stood there, wondering what Faith was doing sitting, wide-eyed, staring at me along with Micah (who for once didn't seem to be glaring at me). I didn't speak, but simply made my way over to Trinity.

"You might have warned me," I complained, running my fingers through my hair.

Trinity grinned and ran a finger down my chest, catching at the water. She laughed. "Thought it'd sober you up quicker 'n' ought if I had to."

"Ha ha. So, how come?"

"She said you offered her a lift. That she'd come on you drinking and taken advantage of you." Her grin told me that she had her own reasons for not kicking the other woman out on her arse. I wasn't sure I wanted to know what they were. "You look good dripping wet, you know that?"

I laughed as she slipped her arms around me. "So do you," I pointed out, reminding her, I hoped, of a photograph I'd carried with me – it lived in a little pocket on the sun-visor of my rig – of her in a very sexy pose, wearing a very wet shirt. "Kept me warm on many a night."

"Yeah?"

"Yeah."

"Well now, does me good to know." I gave her a slow kiss. "Whoa, mister, we got an audience, remember?"

I wasn't sure I cared. Still, given the fact I'd a hangover I wasn't likely to be at my best. "Will you take a rain check?"

"You bet I will. You got something in mind?"

"Maybe." I had, as it happened. I seemed to remember a waterhole on the road to Vesta, but I wasn't about to say anything in case it'd dried up since I'd last passed this way. Given the world we lived in, that was highly likely. I'd thought it a good place to make love once upon a time. Maybe I'd get to find out. "Maybe we'd best hit the road, though; put a few more miles under our belt while we can."

"Good idea. You okay to drive?"

"Sure. You curl up, try to get some sleep." I admit it gave me a good feeling having Trinity curled up on the front seat of my rig, although I wasn't sure I wanted to put a name to the reason why.

I drove as long as I was able, until the sun began to drop low on the horizon. Even the special shades I wore didn't always provide as much protection as I required, and I needed to keep my wits about me because this was a good time for bandits to attack. We wouldn't make it to Vesta for a couple of days and I wanted to put as much mileage under my wheels as I could. When I lowered the visor, I heard a soft, throaty chuckle that made my blood tingle. "Why, Angel, you *were* telling the truth!"

She'd seen the photograph, I realised, and I smiled. "Don't I always?"

She seemed to be considering for a moment before replying, "No, you don't, but you don't actually lie, either." She had a point: there are times when I'm somewhat economic with the truth, like all of us. "Are you gonna keep drivin'?"

"Not sure. Maybe. I don't like this area much. Too many soft spots." By soft spots I meant quicksand. Tricky at the best of times, but more so if, like now, you can't see the markers. That and the fact that bandits had a habit of moving them. Well, let's just say I prefer to use my own eyes and instincts. So I kept on driving, knowing that I could call on Trinity if I needed to, but I can keep awake when I have to without the need for pills, although I take them when I really have no choice, as those of us who travel the roads for a living often do.

Chapter 5

Morning came with the usual blaze of fire, but I waited for good light before I risked pulling over.

"I'll make breakfast," offered Trinity, sitting up.

"Just coffee for me," I said.

"Strong and black?"

"You got it."

She gave me a quick nod and a slow kiss, which suited me just fine. I could risk closing my eyes, I thought, just for a second. But I opened them fast when I heard the door open. I was shocked to see Micah standing there, a mug clutched in his hands, his eyes as wide as ever as he stared at the weapon in my hand.

"Sorry," I apologised. "Habit." His hand shook as he offered the mug to me. "Thanks." I'm not good with kids – never had much chance to be – but I recognised something in him, something of me, the 'me' I'd been at around his age. "Jump up, if you like. I don't bite." I was surprised, I must confess, when he did, staring out through the dusty screen, his eyes avidly scanning the control panel and the map, which showed our position best as I could estimate it. "That's where we are... sort of. Close as we can tell out here. Not a lot of landmarks, see." I saw him smile. Not a full smile, but a beginning. "Want to sit in the hot seat?" I offered my hand to him and saw him flinch away. "Micah, I won't hurt you. I don't beat on women and kids, though I know you're not gonna believe that. I won't say I know how you feel, but I can guess. I was once a lot like you. Have you seen the scar on my back?" He gave a slow nod. He could hardly miss it, seeing as it ran from the top of my shoulder blade down my ribs and almost to my belly. "One day, maybe I'll tell you how I got it. Just believe me when I say I know what bad people can do to kids, okay? Look, I'll get out and walk round, 'kay? You just sit where you are, then scoot over. Don't touch nothin'." He nodded slowly.

When I appeared at the other side, he slipped over to sit behind the wheel. I nodded. He grinned and put his hands on the wheel. I could almost imagine him making engine noises in his head. "That pedal makes it go forward, that one stops it. That lever..." I gave him a quick run through and saw the concentration on his face as he 'drove', his tongue stuck out between his teeth and his brow puckered in concentration. Sipping my coffee, I smiled. "Guess I can leave you in charge, huh, partner?" I asked, knowing that without the key sequence he couldn't start her, and most definitely couldn't move her. "I need to..." I ran my fingers over my jaw and saw him frown. Suddenly, he brightened and nodded, so I slipped out and took my mug with me. I'd go in search of the pool, I decided, taking my gear with me. If it was still there, I'd take a little dip maybe.

I was pleased to find it still there, and still water-testing as safe. A shave would be good, I decided, again running my fingers over my jaw – being the colouring I was I didn't suit a beard, or so I thought.

I'd have jumped sky-high if I hadn't seen the kid's reflection in the water as he knelt to touch the scar on my back. I'd got myself a shadow, I thought, wondering if that was a good thing or a bad one. He jumped back as I turned, expecting – still – to be rebuffed at the very least. "Yeah, that's the one," I said, turning my eyes deliberately back to my reflection so as not to make him worse. "I got that in a fight. Missed my lung, but it could've gone in. He had a knife; I had my fists. No weapons in the mines." I glanced up. "I was taken in a raid, much like I guess you were. Sold to a miner. Long as we worked, it was fine, but if you were sick or hurt... or female…" I wasn't sure I wanted to tell him *that* part. "Guess I forgot the rule that you look the other way, that you don't try 'n' help someone. There was a girl, oh, few years older than you. Some of the guards took a fancy to her. Neither of us escaped – any part of it. You don't need to know. Just there's nothin' so bad you can't come back from, if you got a reason. If you ever want someone… well, you just go 'n' find Faith now; she'll be wonderin' where you are, 'kay?"

He held my gaze for a long moment before reaching out to touch my shoulder. It was as close as he would come to speaking, I thought, at least for now. Then he was gone. I stared into the water for a long time before rising and stripping off my pants. The water was cold at first, so I took it slow walking in. I'd just reached my waist when I realised I wasn't alone. Trinity was standing by the water's edge watching me. She was standing there in her shift, her long hair flowing lightly in the light breeze, just watching me. I wasn't sure whether she wanted me to come out to her, or if she was waiting for me to invite her in.

"It's cold – right?" she asked finally as I began to walk back. "No, don't. I guess

I'm warm enough for both of us right now. Just stay there, okay? Don't move." I froze, puzzled, until I saw the camera in her hand. "Don't think you have it all your way, do you, fella? 'Sides, I want all the ladies to go green with envy when they look at this."

Okay, I thought, feeling a little foolish. Still, fair was fair, I supposed. I had one of her, didn't I? "What do you want me to do?"

"Not a thing. Just stay as you are." Trinity grinned at me. I'd never been a 'pin-up' before, so I didn't know what was required, but I made her laugh. Then she came to join me in the water and the laughter vanished. "I thought you'd be cold," she said, running her hand up my chest. "But you're not." Trinity could warm even the coldest blood. She was certainly heating mine. We were a tangle of hair and limbs, and I didn't care in the least that it was broad daylight and that we were in the open. She could make me forget things like that with only a smile. Which, I thought, could be a bad thing if I were distracted at the wrong time. But right now, she could distract me all she liked.

Trouble found us sooner than I'd liked, but later than I'd anticipated, barely giving me time to put on my pants and almost fall into my boots as Faith came running down the trail to warn me that we had company. I wasn't about to think it was a friendly call, so I ordered them inside, dropped the shields and armed Trinity and myself. I wasn't sure whether Faith was any good with a gun and I didn't trust her with my favourite weapons.

We waited. A group of four, the scope said; mixed vehicles. Bandits, perhaps, or one of the gangs that occasionally travelled the wastes, hitting on any suitable target that came along.

"Angelus, you in there, you prick?"

Charming, I thought. "Who wants to know?"

"C'mon, don't tell me you forgot me, you bastard!"

I frowned and looked at Trinity. I wasn't certain, but the voice sure did sound familiar. And whoever it was evidently knew me. Cautiously, I raised a shield. Then I picked up my crossbow and went to the step. "Morgan? That you?"

"How you doin'?" He stood there grinning. A disreputable mob, I thought, looking at the 'horde' gathered around him. A rag-tag army. I watched them carefully – as carefully as they were watching me. "Nice weapon."

I smiled, holding it so anyone could see it was loaded if they wished. "Thanks. And I know how to use it."

"I know you do; otherwise you wouldn't be holding a loaded weapon like a toy." He spread his hands defensively. "I'm not lookin' for trouble, just being friendly-like."

I snorted. "Yeah. Right. You thought it was a target."

Morgan shrugged. "Not once we got close I didn't. Know your rig, I do. You bound for Vesta?"

"You?"

"Yeah. Big trading fair this time o' year. Never know what's goin' on. Thought we might travel together. Safety in numbers – right?"

"Right." There were more of them than there was of me, so why did they want me around? Morgan I knew from way back. We'd run together once, long time ago. I hadn't liked the guy too much – didn't have no reason to change my view now. I'd heard he liked to play rough with the ladies. And I didn't want to have to use my weapon unless I had to. Not in town, anyway. They have something resembling law in Vesta, and I didn't fancy being banged up for my pains. "You want to tag along, the road's free."

"Fair enough," he replied, waving to his band of merry men to follow him. I watched them go carefully, waiting until they were far enough away before I retreated into my rig.

"If we don't make it to Vesta tonight," I said to the others, "we take it in turns to watch over our posse."

"You don't trust him?" asked Trinity.

"About as far as I could throw him," I replied, shrugging. "I used to run with him, while back. Don't know what he's into these days, but I wouldn't trust him. Stay inside and out of sight, ladies. Micah, don't give him ideas. We're outnumbered, even in this old girl."

I'd made my crossbow safe, but it was to hand, as were guns. I turned to Faith. "You ever used a gun, Faith?"

"Once or twice, time back. My father had an old sawn-off."

"Then you should be okay. Trinity will show you all you need to know, just in case. Micah can be powder-monkey."

"What?"

I laughed. "Bullets – arrows – bolts. It's an old term – when gunpowder was used. You know... canons?" She nodded. "Okay, Micah?" Micah straightened and gave me a salute. I laughed and saluted him back.

I went to find something to wear. I was glad I hadn't had to fire my crossbow because I'd have had a nice bruise to add to my collection. Still, I reasoned, it wouldn't be the first time.

Once I was decent I went up front and sat down. Trinity brought me a mug of coffee, which I needed.

"You run guns with this guy?" she asked.

I nodded. "Once or twice, yeah. Back when I needed to eat, you know?" I'd had nothing back then. Not that I have that much now, materially. But I have all I need, and a nice little nest egg tucked away, if you know what I mean.

"You ever run drugs?"

"I ain't proud of it," I replied softly. "Like I said, I ain't no angel, honey."

Trinity leaned towards me and brushed my hair back with her fingers. "We all done things we don't like to own to. Take me, for example."

"Anywhere, anytime," I drawled lazily. Trinity slapped playfully at my hand.

"You! You're insatiable!" She laughed, a sound I liked. I liked to hear her laugh; because I knew she'd had a hard life. "Whatever do you do when I'm not around? No, don't tell me." She put a hand over my mouth to silence me. "I don't need to hear." I smiled and tried to nip at her hand with my teeth. "Easy, Angel. If you're hungry I'll make you something."

"No, I'm fine," I replied. "Maybe later."

"Sure?"

"Sure."

Her hand rested on my belly, her eyes holding mine. A promise for later, with a bit of luck, I thought, calculating in my head whether or not we had any chance of reaching Vesta. I thought it unlikely, which would mean a watch on our fellow travellers longer than I'd like. Could be a couple of days or more, depending on whether we hit bad weather, which this late in the season was more than likely.

I studied the data, wondering whether I could use bad weather to 'lose' them. Had I been alone, I'd have been more likely to do so than now. But I was considering it, nonetheless.

"Why don't you try to catch some sleep?" Trinity asked shrewdly, running a finger under my eyes. "We'll keep an eye open." I hesitated. "Angel."

"Mm?"

"Why are they so interested in you anyway? They weren't just being friendly, were they?"

"No – I think not." No point in lying. I didn't think they were being friendly any more than she did. I went to stretch out and closed my eyes.

"Is it something you're carrying?"

I hoped not. I couldn't be sure, of course, but I wasn't about to confess even the suspicion to Trinity. Not that I didn't trust her, simply that it was safer that way. "I hope not," I yawned. "Wake me in a couple of hours?"

"Sure thing."

Chapter 6

didn't need her help to wake – I can set a clock in my head to wake me any time – but I was in no hurry to get up. I was enjoying a few moments' peace, collecting my thoughts, when I heard voices. From behind the screen I could hear Trinity talking to Faith. I know it was none of my business, but I hadn't thought they were on speaking terms, so I was curious. All right, I admit it. I was being nosy.

"How long have you known Angelus?" I heard Faith ask.

Trinity lingered for some time and must have been considering her response. "Long time. He was running guns back then and about, oh, sixteen, maybe seventeen. Slender as a rake, but who wasn't back then?" She laughed softly. "I took one look at those eyes of his..."

"They are somewhat unusual."

"And very sexy. Well, I thought so. Still do, I guess. Maybe I liked his youth. Maybe the sense of danger that surrounded him. I don't remember how it changed from... a business arrangement. I'm not sure it ever really was."

There was silence for a while. "He seems a good man."

"He is – but don't let him hear you say it. Ruin his reputation, it will." They laughed together. "But I've seen him in a fight. Don't you go thinking him all sweetness 'n' light; he ain't. He's what he has to be." I heard her curse suddenly. "I said I'd wake him!"

Her head popped around the screen and I opened my eyes – I'm no fool: if she'd known I was listening... "Time to hit the road," I said, sitting up.

"What about your friends?" asked Faith.

I gave a savage grin. "They can eat my dust." But Morgan must have had someone watching, because the instant I showed signs of preparing to move, his people did the same.

My screens told me I was riding into a storm, and I was better prepared than Morgan to withstand a dust storm. It would be tricky, but I could do it. This one I was anticipating to be a real bitch. I suppose I should have warned him; it would have been the neighbourly thing to do, but I wasn't feeling charitable. He'd done the same thing to me, once: abandoned me to a sandstorm. I'd promised myself back then that I'd get my own back, and I'd waited for a long time for this chance.

"Hold on tight; it's going to be a bumpy ride," I informed my companions, dropping my last shield. I was, to all intents and purposes, flying blind, using only my screens. I needed all my concentration, but I'd been at this game long enough to know what I could do – at least, I hoped so.

"Can I help?" Faith asked.

"Just keep me supplied with coffee," I replied with a smile.

"Sure thing. Trinity warned me about you."

"Oh yeah?" I chuckled, risking a side-glance her way. She gave a bark of laughter.

"She warned me about your capacity to down coffee, too."

Oh, we were playing word games, were we? Fine. It would keep my mind sharp. "Well, you know how it is. Sometimes you need endurance."

"Which I gather you have."

"Modesty forbids me from blowing my own trumpet, so to speak."

"Modesty isn't a word I've heard applied to your talents." Slipping onto the seat next to me, she gave a frown and a sigh. "What do those screens tell you right now?"

The laughter was gone from her voice and I accepted that. She was right – this wasn't the time. "Right now? I've got my nose heading into a late season storm, and it's a bitch. Keeping her on the road's gonna be tricky."

"So why—?"

"Let's just say it's payback time."

"For what?"

I didn't reply for a long time. "Disagreement over a division of the spoils, so to speak. Morgan settled the issue by abandoning me with a water bottle and a blanket with a storm on the rise."

"You must have really pissed him off," she offered, surprising me. I had to remind myself she'd grown up in a frontier town so it was unlikely she was as prim and proper as she appeared. Unless it had been a religious community, of course. I'd never asked.

"I guess." I remembered how scared I'd been. I'd been close on seventeen, and not as smart as I'd thought. But I'd found a rocky outcrop barely big enough to call a cave, and I'd curled up with the blanket over my head while the storm screamed and threatened to tear the world apart. It had brought rocks down, blocking me in, and it had taken me an age to dig myself out. It had taken me even longer to get over my fear of confined spaces. But that's another story. As I told her these things, I expected her laughter, but she didn't laugh, which was as surprising to me as me volunteering the information. "Hold on!" I gripped the controls as my rig rocked and bucked – wondering, I'll admit, if I hadn't bitten off more than I could chew.

Finding a way through the swirling clouds wasn't easy, but I managed to keep to the path, although I did feel somewhat battered and bruised by the time the storm abated enough to ease my grip.

"You want me to spell you?" asked Trinity, her face peering through at me.

"No, it's okay. I'm heading for Swallow's Gap. We should be able to find a sheltered spot there to ride the rest of it out."

"Can I get you—?"

"Honey, if I drink anything else my kidneys'll be floating," I chuckled. "'Sides, I'm high enough on caffeine as it is."

She laughed softly. "Faith?"

"No, thanks, I'm fine. Micah okay?"

"Sure. He's sleepin' right now. We played chess for a while."

I was about to say that I didn't know she played chess, but thought it better to keep my mouth shut. If she'd been awake, she might just have heard what I'd said to Faith. If she hadn't, I wasn't about to tell her. Call it vanity, if you like. "Who won?"

"He did, dammit," she groused, then chuckled. "I'll see what there is to eat, 'kay?"

"Fine by me." I wasn't going to turn down a chance of a meal, was I? I was starved, to tell the truth.

The Gap was a formation of rocks that I knew well, with lots of ways in and out. Plenty of places to hide. As the light went down, brought on early by the still present winds, we ate together. Conversation was light, and while the women took care of the domestic side of things, I went out to check my rig. I elected to sleep on the bench seat of my rig because I might need to hit the road fast. If I was hoping for a little solitude, I didn't get it. In the darkness I inhaled traces of Trinity's perfume on the air as she slipped in to join me. In the absolute darkness I felt her touch, knew she was teasing, touching to stir the senses more than simply to locate. I felt my clothing give way to her fingers, and the softness of her mouth, her smile.

"So that's why you had the shakes if the candles went out," she said softly against my skin, leaving me in no doubt that she *had* overheard. I felt her silent laughter as her mouth began to work its magic. "No, lie back. Let me enjoy you."

"Not fair." I shuddered; gritting my teeth as she repeatedly drove me to the edge and brought me back. Damn the woman; couldn't she give me a little time to catch my breath? What was she trying to do to me? Trying to drive me out of my mind? No, I thought, grasping at sanity. Simply asking me to trust her, to let her give me pleasure because it gave her pleasure to do so. Fair's fair, I told myself, allowing my body to relax. After all, I'd asked the same of her, hadn't I? "Can't I play? Just a little bit?"

"No."

Well, that told me, didn't it? But when she kissed me, I couldn't do anything else but kiss her back, could I? She didn't object, so I let my mouth play.

Sleep, when it came, was deep and dreamless – which was just as well, because anything else would have found us on the floor.

Chapter 7

I t was a relief when Vesta came into view, because I was going to have to do some serious maintenance work on my rig. She coughed and spluttered her way into town. Luckily, I knew of a workshop where I could do any work I needed to. At least, I hoped so. As I jumped down, the doors of the battered old workshop flew open and a large bear of a man rushed out, enveloping me in a rib-crushing hug that knocked the breath out of me. "You fucker, where you bin?"

"Around," I winced. "How's business?"

"I makes enough," he said, "to keep body 'n' soul. The old girl sounded bit sick. What you do to her?"

"Rode in on the storm, what else?" I chuckled. "Can I use your space?"

"Any time, man, just nose her in."

As I did so, Trinity, who had been asleep on the front seat, stretched and sat up. I saw Rom's jaw drop and grinned in sympathy: Trinity's likely to do that to a man.

"Trinity – Rom, the best mechanic I know."

"Ma'am." He bobbed his head in greeting. "If you want to freshen up."

Trinity toyed with being polite but didn't fight too hard before surrendering. "You don't have a tub, do you?"

"Just so happens I do." He grinned at me and winked. "If yer trust me with yer lady, man?"

I raised an eyebrow in Trinity's direction. "Oh, I think she can handle herself."

"If she can handle you, guess that's so. This way, ma'am."

With a flourish, he escorted her to the bathroom. With a sigh, I rolled up my sleeves and got to work. I had a feeling I was going to need that tub after Trinity, so I hoped she'd leave me some hot water. Even warm would do, I sighed, wiping my face with an oily hand and sneezing as dust went up my nose. When Rom came back, he was rolling up his sleeves to help me. "So, c'mon. Fess up. How did the likes o' you catch a looker like that?"

I gave a lazy smile. "Just luck, I guess."

With a snort of derision, he slipped under the rig to join me. "Somehow, I thinks that's not all of it. Say, you gotta harem in that thing?"

"No, why?"

"Just cos I can see a pair o' feet."

I shuffled and squinted. "Micah? What's wrong, kid?"

Micah knelt down and shuffled under. I winced as he dug me in a very delicate spot before planting his elbows in my belly as he handed me a note.

"I can't read it," I grimaced.

"Can't he just—"

"Micah doesn't talk," I said quickly. "Do me a favour, kiddo. Shuffle back and let me get out?"

With a quick grin, Micah did a rapid reverse. The note, of course, was from Faith. "She's gone to look for a ride? At this time of night?" I swore. "The crazy bitch!" Wiping my hands rapidly, I bent down. "Tell Trinity I've gone lookin' for Faith, will yer?"

"You wants backup?" offered Rom.

"No, it's okay. Micah, my coat."

He nodded and ran back inside and brought my long coat to me. In the pocket was a small gun. As I said, there's a rudimentary law in Vesta, and carrying a weapon in public wasn't likely to go down well.

As Micah fell into step beside me, I held out a restraining hand. "No, Micah. It's not a good idea." I saw the look in his eyes, the fire. I knew the look, and that he'd follow me whether or not I wanted him to. "Just keep out of my way." If I was going into a fight, I didn't want him hurt.

Vesta is a strange, sprawling sort of place – the largest settlement I know of, in fact; a mixture of ramshackle buildings and lean-tos, mud-stoned, some salvage knock-ups. It has a certain charm. Among the trading markets, the whorehouses and inns, arms dealers and cattlemen, the place somehow works. Faith would have gone to the main square, where among the inns the travellers gathered, where she might be able to find a lift somewhere 'civilised'. I didn't know where she was planning on going, or even if she had an idea. I couldn't recommend anywhere, because there was a lot of places I hadn't been, and a lot of places I really wouldn't go and even fewer places I would consider calling home. Still, her needs were probably different from mine and I couldn't dictate to her, could I? I felt a moral duty though to at least make sure she got treated right – maybe my 'name' was having an effect, ha ha.

It wasn't hard to find her; it only took a few questions. I saw her sitting with a group of men and had to admit I admired her nerve – they were a disreputable looking mob. As I made my way across the crowded floor, Micah at my heels, the crowd parted for me. I have a certain reputation, I suppose. One or two called my name, one or two signalled acknowledgement by nodding their heads, one or two I really didn't want at my back, if you know what I mean.

"Angelus. You were busy."

"Coulda waited. Gentlemen, this lady's a friend of mine. I trust you've been polite?" They assured me they had been, and I chose to take them at their word.

"The kid shouldna be here—"

"The kid's with me," I said. "He leaves with me and not before." Finality. I wasn't about to let him wander around alone at night, no matter what the rules were.

"And if I say other?"

I turned my head slowly at the sound of a half-remembered voice. He'd been a lowly officer last time I'd been in these parts. Seems he was a deputy now. "Sorry, Max, but I ain't leaving him alone outside. He won't touch no stuff, and he'll keep outa trouble. My word."

"Your word good?" My companions stiffened in righteous outrage. "Guess so." He grinned. "You carrying, Angelus?"

"I know the town rules." Ambiguous: no denial, but no admission either. Fortunately, he didn't press – but I knew he knew I was.

"Good enough. See you keep them."

He hovered by the bar, chatting to the guy who ran the inn, keeping an eye on proceedings.

"Look, I need to see a man. Business. You deal with this lady right or you'll be hearing from me, right?" They all agreed, of course. "I won't be long, Faith. Don't leave here without me, right?"

"As you say, Angelus." I gave a quick nod and went on my way. Micah followed me, which I found curious. I'd have expected him to stay with Faith, and I wasn't sure I wanted him with me. I guess I could've ditched him, but I didn't.

I suppose I could've waited for morning, but certain business needs to be done under cover of night. And I was concerned that Morgan and his gang were going to turn up. I'd probably pissed him off sufficiently to make him more than a little aggressive, so I was expecting trouble when next we met.

As I made my way through the darkened streets, I had my gun in my hand and my other hand clutched Micah by the arm. I didn't want to have to go hunting for him in the shadows.

Knocking on a door after checking we were alone, I waited for the inspection shield to slide back. At the sound of bolts being drawn, I took a couple of steps back, dragging Micah with me. The door opened to reveal a small woman robed in red. I gave a half bow of respect.

"Angelus. I'd almost given up hope." She moved back to allow us entry, closing and locking the doors behind us. "You have it?"

"As much as I could. I fear it will not be enough." I hesitated. "I am sorry if I have failed you, Sister."

She smiled gently and extended her hand. "Even a little is more than we have," she said as I placed the small box on her hand. "Your son?"

I laughed. "No, just a travelling companion. I found him and a woman in the ruins of a slaver."

"God looks kindly on a good Samaritan, my son," she smiled. I grimaced and made a half-hearted protest. "Just because you do not believe in him, my son, does not mean he does not believe in you."

I accepted her rebuke gracefully. There were a lot of believers... after. And a lot of those who lost their faith, too.

The contents of the little box I'd handed to the sister was not much to the eye – six small vials containing a pale blue liquid that would keep a little boy alive a little longer. The little box was worth its weight in gold, as they used to say – or a king's ransom – and, I believed, what Morgan had been after. I believed he'd wanted to use the little box to hold the Sword of Damocles over the head of the boy's father – what passed for the authority in Vesta, known as the Mayor – to bend the rules in his favour. Me? I didn't have an axe to grind. I'd never met the boy, and as far as I knew, I'd never met the father either. But I'd met Sister Martha, and I'd a soft spot for the old battleaxe. Okay, I'll admit that at one time it'd been in the nearest patch of quicksand, back in the days when I'd been an unruly runt and she'd been the only law I'd bow to. It was Sister Martha who'd stitched me up before now, so to say she knew me intimately wasn't an exaggeration. I'd been out of my head with fever once, violent as all hell, strong as an ox, she'd said, but somehow she'd been able to bring me back. So any favour she asked of me I'd do, even accepting a lecture on faith that I knew would be forthcoming. I'd lost any faith I'd had under the lash, I'd told her many times, and her reply had always been 'just because you have chosen to forget God does not mean he has forgotten you,' and who was I to deny her? After all, she was on first-name terms with the Almighty – or so she'd once claimed. Our paths had crossed many times over the years and would again, with luck, for many years to come. Anyway, as I'd always said, if God did exist, I'd have her to put in a good word for me, wouldn't I?

"I cannot thank you enough, Angelus. Will you stay the night?"

"No, thank you, but no. I have to get back to my rig. I have to make a collection on the way back, and I don't dare leave it too long. Do me a favour, Sister; put that somewhere safe."

"I will. Somewhere *very* safe. Bless you, my son." She pulled down my head to kiss my brow. "Until we meet again, I will pray for you."

I bowed my head and waited for her to unlock the door, waiting until I heard the sounds of the bolts again before moving away.

As we made our way through the streets, I caught at Micah's hand. "Don't you go spreading this about, mind. You'll ruin my reputation." I caught the quick flash of his teeth as he smiled.

Fortunately, Faith hadn't got herself into too much trouble, but she hadn't managed to negotiate herself a lift either. We'd try again later, I assured her, and took her back to Rom's place, and my rig.

Rom had arranged security for my rig, a room for Faith and Micah and offered his own room to me. I declined, which upset him a little. I preferred to sleep in my rig, and only a beseeching look from Trinity had persuaded me otherwise – okay, that and being bodily lifted off the floor by Rom and deposited in his bedroom!

"Business go okay?" asked Trinity, pulling my coat over my shoulders.

"Yeah. No problems."

"You're not gonna tell me, are you?"

"No need for you to know, hon," I replied. "Old promises."

She smiled and brushed my hair back. "Okay. C'mon. You wanna take a quick shower?"

"I think I'd best," I said. "I had to cut and run quick like."

"Faith okay?"

"No worries. No luck yet. We'll see." I separated myself reluctantly from her and headed for the bathroom. I half hoped she'd join me in the shower, and half hoped she wouldn't. To tell the truth, I was bone tired. I guess I'd been on the road too long. I never stayed in any place long, not even when I paid Trinity a call. But sometimes you just know your battery needs recharging, right? I returned, drying my hair, to find her stretched out on the bed.

"You okay, Angel?" she asked, frowning.

I sat down on the bed and began to sort out my hair. "I think I'm getting old," I laughed softly.

"You do feel a little tight." She dug her fingers into my neck and shoulders. "You should let me drive more."

"Guess I've been on the road a while."

"Guess so." She planted a kiss on my shoulder. "Lie down. C'mon." I didn't need any encouraging. I lay down, closing my eyes with a sigh. I could feel her practised fingers soothing me into sleep.

I awoke feeling refreshed. Trinity was still asleep and I moved carefully so as not to wake her simply so that I could look at her in sleep, devoid of make-up and her 'public face'. "I have a reputation to uphold, too", she'd once said when I'd asked her why she used so much make-up in public. I'd told her she was beautiful enough without it and she'd laughed gently, caressed my face with a hand and kissed me lightly before saying, "You're young. When you get older you'll understand." She wasn't that much older than me, I'd discovered – well, if I was as old as I thought I was she wasn't – but that wasn't what she was saying. She was saying that she was a whore and she had to look her best for her clients. Later, when she'd been caring for her girls, she'd still had to look her best, giving them something to look up to, she'd said. I always thought it was a disguise. That her public face hid the woman I knew lay beneath. I didn't know if I'd ever told her my thoughts. I guess we hadn't talked much sometimes. Maybe we both had our masks, I thought as I looked at her, waiting patiently for her eyes to open, waiting to see her smile.

I wasn't disappointed. Her smile, when she saw me, was everything I hoped it would be. Life was good, I thought, as I relaxed and drew her to me. Which probably meant it was about to fall apart.

Chapter 8

Trouble came my way in the form I expected, vis-à-vis Morgan. I was stretched out under my rig when I saw a pair of boots appear, followed closely by a second. I was unarmed except for a wrench, which wasn't likely to be much use, and there was little I could do but avoid striking my head as they hauled me out. Lying there looking up at two of Morgan's 'hoods', I waited, not wanting to make any sudden moves.

"Morgan's none too pleased with yer," said the first. "Nasty trick yer pulled."

"No worse 'n what he did to me," I responded evenly, keeping my voice soft and my attitude non-threatening – although it's hard to appear threatening while lying on your back! – "but I guess he didn't mention that, did he?"

"Git up. He wants to see yer."

I hesitated, then heard the soft click of a door. So did they. While I admit the sight of Trinity in a shift might be enough to give any full-blooded male pause, the sight of Trinity in a shift and holding my crossbow most certainly is! I didn't know if she knew how to use it, but more to the point, nor did they, and she held them at bay long enough for me to rise and take it from her. "Much as I'd like to accept Morgan's gracious invitation, I'm a little busy. I'd advise you to get the hell out of here and tell Morgan I'll be in 'The Hunter's Moon' tonight if he wants to talk man to man."

I saw the first man swallow and glance cautiously at the second. "I thinks Morgan'll say it's a deal," he said, glancing with more than a little appreciation at Trinity, who had retreated behind my back for shelter. I raised the bow to give them a hint that it was time to leave, which they did. I stood, watching them go, forgetting Trinity for a moment. Until she bit me on the neck, that was.

"Ouch!" I exclaimed, trying to turn.

"Don't."

"Huh?" She had me puzzled, I'll admit. I felt her teeth nip my ear and her fingers brush my hair from the back of my neck. "Honey, I'm dirty—"

"I know." Her voice vibrated through me, making me shudder. "Lock the door. I'll soon wash you down."

I groaned. "I need to put things away, tidy up." My excuse sounded lame, even to me.

"No you don't. Not yet." Her smile grew wicked as she allowed me to turn, almost coy as she rubbed the ball of her hand slowly over my chest. "Or maybe you should, but quickly. The dirtier you are, the longer it'll take me to wash you clean, and there's a lot to be said for anticipation – right?"

I wasn't about to argue with her, although when I walked into 'The Hunter's Moon' later I felt as if I wished I had. Part of me regretted agreeing to bring her along because she was wearing me out; part of me couldn't believe my luck.

I nodded to the barman and settled myself in a strategically useful position: I needed to see people enter and leave, needed my back covering, all the things it would have been nice not to do while out for an evening's relaxation. Deep down I really didn't expect Morgan to be after blood. I thought it was mostly for show. I didn't want to play 'King of the Hill' with him. I wanted to do my business and get out of Vesta. I didn't like towns much, not really. I tolerated them because they were good for business, good for people, I supposed, but whether or not they were good for me... The barman nodded once and I settled myself in what, I hoped, was a comfortable position, one hand resting on the table next to the mug of local firewater, my other hand close to my gun. I had knives in my boots, too, in case the law turned up. Max might not push the issue; he knew I was likely to be armed, of course, but flaunting it in public was a bad idea. After all, he had a reputation, too.

As Morgan weaved his way towards me, he had the grace to leave his 'goons' behind. Well, at the bar, to be precise. He came to a halt before my table and stood looking down at me, thumbs hooked in the belt of his pants. Slowly, a smile came to his craggy face. "Nice one, you little prick. Seems I taught yer somethin' after all."

I gestured for him to sit and offered him a drink, which of course he accepted. "Guess you did. Survival."

He inclined his head and smiled again. "A good lesson to learn." Morgan drank and cradled his mug as he looked at me speculatively. "You made your delivery, I guess?"

"I did." I met his gaze evenly.

"Fair enough. No contest, then." He relaxed. "I'm kinda glad. Felt guilty... you know... a kid..." I inclined my head in acceptance of his word. Whatever his faults, I'd never known him to lie. "Seems you have company. My boys gave me a report."

"I'll bet they did," I responded dryly.

"Lovely lady, long red hair. I thought you travelled alone."

"I do. Usually."

"Still, if the lady's half the looker my boys described..." He leered cheerfully. "Can't say I blame you. So, where you bound next?"

"Don't know," I replied truthfully. "Depends where the wind blows. Why?"

"Guess I'm at a loose end. Lookin', you know?" I knew. I poured us another drink. We sat and talked, of the past, mostly, because neither of us had much hope for the future. The storms were getting increasingly severe. I'd heard it said that it was a cycle; that it might drive us underground again for who knew how long. I hoped not. I didn't think I could face that. "You thinkin' o' settlin', Ang?"

Startled, I almost choked. "Not likely."

"Just wonderin'." He settled back, stretching. "Seemed... you travellin' with a lady..."

I laughed softly, brushing my hair back behind my ears. "More than one, but your goons didn't see everything. Transport, you know. I couldn't settle, you know that. Couldn't go below again."

He nodded thoughtfully, frowning. "You... you 'kay, kid? You look... dark." He gestured under my eyes. "Or is that just yer lady wearin' yer out?"

I chuckled. "You got it."

"You take care o' yerself, yer little prick. It'd be a duller world without yer. Now, I don't know 'bout you, but I'm knackered. I'll see yer later?"

"Bet on it."

I made my way back to Rom's place and pretty much fell into bed. It seemed only a moment later that I felt myself being shaken awake. I groaned. "Huh?" I didn't receive an explanation other than another, harder shake, so I reluctantly opened my eyes. Micah. That explained it. "What is it, kid?" He gestured frantically towards the door, pantomiming for all he was worth. "Visitors? We have visitors?" He nodded vigorously. "Toss me my pants." He did so and I slipped them on, running my fingers through my hair as I looked around for where I'd dropped my boots. Picking up my crossbow as I passed, I headed for the door. "Stay inside," I ordered before opening it. I don't know what I expected to see, but it wasn't the Mayor's personal guard standing in the doorway of the repair shop.

"We apologise for waking you. The Mayor has asked that you join him for lunch. He has a proposition that might interest you." The man gave a half-disguised grin. "If you need to..."

I ran my hands through my hair. "Guess I'd better, huh? Are you waiting?"

"If you don't mind."

"Micah, show these gentlemen where to sit. Get them anything they need." Micah smiled and, with perfect aplomb, escorted the two men to Rom's office. I sorted myself quickly, even tying back my hair – something I rarely do – before picking up my coat and slipping it on. "I trust Micah has taken good care of you?" I asked as I walked in.

"Excellent care. Your son?"

"No." I shook my head. "Just a friend. Micah, when someone comes back, tell them where I am, then they don't send out a search party, huh?" He grinned and nodded vigorously. That wasn't just for show; it was a matter of expediency. We were taking a trip across town, and that could be dangerous even in such company given the area we'd probably pass through. Also, with the likelihood of another storm, I didn't want anyone to worry if I was late back or to come looking for me and put themselves in danger, particularly Micah, who couldn't shout for help if he needed it. He caught at my sleeve, his eyes wide with concern. "It's okay, Micah. I'm not in trouble. Take care of the place while I'm gone, huh?" I wondered briefly where Rom was, but he'd probably gone out for parts or supplies. Trinity and Faith could be anywhere. Probably shopping. Micah gave me a half bow and I smiled encouragement before following my escort out of the door. I was relieved to hear the bar being put on the door as we moved away.

The quickest way to the Mayor's place was straight though an area known as The Gallows. That wasn't actually its name, of course, but that's what the locals called it.

"Storm rising," commented the senior of the pair, whose name, I'd discovered, was Nev. "Best make tracks."

He had a point. Given the heaviness of the air, making all speed did seem a practical idea, as it tended to precede a mag-storm. The dust would come next, and with it the lightning. Occasionally, a twister would ride on the wind. That's when it got really interesting. Heading through The Gallows wasn't wise, but it became increasingly imperative as the storm began to rise. I covered my nose and mouth and ran along with them, dust stinging my eyes. We made it, but only just. As we crashed through the Mayor's door we were all but unrecognisable.

"Nev, Trey, get yourselves cleaned up. You are the messenger – Angelus?"

"And you are?"

"Tomas, the Mayor's private secretary. I must apologise on his behalf for dragging you out into a storm. Perhaps you would care to freshen up?"

"I'd love to, thanks." I needed to get the dust out of my mouth at the very least.

"If you would follow me?"

By the time I re-emerged, I felt halfway human again. Tomas was waiting patiently. He smiled as I appeared. "An improvement, I think, if you do not mind my saying so."

"I don't mind at all," I replied. "If there's the possibility of a drink..."

"Of course." He smiled. "What would you like? Juice? Coffee? Water?"

"Water would be wonderful," I said in reply. "Thank you."

He nodded and led the way into the nearest room. It was, as they say, comfortably appointed. I admired his taste in artwork and was looking at one when the door opened again.

"Good, isn't it?"

I half turned and smiled. "It's fantastic. Who's the artist?"

"I'm told it's by a lady by the name of Eliane. I love the feeling of light."

I nodded. I don't usually go for so-called modern art, but this was special. I sipped my water and stared at the painting. There was something about it, something I couldn't name. Maybe I'd seen it before, or something like it. I found it hard to draw my eyes away. "You wanted to speak with me, I think. A proposition?"

He nodded. "Take a seat. Let's talk." He gestured towards the comfortable-looking couch. "Are you certain I cannot offer you anything more?"

"No thank you. Water's fine." I wondered if I ought to call him 'sir' or something. He seemed to read my thoughts because he grinned.

"As long as Tomas isn't here, please call me Dan."

"Tomas would be most offended?" I offered.

Dan, otherwise known as Mayor Daniel Truman, chuckled. "That he would. I wanted to meet you because of what you did." I raised a brow, although I knew to what he referred. "Sister Martha grassed on you."

"I thought their lips were supposed to be sealed or something," I grumbled.

"Actually, I think that was priests. Maybe I'm wrong. To be true, it cost me a donation." I grinned. Served him right. "But I'd have paid ten times over for what you did for my son."

"How is he?"

"Dom's doing good. I don't know how long he has, but—" His voice caught. "One day at a time, right?" I nodded. "Anyhow, you have my thanks for what it's worth. If ever you need a favour."

I studied him. I knew what a politician's word could be worth, but I accepted it graciously. You never knew, after all. "I'll bear that in mind."

"Would you like to see him?" he offered. "He'll be awake... doesn't sleep much... the pain... I was told you had a boy with you. Your son?" I explained again about Micah, about how I'd come on him and Faith. "Ah. Interesting. Shall we go see Dom?" I didn't see how I could courteously refuse, so I nodded. I wondered what he wanted. He led me up the curved staircase to a bedroom. In the sitting room outside, a young woman sat. She smiled as we approached. "Is he awake, Maggie?"

"Playing games. Go on in; I'm sure he's heard you."

We went into the boy's bedroom. Not a hospital room like I'd expected, I admit; a boy's bedroom as untidy as any boy's. His face split into a grin.

"Dad! Gonna let me thrash you again?"

The father grimaced. "Beat me at chess and has never let me forget it. Dom, this is Angelus. Angelus, my son Dom."

"Pleased to meet you, sir."

"Angelus," I said, taking his offered hand. It had the pretence of strength, I thought, but no real substance.

"Angelus is the man that brought you your medicine," he said, glancing at me.

"Thank you, Angelus. It's not nice, but Dad always says that you're not supposed to like medicine."

"Your dad's right," I replied, glancing at him. "If you liked it, you'd take too much and it would make you very sick."

"How can something that makes you better make you sick?" he asked.

I rolled my eyes as his father suppressed a smile. "It's like if you eat too many sweets. You get tummy ache if you eat too many sweets."

"Oh, I get it. Do you play chess, Angelus?"

"I used to. Haven't played in a while." Bad move, I told myself, as I saw the positively evil grin on his young face.

"Oh good. I mean that you play."

"Like hell you do," I laughed. "One game."

"One game," he agreed.

Four games later, I made my way downstairs. We hadn't been playing that long, I realised. He was a very good player indeed. "We drew two each," I told Daniel Truman. I wondered if he'd been weeping. I suspected he had but pretended not to see.

"He's a good kid. All I have left. The fever took his mom and left him in constant pain. He catches a chill, it could kill him, you know? I tell myself to be grateful for what I'm given, but..." I nodded. "I've heard a lot about you, Angelus. I've heard that you're a good man, as Sister Martha would attest. I've heard that you're dangerous. I guess both are true. You live on the road; you have to be able to defend yourself. I'm no judge. I have a favour to ask." Here it comes, I thought. "You might need something stronger to drink," he said, pouring something from a grand-looking decanter into two glasses. Real crystal, I thought. Probably very old. "A proposition, as I said. What you may not know is that the fever is back." I started. I knew the fever to which he referred, of course. It had taken his wife and almost his son. "A group of settlers out near Hoods Canyon began showing signs about a month ago. Self-imposed quarantine, but they're running out of supplies fast – medical supplies, food, fuel. I need someone I can trust to run supplies out to them. If people here find out, I'm afraid they'll take action, you know?" I nodded. I knew only too well. "I'll pay you whatever you ask, of course. Take that as read."

"Why me?" I asked, curious.

"Because I've heard you're immune, because I can trust you not to cheat me, because you've got the guts to make the run. Choose your own reason." He held my eyes for a long time.

"I don't know whether I'm immune or not," I replied slowly. "Only that I had it once, long ago, but I remember. I need to make a few arrangements first," I said. Namely, to persuade my travelling companions to stay behind. "I can leave after sundown, if you'll have the gates opened for me. Best to slip away under cover of night, if you know what I mean."

He closed his eyes and muttered something I guessed might be a prayer of thanks. "Name your price."

"Fuel and food," I said, startled – and perhaps a little insulted – that he appeared to assume I'd want money.

"That was what Sister Martha said you'd say," he said with a smile. "I apologise – I thought you'd want money."

"Don't sweat it. Chalk this one up to Sister M for services rendered."

"I won't ask," he said, rising and offering his hand. "I'll see that the wheels are smoothed for you and that you're ready to go at the earliest. Thank you seems inadequate." We shook hands. "Take care of yourself. When you get back, come see me and Dom."

"I will," I promised, turning as the door opened.

"Ah, Tomas, I have some errands for you. Are Angelus's escorts waiting?"

"Yes, Mayor."

"Until we meet again – good luck."

"I've a feeling I'm gonna need it," I grinned. "C'mon, guys; let's hit the road."

My escort did not need encouraging, and had me back at the workshop in no time flat. I found them waiting for me: Trinity, Faith, Micah and Rom, all eager to hear what had happened. I wasn't sure what to tell them, but in the end I settled for the truth because I trusted them to keep quiet about where I'd gone and why. What I didn't expect was their pronouncement that they were coming with me. "Oh no you ain't. This ain't no joyride—"

"You might need muscle..."

"You need another driver..."

I raised my hands for silence before Faith could add her voice to the onslaught. What Micah had in mind I wasn't sure, but he looked ready to join in.

"Look, I appreciate the sentiment, but I can't allow—"

"Now wait a moment, mister. You have no right to make decisions for us. You can kick us out – sure you can – but friends don't do that."

"Friends don't take friends into a plague zone either."

"The fever isn't—"

"We don't know that it *is* fever. Sure he says it is, but he could be wrong. We take precautions. My precaution is that I make the trip alone. Okay?"

"Like hell!" Trinity stood, hands on hips, glaring at me belligerently. It gave me pause. Trinity in a fury is able to do that. As we stared each other out, I was vaguely aware of Faith ushering Micah and Rom away, leaving us staring at each other like dogs with hackles raised. "Angel, it's my risk to take. You need someone along, a hired gun, if you like, a second driver. Besides, you need someone to keep you warm at night."

If I looked at her much longer I'd weaken. I knew it, and she knew it. If I took her along, I'd hate myself. If I didn't, she'd hate me. But she'd be alive. Slowly, I drew my shades out of my pocket and slipped them on. "If you're still here when I get back, you can make me pay. The answer's still no." Then I walked away towards the back of my rig, feeling her eyes boring into the back of my neck.

She'd make me pay all right, one way or another, and I wasn't sure how much I was going to like it. But she'd be alive.

To tell the truth, I was glad to hit the road again. Being alone was cool: I had no one else to account for, no one to care whether I combed my hair or shaved. But at the same time, I guess I missed the voices. I'd even got used to Micah, his presence at my elbow every chance he got. I wondered if he'd talk one day. I hoped so. It was a hard enough world when you *could*.

Chapter 9

t was a long drive out to Hoods Canyon. It would take me several days of hard driving to get out there, and I had to keep my eyes open both for storms and for bandits. Then there were the wolves, or what had once been wolves, I'm told. Hoods Canyon had once been the site of a research laboratory, so the records said. I wasn't sure what sort of research, but I'd put my money on the likelihood that whatever research had been going on there hadn't been for mankind's benefit – in the end, anyway. Even if they'd had a hand in the weapons that had almost brought an end to us all, it didn't matter any more, any more than the reason it had started – other than as a lesson, perhaps. Some said it had been biologicals, some said it had been atomics. But it didn't really matter any more. Whatever had been used, we had to make sure it never happened again. I don't know whether it had been accidental or deliberate, but the end result was what we had been left to live with.

The wasteland was the stuff of nightmares: a ravaged landscape dotted with what had once been trees but which were now no more than leafless stumps with all the appearance of stone. Not a breath of wind stirred, but a storm was capable of rising in moments, so I had to keep a watchful eye on the horizon as I took a stretch and a spell away from the wheel. I briefly considered hunting, but decided against it. Contaminated meat.

The back of my neck prickled and I turned around slowly. Although I could see nothing, I knew I wasn't alone and raised my crossbow instinctively. They wouldn't attack in daylight, I thought, but light was failing fast and I was some distance from my rig.

They were clever, I had to admit: trying to herd me away from the shelter of my rig. I wasn't going to compound my mistake by allowing myself to be forced away from safety... except that I did. They were more than clever: they were intelligent.

I took two of them down and wounded a third before they got close. Then it was knife against claw and tooth. As I dragged myself into my rig, I began to wonder if I'd been wise to leave my little gang behind after all. They'd have been useful right then.

The wound to my leg was the worst and needed stitching as well as soaking in antibiotic powder. By the time I finished I was feeling decidedly worse for wear. Even cleaning the wounds might not be sufficient, but I wasn't a novice at the task so I hoped I'd be okay.

After an unsettled night's sleep, I set off at first light in the hope of reaching the settlement before sundown. Driving hurt, but painkillers took the edge off. I don't like taking them, but sometimes you have to do things you don't like. It kept me going to the edge of the settlement.

I drew to a halt outside the wire fence and waited. They knew I was there, of course. I'd seen the glint of light off lens. They weren't about to let me in; I didn't expect that. But I simply wasn't about to leave my package out in the open without someone at least close enough to retrieve it.

I saw the small vehicle heading my way and waited until they were close before leaving my rig.

"Don't come any closer," the female driver said as she dismounted and walked towards me. "For your own safety. You'll be okay if you stay where you are. Is that our medicine?"

"I guess so. I was asked to bring it and to deliver it to a Dr Owen. Is that you?"

"Zoe Owen, yes. And you are?"

"They call me Angelus."

She smiled and tucked a stray lock of hair behind her ear. She didn't appear to have the fever, but you never knew. Her eyes were a little on the bright side, but that could just have been the light. "I have heard your name, Angelus. You are the Messenger."

I smiled. "Among other things. Just a delivery boy."

"Well, I doubt you have ever carried a more important message." I knew a man who might dispute that, but I said nothing and simply smiled. "If you place the box down, I will collect it as soon as you are gone. Forgive me for not inviting you inside, but..."

"I'm probably immune," I said, "but I could carry it, I guess. Is there ought you need?"

"We are self-sufficient, for the most part. You give us hope. I would like to shake your hand one day, Angelus. Perhaps we will meet in better days and I can thank you for the hope you bring, whatever the result."

I nodded, understanding. For some it might already be too late. "I'll look forward to it."

Placing the box where she had indicated, I retreated to my rig. With a last look back, I climbed aboard and hit the road. I wanted to put as great a distance between us as I could before dark. Not because I feared the fever, but because my leg was beginning to hurt like hell.

Chapter 10

Truth is, I don't remember much about the drive back to Vesta. I don't remember a thing after nightfall that day until I woke up in a bed I didn't recognise. I felt as weak as a kitten and my mouth felt as if something had died in it. I'd been shaved, I realised as I ran my hand over my jaw, and my wounds tended to because the dressings were new. Which drew my attention to my leg. My leg, I thought, which didn't ache any more. Uneasily, I tugged at the sheet because I was tangled in it, trying to rise enough to look. The effort left me exhausted and I lay for some moments trying to summon the strength to try again.

"Ah, you're awake."

"Faith?"

Her smile broadened. "You know me. Good. You didn't for a while. Know us, that is. Let me tell Trin you're awake."

"Just a moment. Where are we? How long have I been here?"

"In the Mayor's house. We found you about a week ago, in high fever. We thought at first it was the fever, then we found the wounds. The one on your leg was poisoned. For a time we didn't think you'd make it. Trin's been with you most of the time. She's sleeping. I'll go wake her."

That was about the longest speech I'd heard her make, I realised. "Let her sleep. I'd like a drink."

"Coming right up," she smiled. "Just rest."

I'd just close my eyes for a moment, I thought. Just for a moment...

When I opened my eyes, the room was bathed in sunlight. Trinity was sitting in a chair next to the bed, watching me. "If you'd taken us along, this wouldn't have happened," she pointed out logically. "Let me help you sit up, if you still want that drink." I did. She helped me, supported me and helped me drink. "Easy now. Don't drink too fast. That better? Lay back now. I need to check your leg." She eased me back and went to pick up the dressing pack on the table next to the bed. Gently, she cut off the old dressing and checked the wound. It looked healthy, I suppose, if that's the right word to use. It wasn't angry, black or anything, which I guessed was good. "Lookin' good. Just stay off it for a while; you'll be fine," continued Trinity as she probed the wound gently. "You know, I think we'll leave it uncovered. Do it good." She ran her eyes slowly up my leg, mischief tugging at her lips. "You know, I gotcha just as I want you – in bed, naked – but I guess I prefer you strong enough to fight back."

"You promised to make me pay." I reminded her unnecessarily. Trinity wasn't one to forget.

"I know, and I will. Later." She bent to kiss me slowly, gently. "Take that as a reminder, in case you've forgotten."

I hadn't, of course, but I didn't have the strength to make the point.

I felt myself drift away and didn't fight too hard. When next I woke, I found I had another visitor. This time it was Dom Truman in some kind of special chair.

He smiled as my eyes opened. "I asked nurse to bring me in. I hope you don't mind."

"Come to thrash me, Dom?"

He grinned. "Mustn't. Got my orders, I have. Not to tire you. So you'll have to wait... or I will. How's the leg?"

"Stiff, but healing."

"Good, I'm glad. Dad told me what you'd done. You were very brave."

"He wasn't supposed to tell," I muttered defensively.

"Oh he didn't voluntarily."

"What did you do to him?"

He grinned slyly. "Tickled his feet with a feather."

"That would do it." I chuckled despite myself.

"I could ask nurse. She might be able to think of something... you know... so you could exercise."

I had my own thoughts about exercise, but I wasn't about to voice them in front of a kid.

As if on cue, the door opened and a woman came in. "Master Dom, time you were leaving. I hope he hasn't tired you."

"No, he's been the ideal visitor."

"It'll be a first time," she smiled, taking hold of his chair. "I'll be in big trouble if you're caught."

"Oh, don't worry," I heard him say as the door began to close. "I can handle my father."

I wanted to get up. A few moments wouldn't harm, would it? I disliked idleness: it reminded me of something I'd rather forget. But most of all, I didn't like being reminded that I wasn't invulnerable, I guess. I could make it as far as the chair, I thought, where I could see a pair of boxers. Better than nothing, I guessed. But it was a case of the mind being willing and the flesh being weak. It was harder than I'd imagined, reaching that chair, and the effort taken to put on even that one piece of clothing almost did me in. I hadn't realised what it had taken out of me until I saw their faces – Trinity, Faith and Micah – when they discovered me on my knees, using the bed for support and trying, for the fourth time at least, to raise myself to my feet.

"You stupid bastard," was the least Trinity called me as she ran to me, as she and Faith slipped their arms under me and man-handled me onto the bed, where I lay, exhausted. Whatever she called me, it wasn't half what I called myself. "If you wanted your drawers, all you had to do was ask. But no!" she stormed. "You macho prick, do you know—"

"Trin." Faith reached out a cautionary hand and caught at Trinity's arm. "Of course he doesn't."

"Suppose... suppose you enlighten me," I said, holding Trinity's gaze.

"You were half dead when we found you." Faith explained. "The poison was in your blood. Your leg was a mess. We thought for a while it might have to come off. You'd done everything you could, but it wasn't enough. You lost a lot of blood when they cut you open." Faith stubbornly continued despite a warning glance from Trinity. "He deserves to know! If it wasn't for the Mayor's pull, you wouldn't have made it. He called in a few favours, got you medicines, blood. We sat with you, bathed you, mopped up after you." She grinned. "Even Micah."

I tore my eyes away from Trinity's accusatory stare and smiled at Micah, who hovered behind Faith, for protection, perhaps. "I'm grateful. I am. Truly. It's just I hate—"

"We know."

Faith drew Micah out of the room at Trinity's signal, leaving us alone.

"You talked. Well, groaned mostly." A tentative finger stroked the scar on my rib cage. "There's no shame in weakness, Angel. You can't help it, so don't sweat it. You've done enough." I gave a weak smile. "It's damned frustrating for me, too, you know."

"What is?"

Trinity gave a half smile. "Having you at a disadvantage. I could get to like it, if it wasn't for that."

Strange woman, I thought. "You into domination? You never said."

"I don't need to tie you down, do I? Simpler that way." Her fingers brushed back my hair. "We almost cut it off, you know, but we decided not to." I didn't comment. It would have grown again, after all. But Trinity liked my hair long. "You should sleep. Is there something I can get you? A drink, perhaps?"

"How about a kiss?"

"That won't help you sleep."

I didn't want to sleep, not really. I still had the feeling that if I slept I wouldn't wake next time. Strange, but there you are. "It will."

Looking at me suspiciously, Trinity leaned down to give me a kiss. I held her close, enjoying the feel of her body against mine.

"Angel, you're shaking." She pushed against me, but I held her firm.

"You feel so good. There's nothing I'd like more than to ask you to lock the door and make love—" I was about to say that I'd never be able to, when Trinity slipped out of my arms and locked the door before I was able to finish the sentence. I felt my throat go dry as she returned to the bed and began to undress. Very slowly. Her smile was seductive, and I began to realise I'd been missing out on something.

"Pretend you're a paying customer," she said softly, swaying. "You don't need to do nothin', mister 'cept enjoy. Let me give yer what yer need, darlin'."

"And what do I need?" I asked hoarsely, wetting my lips.

"Me."

Chapter 11

slept, shall we say, like a baby. When I awoke I felt great. I even made it to the bathroom and back, using the crutches that had appeared by my bed courtesy, I assumed, of Dom.

The next time he came to visit we played chess. He beat me, but I didn't mind. Then he offered me a race down the corridor. I must have been insane to agree. We must have looked a strange pair, him in his nightshirt flapping wildly as he tore along the corridor, me wearing boxers racing after him on crutches. And we must have looked more than a little guilty when we came face to face with Dan Truman at the other end.

"Young man, I hope you have an explanation for this insanity." He glared at his unruly son.

Unrepentant, Dom grinned. "It was his idea," he said.

"It was not!" I wasn't about to take the rap! "It was—"

"I can guess whose idea it was," he replied dryly, calling for Dom's nurse. "Take him and put him back to bed. And confiscate his wheels!"

"Dad!"

"Next time you might think twice about dangerous driving," he said, trying not to smile. "You see, Mr Morgan? I told you he was recovering."

I clung to my crutches and glared at Morgan, who was grinning at me. I must have looked a mess, to say the least.

"You gettin' careless, kid. 'Fore long, you'll be able to join 'em up," he said as he gave me a bear hug.

"Well, you know me. Always a sucker for kids 'n' animals."

"Told yer not to feed 'em." He ran a critical eye over me. "Only you'd take on a wolf pack, you stupid prick. Serves yer right. Get back to yer bed. Don't make me waste any more fuel."

I laughed softly, nodded once and began to pivot. I wanted to hear what he'd done later. The real version, not the sanitised one he'd probably given the Mayor. I'd thank him in my own way when I could return the favour. That was the way it worked. For all my air of bravado, I was still shaky, and hated it. I guess it was almost a phobia with me, and I was prepared to do anything to get back on form. I'd eat anything, drink anything they gave me if they told me it would work, although my illicit races with Dom were curtailed by his father, and I had to agree to the wisdom of it.

I visited him when I could, sometimes with Micah. Dom was teaching Micah to play chess, which relieved me of the responsibility. When I could, I hobbled down into the small garden, desperate by that time for fresh air. One or two of the Mayor's staff greeted me as I passed and enquired after my health, much to my surprise. I'd made it to the wall of the tiny pond – a luxury in this climate – when I realised I wasn't alone.

"Hi, you little prick," Morgan greeted me in predictable fashion. "You're looking better."

"I'm getting there," I admitted. "You shippin' out soon?"

"Yeah. Me and the guys are running supplies out to the mine at Vargas."

I nodded. I'd done it myself once or twice. The mine was a deep one and much of the settlement was underground. It was rough country, a roughneck town. "Watch your back."

"Oh, don't worry; that's what the guys are for."

"You trust them that much?" I asked.

Morgan didn't reply, which spoke volumes. I'd said to Trinity that I didn't trust Morgan, but that wasn't entirely true. I'd trusted him once. Before he'd dumped me, that is. He must have been reading my mind, because he gave a soft laugh. "We've had our time, ain't we? Guess I owe you an explanation."

"For what?"

"You know. You was a cocky prick, you know, a nasty piece of work. Good with weapons, and your fists. But you didn't take well to orders. We were going into a situation where I couldn't trust you not to start a fight. Dumping you seemed the best way at the time. Knew you'd make it, I did, but guess I shoulda explained."

"I wouldn't have listened, not then," I admitted. He was right. I'd have caused no end of trouble, most like.

"So I guess we're even?"

"Guess," I agreed. "What happened – really? Where'd you go?"

He didn't pretend to misunderstand. "Out to Maxim's," he admitted, waiting for the explosion. I didn't explode. It wouldn't do any good after the fact, and I didn't have the energy. Xavier Maxim was a dealer, I guess. A supplier. Of anything and everything – for a price. He had a place out in the desert north of Vesta, outside the Mayor's jurisdiction, of course. Maxim was a law unto himself, and you didn't cross him if you wanted to live. If you went to him, you paid the price he asked or you didn't buy. There was no negotiating. And for the drugs I guessed Morgan had gone for, Maxim would have asked for blood, given the fact that it was Dan Truman who was asking.

"Did he know who—?"

"I didn't tell him. All I did was carry the note the Mayor gave me. You've crossed swords with Maxim once or twice, haven't you?"

"Yeah, you could put it that way. Didn't use to care too much where he got his stock, you might say. Tried to separate me from something I was carryin'. When I didn't lie down and beg..." I shrugged. "Another time, we were both after something and I outbid him. He make it difficult for you?"

"Naw, not really. Didn't say much, really. Just looked at the note, smiled and produced the goods. If you wanna know what was in it, you'll have to ask the Mayor."

Who wouldn't tell me, I had a feeling. At least, not yet awhile. "Thanks anyway." I offered my hand.

"I'll see you later. I see your 'nurse' watching. Time you were goin' back ter bed, kiddo." He leered and laughed. "Can't say I blame you none."

I glanced over my shoulder in the direction of his gaze and grinned. Trinity was standing there, of course, hands on hips, glaring at me. I made my way slowly to where she stood. "Have I been a naughty boy?" I asked lazily.

"You know it."

"Are you gonna punish me?" Was I hopeful? Guess I was.

Trinity was laughing softly as she leaned towards me, digging her fingers into my scalp as she kissed me. "Maybe," she laughed, teasing, tugging at my hair to draw me inside. "You on speaking terms with him now?"

"I guess."

"Good. He went all out for you. Ask you to 'run' with him, did he?"

"No."

"Not yet. He will, I think."

She might well be right, I thought. I could do that – ride shotgun, that is. It might be just what I needed in the long term. In the short term, well, Trinity and I were doing just fine.

Chapter 12

My only gripe about riding out with Morgan was that I was riding with him and not using my own rig. The old girl's not the fastest rig, certainly not the newest, but she's mine. I don't own much else, I guess. I'm not sure how happy Trinity was about letting me go wandering off so soon after almost coming to grief, but both she and Faith waved us off with a seeming good heart. I gathered that Faith had a job serving in one of the more reputable inns. She'd be kept an eye on, I was assured. I guess I felt responsible for some reason. Maybe I was developing a conscience in my old age or something. Trinity suggested a bang on the head might have had something to do with it!

Morgan had a couple of his goons riding in the back – I didn't envy them – another on the back seat of the extended cab and me up front with him.

"That's some weapon you have there. Who made it?"

"Kaz."

"Kaz? Deepstar?" I nodded. "Carved a stock for me once; beautiful piece of work. Thought it looked familiar. You used it yet?"

I gave a bitter smile. "Not on anything human."

"You good with it?"

"Not quite as good as I should be, I guess," I ran a hand over my thigh.

He nodded, understanding. "That healed yet?"

"More or less. Goes out on me from time to time. According to Trinity, it's muscle wastage or something."

"Oh. Well, I guess she'd know," he grinned. "Enough to make any man weak, she is. You're a lucky kid."

"Not so much of the 'kid'," I chuckled.

He raised his hand in appeasement and laughed. "No offence. Guess I forget time's passed. When you get to be my age..."

I laughed. Morgan wasn't ready to push up the daisies quite yet. I didn't think he was that much older than I was, but I could've been wrong. "And what's that, oh wise elder?"

"Pushin' fifty, if you wanna know." That surprised me. He didn't look it, and I told him so. "You can ride with me again," he chuckled.

The trip out to Vargas was pleasant enough, even relatively smooth. No storms, for once, to slow us down; no bandits; none of the trouble we'd been expecting. Which made us both uneasy, for some strange reason. Perhaps it was living on the edge, always expecting trouble and finding it that made us so. I couldn't say for sure. I was almost happy to see the familiar mounds of Vargas appearing on the horizon. Strange, since if there was anywhere I hated, it was Vargas. Too many memories.

"You okay, kid?" asked Morgan with a side-glance my way.

"Yeah."

"Liar." Morgan knew enough of my past, but by no means all. Few people knew all. Except one person, I thought, as I made my way towards one of the bars.

I knew the voice long before I saw the owner of it. Even after all this time, just the sound of that voice could turn my insides to mush. 'The voice of an angel', they'd once said. I'd agreed. I guess I still did. It'd been several years since I'd seen him: seven years six months and three days, give or take. He hadn't changed much. His hair was short, spiked, as black as night, and he knew I was there. Somehow, in the way he'd always known. A note faltered in his voice – subtle, but if you knew the song like I did...

Dante. His name, like mine, was not the one he'd been born with. Dante and Angelus. Angelus and Dante.

I left my prop – the wall – reluctantly, because I knew my knees were going to let me down. Although I'd thought myself more than capable of greeting an old friend without my legs giving way, I do like to look my best. A few old friends greeted me as I made my way across the room, but I was aware of only one person. Strange, really, I thought. Perhaps it was residual weakness and being too long off my feet that made me feel light-headed.

I needed a drink, I decided, and detoured to the bar. The fiery liquor made my eyes water but I really didn't care. Perched on a stool, I considered getting drunk as I listened to his voice and stared into the golden liquid.

"How about buying an old friend a drink?" asked a voice close to my ear. I raised a hand and signalled to the girl behind the bar. "Cat got your tongue?" he teased playfully, fingers reaching for the glass with only the slightest hesitation. "Just got in?"

"Yeah. Came in with Morgan."

"Ah. Where's your rig?"

"Back in Vesta. Had a little accident."

"Serious?"

"Still here." I replied carefully. I saw his brow crease.

"That sounds like you might not have been." I didn't speak and knew he'd keep pushing. There was a time and a place, however. He seemed to understand, because he said, "I've got one more set then I'm free. Don't run away." His smile was almost intimate as he made his way carefully to his 'spot'. "This one's an old one," he announced, "for an old friend. It's called 'Shadow and Light'."

While he sang, I got steadily drunk. Too many memories, I guess. I even considered slipping away, but he knew the place considerably better than I did. He'd find me.

"C'mon. Let's get outa here," he said finally. I raised my head slowly, refusing his offer of help. It wasn't that I didn't want him to touch me; it was that I wanted it too much.

He didn't seem to sense that, which was strange, as he muttered, "Suit yourself." He waited for a moment, sighed and growled, "Don't be so bloody-minded," as he slipped an arm under mine to support me as he hauled me to my feet. He was stronger than he looked. It felt good, I thought, fighting a spinning head and a desire to lean against him for support simply to *feel* him. "Easy now," he grinned, leaning me against a wall as he reached out to feel for the door release. "Not going to pass out on me, are you?"

"No. Course not."

I felt his hand rest against my chest and heard him chuckle. Despite the semi-darkness, it was still too public. These were still somewhat conservative times in some places. "Talk to me, Angel. You've hardly said a word. Tell me where you've been, what you've done... if you've missed me." I didn't want to talk. I didn't want to think. I told myself oblivion was what I wanted, but it wasn't. "Would it help if I turned out the light?"

"It doesn't matter," was my reply. I didn't care and I knew he wouldn't. His world, after all, was permanently dark. Dante was blind.

"What are you wearing?" he asked, closing the door.

"The usual," I replied. "Black pants and top. Why?"

"Nice to know some things don't change," he laughed. "You okay? You sound different."

"I do?"

"Yeah. Don't know why. I hear you've been ill. Someone said you were dead, but I knew you weren't."

"I almost was."

"Ah. That explains it."

"It does?"

"To me."

"Oh."

An awkward silence fell. I'd never felt that in his presence before.

"What happened?"

I told him and he listened gravely.

"Who cared for you?"

I told him that, too.

"So you're still with Trinity?"

"Or she's with me. I'm not sure which."

"That's good."

"Why?"

Dante smiled. "I wouldn't want you to be lonely."

I didn't know what to say. "I ought to go," I began feebly, hating the distance between us but at the same time guiltily grateful for it. I wanted to close the distance between us, but I wasn't sure what lay behind those beautiful eyes of his.

"No. You really shouldn't." His voice, like velvet, was suddenly closer than it had been. "You really shouldn't..."

Chapter 13

"That's an interesting new scar," remarked Dante, his fingers tracing the line with a feather-light touch. Somewhere along the line I'd lost my clothes out there in the dark. I didn't mind the dark so long as I wasn't alone in it, and Dante had once been used to my screams in the dark – for a variety of reasons! I first met Dante in the mines. He helped me heal my wounds. I helped him survive. It had been a fair exchange. Somehow we'd survived, and somewhere along the way it had become something more. We'd drifted along together for a while. When I'd hit the road with my rig, he'd hit the road with his voice. Did Trinity know about Dante? Yes. Did she know everything? Maybe. I've never kept our friendship secret from her, no more than I had my friendship with her from him.

"Glad you think so."

"Are you sober now?" His voice was light, almost playful. "Hm?"

"Oh hell!" I groaned and he laughed. "I'm getting there," I admitted.

"Do you want any help?"

Did I want any help sobering up? His laughter told me he remembered a few ways that might accomplish that. Perhaps sitting up wasn't a good idea, because it gave him the opportunity to slip his arms around me from behind. "I'd forgotten how good it felt to hold you," he said against my ear. "And to be held by you. For old times' sake?" There was a touching appeal in his voice, and the warmth I'd always known.

"If you weren't holdin' so tight..." He eased his hold, enabling me to breathe, and then promptly took my breath away with the kind of kiss you definitely don't give someone in public!

Waking, I was surprised to discover I wasn't suffering from a hangover. I was reluctant to open my eyes because I wasn't looking forward to darkness, but I discovered the room bathed in soft light. Dante was curled up on a couch looking at me; well, in my direction at least.

"I thought you'd never wake," he said, knowing, as he always had, when I opened my eyes. "Can I get you breakfast?"

"I'm okay."

He laughed softly. "You're more than okay," he said, pushing himself to his feet. He had a tattoo like mine on his hip, I realised.

"Come back to bed," I asked him, surrendering to the inevitable.

He made the pretence of hesitating, gave a whoop of laughter and almost catapulted me off the bed when he jumped on it – and me. I almost regretted it, as the pain shot through my leg. Instantly contrite, Dante proceeded to apologise. Repeatedly.

It took my mind off being underground I had to admit. Dante understood and told me, "I'm in permanent darkness, my Angel. The mine was no different for me. The only brightness ever in my life was you. Maybe you don't want to hear it, but it's a fact nonetheless. You always told me not to lie." I had, I knew. I waited for him to continue. "If you walk away from me again..." I heard him curse as he choked it back. "I'm sorry. I know that's not what you want to hear. No ties, we said. Keep it light. I guess I'm just so happy to see you again."

That hurt for some reason. If anyone else had said it, it would not have sounded strange, perhaps. It wouldn't have hurt. I'd never thought about his blindness, I guess, not in a long time at least. Dante was just Dante. "Believe me; I'm happy to see you, too. You haven't changed much, you know."

"You have. Scars you didn't have before. Your hair's longer. You lost weight?"

"Guess I must have. Fever."

"That'd do it. Nice abs, though."

I chuckled. "You want to come with me?" I found myself asking. I felt him go still.

"You mean that?"

"Would I say it if I didn't? You can't stay here forever. I'm heading back for my rig. Don't know where from there, yet. Depends on what comes, I guess."

"Still footloose," smiled Dante. "I guess we could travel together awhile, like the old days. What're you gonna tell Trinity?"

I sighed. "Damned if I know."

I had been hoping I wasn't going to have to face that any time soon, but Morgan's announcement that we were leaving pronto made me wonder what business he'd been conducting that I didn't know about. I probably didn't want to. I had enough problems of my own without adding any of his, after all.

All the way back to Vesta I kept expecting something to happen. Maybe I was becoming paranoid, I thought. Looking for baddies behind every rock. I was aware of Morgan's eyes from time to time as I drove. Speculative, wondering why I was silent and watchful. When we changed places, I sat with my crossbow to hand up front with Morgan. I knew he was wondering why I wasn't sitting with Dante, why I'd barely spoken to him.

My thoughts were far away. I was thinking we were developing into a rather motley crew as we closed on Vesta: me with my unpredictable leg, Dante who was blind, Micah who couldn't, or wouldn't, speak, and perhaps even Trinity, a whore. Only Faith seemed – I hesitate to say it – 'normal', which made me wonder, if she was still around, well, *why*?

I was wondering what I was going to say to Trinity and how she was going to react. Knowing about someone was, after all, very different from coming face to face with them. I was surprised that Morgan had remained silent; he wasn't usually so tactful.

As we drew into Vesta, the night was drawing in in its usual lurid fashion. "Just take care," was all that Morgan said as he jumped down from the rig. Vesta was, because of the nature of the place and its transitory inhabitants, quite relaxed in attitude morality-wise, but even so...

"You know me," I replied.

He gave a half smile. "That's the trouble, you little prick. I do." He gave me a slap on the arm. "See ya," he winked.

"Yeah. See ya." I took Dante by the arm. "Just lean on me," I said, knowing how strange he would find the openness of Vesta after underground Vargas.

Getting him to Rom's, where I'd left my rig, wasn't hard. Coming face to face with Trinity was. Dante tensed when I did, moving closer to me instinctively. I hadn't wanted to be public, but it could have been worse. She came over to us, her eyes softening when she read mine. "No need to be so protective, my Angel," she murmured as she kissed me. Then, to my surprise, she touched Dante on the cheek. "Welcome to Vesta, Dante. I'm Trinity."

"I could say, 'we meet at last'," he smiled, "or something equally dramatic."

"Long time comin', I guess," she said dryly, her lips twitching. "I think we're gonna need a bigger bed!"

I gave an uneasy laugh. I hadn't thought how we were going to handle this. I hadn't wanted to. I guessed I was going to have to, as Trinity slipped her arm through Dante's and drew him away from me.

"Butt out, Angelus," she said, smiling sweetly. "We're gonna pull you to pieces and you don't wanna hear, so..." Dante flashed me a quick, reassuring grin before leaving me standing open-mouthed.

I didn't have much to do except go and get drunk, I decided, because I sure as hell wasn't going to get between them.

"You hidin'?"

I looked up to see Faith on the other side of the bar. I hadn't realised where I was. "Whatever gave you that idea?" I articulated slowly, precisely, because I was halfway paralytic by then.

"I rest my case," she grinned, leaning across the bar towards me. "But you're only making it worse."

"I am?"

Faith lowered her voice. "Ain't none of my business, but you take care, huh? Could be a world o' pain headin' your way."

"Nothin' new, honey," I sighed, smiling weakly. But I understood. Public or private wouldn't matter if things went bad.

"You find your way back okay?" she asked. "If you wanna wait..."

I shook my head. "No, 's fine. I'm okay." I wove my way back without too much difficulty, because this part of town was reasonably safe. Should it prove otherwise, I had my knives. Which, to put it mildly, I almost used when I entered the bedroom we were using and found myself 'attacked'! Darkness, a tangle of limbs, and laughter.

"You're drunk!" Trinity accused as I attempted to fight off her hands.

"Bad habit he seems to be getting into," remarked Dante. "You wanna sober him up, or...?"

"Oh, definitely 'or'," chuckled Trinity, grabbing at my hands as I made a vain attempt to stop them both undressing me.

"I can do that myself," I muttered defensively.

Dante ran his fingers unerringly over my collarbone to brush back my hair. "Sure you can, but this is much more fun."

"Stop squirming!"

How the hell could I? I had Trinity working on my pants and Dante had his lips on my throat. Vanity told me I ought to at least try and fight back, but I still didn't have the two of them right in my head. I hadn't reckoned on this – any of this – and I couldn't see how they'd be comfortable in each other's presence this way. Time to surrender? You bet. For now at least. "I'm all yours," I said, forcing myself to relax, to lose myself in Dante's mouth. If I wanted to touch in return, that wasn't to be permitted, at least not in the short term, and I had the feeling it was going to be a long night, what was left of it.

We awoke in a tangle of limbs, sheets and hair. I had Dante on my left, his head in the crook of my shoulder, hand on my chest, and Trinity on my right, her hand on my groin. Her smile told me she knew exactly what she was doing.

"Do you know a better way to start the day?" she asked, straddling my hips. Dante, having vacated his position at my shoulder, chose to brush my hair from my face and began to kiss me very slowly. At some point I must have fallen asleep, because I remember nothing else for a long time.

Chapter 14

When I opened my eyes I was alone, which surprised me somewhat and alarmed me more than a little. I wondered where Dante was, and with whom.

I showered, dressed and decided to raid the kitchen. I was starving, to tell the truth. I was halfway through my second helping when I heard a crash behind me. Given the language, I was unsurprised to see Dante standing by the kitchen table rubbing his thigh.

"I'll get used to it eventually, I guess," he grimaced, extending a hand to feel his way. When he came into contact with me, he gave a chuckle as his fingers fluttered over my skin. I turned into his embrace, which was probably not a good idea – or was an exceedingly good one, depending on your point of view I suppose! – given the fact that I was wearing only a thin pair of boxers. We were in the middle of a decidedly steamy clinch when we heard a sound – a door opening – and broke apart to see Micah standing in the doorway, his mouth open, eyes as large as saucers.

Shock froze me on the spot. I'd never for one moment thought of Micah being in the place.

"Who is it?" asked Dante, sensing my concern. To my surprise, he turned so that he was standing in front of me, to all intents and purposes protecting me. The irony of the situation didn't escape me.

"Micah..." I began.

He didn't speak, of course, but the shock seemed to fade from his face to be replaced by a faint smile, almost shy. I didn't know what to do, what to say, but was saved from needing to do so by his disappearance through the door.

"Who is Micah?" asked Dante softly. "Oh, the child. What did he...?"

"Enough, I guess," I replied dryly. "I'd better get my pants on before someone else walks in." He released me, catching me by the arm as I began to move carefully past him.

"Give him time, Angel. Don't follow him."

"I wasn't about to," I admitted. I didn't want to make matters worse, if that were possible. While I admit I'm not always one for 'hiding my light', as they say, I didn't want to be accused of corrupting a child.

While my head told me it was barely past breakfast, my eyes and the clock told me it was almost evening and I had an appointment to keep with the Mayor. As I showed up at his door, I was admitted by his secretary and conducted to his office. "How's Dom?" I asked as I took the offered chair.

"A little tired, but so far so good. And your leg? Are you able to drive?"

"No problem," I replied. "So. What do you have for me?"

He smiled. "Have you ever been down to Glenn Creek?"

I frowned and shook my head. "Not that I remember. Bit out of my usual routes." If it was where I thought it was, it was out of almost *everyone's* usual routes! I'd heard of it, though. Some called the men and women who'd gone out there brave, others had called them insane. The Creek was at the edge of the wastes; the last outpost before whatever lay beyond. No one, as far as I knew, had ever been beyond that place, or if they had, had returned to tell the tale.

"I have a favour to ask of you, as a favour has been asked of me. They need supplies and weapons in a hurry." That wasn't all they needed, I discovered. Someone was proposing an expedition 'beyond'. There'd been rumours for years of something out there; some said a fabulous city, some said a mine; Eldorado, perhaps; the Garden of Eden. Who was I to know? They wanted hired guns, an escort into the wilds. An adventurer, as Dan Truman put it. "Interested?"

I was, I had to admit. The prospect of discovering what lay over the next horizon... And it would do to get me out of town for a while, if I needed an excuse. "Sure I am."

"If you want to discuss it with your merry band please do so, and we will talk again."

This time when I inspected my rig it was with a view to checking its suitability for that kind of terrain. It was well armoured, well protected. The old girl looked in good shape.

"You hittin' the road again, Angelus?" asked Rom, wiping his hands on a damp cloth. He'd been working on a motor over on the workbench.

"Think so."

"Guess yer never stays long," he smiled. "Maybe one day you'll find yer place.

When you goin'?"

I shrugged. "Don't know yet. Need to restock. Few days, maybe."

"I'll give the old girl a final check 'fore."

"Thanks. Appreciate it."

I'd have to tell the others, I thought, although I really didn't have much of a clue as to how many that would include. I found Trinity and Faith in the kitchen, which was handy. I didn't know where Dante was, or Micah, but the two women had evidently been talking because they went suddenly silent. "What?" I asked. "WHAT?"

"Nothing," smiled Trinity, glancing up from the pot she'd been stirring. "So, what's cookin'?"

"I'd've thought you'd know better 'n me," I chuckled.

"Ha ha. You been to see the Mayor? Business?"

"Uh-huh."

"You goin' alone this time?"

"Don't know," I shrugged, pulling up a stool. "Where's Dante?"

Trinity grinned. "He wanted to get out of the place, to feel fresh air on his face, he said. Go shopping. I suggested Micah take him to the market." That would have been something to see, I thought. "Don't worry; Micah'll take care of him."

That wasn't the reason for my unease, but confessing the real one wasn't easy.

"Micah... Dante wouldn't—" Faith was looking worried.

"Of course he fucking wouldn't!" I snapped fiercely. "What do you think he is?" I gestured wildly. "Scratch that. I don't much care what you think he is, or what I am!"

"Angelus, I'm sorry. I didn't mean to imply..." Faith shook her head. "I'm grateful for all you've done for us, for Micah and me. So, tell us. Where this time?"

"When they return," I said firmly. "I don't want to have to repeat myself, after all."

Trinity wiped her hands and crossed over to me. "I'm getting worried, though. They've been a long time."

I smiled. "Dante may be blind, but he's not helpless."

"Has he always been blind?" asked Faith.

"Yes... or as long as he can remember, that is. The fever. Guess it had different effects on different people."

"You always claimed... the mine... that scar..." I knew what Trinity was about to say. Confession time, I thought. Painful memories. "It wasn't a fight over a girl, was it?"

I gave a sigh. "No. Of course it wasn't."

"Won't you tell us what really happened?" she asked. Her voice was soft, gentle, so full of sympathy that I knew she suspected already.

"Must I?"

"I think you should. If only to lay the ghosts to rest."

My lips contorted. "Sure it's not morbid curiosity?"

"Angelus!"

I waved my hand in apology. She didn't deserve that. "Sorry."

"I should think so." The voice turned all our eyes to the door in surprise. Dante stood there, his hand on Micah's shoulder. "Because Trinity cannot help that she loves you, too." He gave a soft laugh. "Or should we not speak that word in the company of friends? I'm not ashamed, Angel. Are you?" He didn't give me a chance to reply, bending simply to whisper in Micah's ear. Micah smiled, nodded and took the packages from him. "If you'll not tell, I will... or as much as I can, or they would hear. I was little older than Micah when I met Angelus. He became my friend, my protector. And in the darkness I was his eyes. It did not matter to me, you see, how dark the world was. It had been so for me as long as I could remember. I've never seen the light, but it causes me few difficulties when I'm familiar with a place. Angelus never treated me different, never held my... nature... as a barrier to the friendship he offered. I didn't seduce him, if that's what you're thinking. In the beginning, it was..." He swallowed convulsively and I silently begged him to stop. He didn't have to do this, I thought, feeling my heart wrench. It must have shown on my face, because I saw Trinity shake her head, indicating that I should allow him to continue – that he needed to continue. "It was good to be held in the dark; it drove away the fear. A kiss or two... somewhere along the way it became..." Dante gave a deep sigh. "They came one night. I remember their laughter, and the pain and Angelus's screams. What... what they did to him is his tale to tell, if he will. I sometimes wonder if what I imagined was worse than the reality. When... when it was over, I realised how Angelus had fought, how badly they'd hurt him. It was the first time I'd regretted not being able to see, because I wouldn't suffer anyone else to touch him. Hence the 'interesting' scar." He gave a weak smile. "It took a long time for him to heal. Later—"

"Later, I went after them," I continued, my voice cold.

"What did you do?" asked Faith softly.

"I cut their throats." Finality in my voice brought silence for a while.

"How old were you?"

"By that time? Sixteen, give or take," I replied. "Not long after, I met Trinity, and life got complicated." That was one way to put it, I thought. Unprepared to bare my soul any more, I stood up.

"Angel."

"Mm?" I turned back to face Trinity.

"You've just time to wash up before we eat. Then you can tell us where the hell you're dragging us this time."

Hell, I thought, was not a bad guess.

I made my departure after Dante, Micah and the packages with more than a little relief. Anything was better than continuing the soul-searching.

Dante smiled at me as I closed the door. "Micah is a good guide," he said. "He found everything I needed."

"What was that?"

"Clothing, new strings for my instrument." Did I mention Dante is also a skilled musician? "...A gift for you."

"For me?"

"Your birthday."

"My what?" I'd never been sure when my birthday was. Few of us were, after all. "Oh." Curiosity got the better of me. "Can I have it now?"

"You can have part of it," he responded with a knowing smile. "The rest will have to wait."

I liked the sound of that. "Seems fair."

His hand sought a small package, which he offered to me. A chain, I discovered, heavy, intricately wrought.

"It's beautiful." I let him fasten it about my neck. His fingers lingered on my collarbone and he gave a reluctant laugh.

"If you'll take a rain check..."

"I'll take a kiss for starters," I replied.

His smile was beautiful. "Any time."

Chapter 15

When I told them what I was planning, they listened gravely. I wasn't sure whom I was including in the 'offer', to tell the truth. I'd kind of got used to my little band, my crew.

"That's all I know for the moment," I said. "If you want me to drop you anywhere on the way, Faith, I will. Or you can come along, if you want to know what's over the next horizon. Micah can remain here, with Dom, if you wish. The choice is his – or yours. Trinity," I sighed. "You're always welcome, if you still want me."

Trinity snorted. "I'm not as easy to drop as yer accent."

I blinked. My accent had a habit of changing, depending on where I was and whom I was with. I grinned. "I wasn't sure—"

"Yer never kept Dante a secret, and even I know first love's not easy to forget. You need both of us. Maybe even all of us, 'kay?"

There wasn't much I could say to that so I didn't try. I suspected Trinity, too, had her secrets. Maybe one day she'd tell me what they were. If not... well, that was her business not mine.

Later, Dante played while I sat on the step of my rig and listened. Too many memories, I thought, wondering where my life was taking me. I'd always run from commitment, I suppose, and now I found myself not only with two lovers, but dependants of another kind. Time I grew up, I laughed to myself.

I became aware that I was not alone and I looked up to see Trinity standing before me with a bottle of liquor. "You look as if you need to get drunk," she said.

"I seem to be doing a lot of that lately," I sighed. "I'm pretty screwed, I guess."

She squeezed next to me and laid her head on my shoulder. "No more 'n the rest of us, honey. You've just been sailing along on yer own, 'n' now you've come up sharp. Yer sure yer want me along?"

"Only if yer want to," I said. "It could be hard. No rescuer if we come unglued."

"Well, you'll just have to do what yer always do, won't yer?"

"What's that?"

"Come up smellin' of roses." She ruffled my hair and smiled. "Comin' in?"

"I think I'll sleep out here tonight. If yer don't mind. I need to think."

"Sure, hon. I understand." She gave me a kiss and left me. I was grateful.

My rig had an extended cabin, the back part being where I transported stuff. In the back of the extended cabin were a couple of small bedrooms, the galley and all, the front being two rows of seats where I occasionally slept when it seemed expedient to do so. I'd occasionally had company there, which usually called for inventiveness. I wondered how I was going to manage in what was likely to be a curious domestic arrangement for all of us.

Settling in the small room I regarded as my sanctuary, I took a drink. It tasted good.

"I think you've drunk enough." I felt the flask being taken from my fingers and did not resist. Dante settled his weight onto the edge of the bed and felt for the table beside it, on which he placed the flask. "Trinity sent me," he offered into my silence, turning his head my way. "She thought we needed time together. Was she wrong?" I didn't reply. Nor did I move as his fingers sought and located me. "Are you angry?"

"No."

"But you wanted to be alone."

"Yes."

"Do you want me to leave?" I didn't. Not really. I reached for his hand, raised it to my lips and, with a sigh, closed my eyes. He didn't move. "If I caused you hurt, it was not my wish other than to heal. I'm talking too much. When I'm nervous, I talk."

I laughed softly. "I know. I remember that you talked and talked..."

"And the only way you could stop me was to kiss me." We laughed together. As I sat up, Dante stopped talking. He had his head tilted slightly to one side, as he does when he's curious. I reached out to kill the light, plunging us into absolute darkness. "Angel." I felt my way up his arm, running my fingers over his face, his mouth, as he sometimes did with mine. He knew I hated darkness, often had some glimmer of light somewhere, and I felt him sigh. "What do you want of me?"

"Nothing," I replied. "Everything. How the hell do I know?" I set about undressing him slowly. Slowly, because I was enjoying it, and so, I hoped, was

Damnation Day

he, and also because, of course, I couldn't see a thing. I wasn't thinking sex any more than I believed Trinity had been when she'd 'arranged' this. I simply wanted to hold him – or be held by him, I didn't mind which – because it would lay to rest the memories that had been unearthed of things neither of us had said. I stroked his hair, ran my fingers over his face, his mouth, the body I'd known so well and I guess still did, and we held onto each other until morning came. Waking up with my head on Dante's chest and listening to his breathing was good. I could feel the steady beating of his heart beneath my hand. A few moments of peace in my crazy world, I thought, giving a sigh. I ought to move, I knew. I needed to make arrangements for our little expedition. I needed to do any number of things. But none of them were appealing at that moment. I was happy to let the world go on as it would, and to step aside for just a few moments.

"You okay?" asked Dante softly, stroking my hair lightly.

"Yeah."

"No more demons?"

"Not right now," I admitted, pressing my lips to his chest. "Are you hungry?"

"You makin' breakfast?"

"I might."

"That'll be a novelty."

"I'll have you know I'm a good cook!" I laughed, digging him in the ribs.

We wrestled a little, but nothing serious. We were in something of a tangle when the door opened to reveal Trinity carrying a tray. We must have looked a sight because she cracked up laughing.

"You should see yourselves," she giggled. I grimaced. Dante's hair was stuck out all over the place, but mine was tangled, wild, over my face. "We have visitors."

"Oh. Do we want them?"

"Probably. It's the Mayor."

"Oh fuck!" I struggled to untangle myself from Dante and the sheets to find something decent to wear. I didn't have the time to do much other than make myself tidy, because you don't keep someone like the Mayor waiting, even if you might, loosely, call him a friend.

"Good morning, Mr Mayor," I said politely as he rose to shake my hand. "How can I help you?"

"Just thought I'd drop in with the stuff you wanted. I have a meeting down the way." He shrugged. "I don't suppose there's a chance of coffee, is there? Right now I'd kill for one."

70

"Sure thing," grinned Trinity. "Wouldn't want you to commit no crime, Mr Mayor."

"You know, this is quite a guy, my dear."

"He's got a big 'nough head already, sir."

"Maybe he's gotta right."

Trinity glanced my way. "Maybe he does at that."

"Good coffee. Best be on my way, I guess. Good luck. I'd kind of like to know how it turns out, you know? The world would be a duller place without you."

I took his hand again before he followed his escort out. Time to hit the road, I guessed. To seek out new pastures. "Let's get the show on the road," I said.

To tell the truth, I wasn't absolutely sure how well my leg would stand up to the inactivity that came with long-distance driving. Or rather, when I got out of the driving seat, whether it would hold me up! Okay, much of it was undoubtedly psychological, being born of an acute dislike of weakness in myself. I'd been lucky, you see. Apart from a couple of occasions in my life, I'd never really been hurt. Well, three if you count the fever. I didn't count fistfights or the occasional knife wound. They only counted as minor inconveniences.

Chapter 16

We were stocked to the gills with fuel, supplies, weapons, everything it and the trailer now attached at the rear could hold. There was a small depot halfway where, with luck, we could supplement our stocks, but after that... well, no one knew. Trinity kept me supplied with coffee while I drove, and often as not the entire crew occupied the front with me, except when I drove at night; then it was usually either Trinity or Dante or occasionally both.

The landscape was bleak and burned, with less and less vegetation the farther south we travelled. Just north of the supply station we were forced to 'dig in' because of a sudden storm, and I was just settling down for a – hopeful – night's sleep when I was surprised to be landed on by Micah scrambling over the seat. I gave a sharp exhalation of breath and, I admit, swore vehemently, because he came down on my belly with a fair proportion of his weight. We lay there, almost eye to eye for what seemed like a long time before he scrambled off me and I struggled to sit up.

"Micah? Is something wrong?" I asked. With only the system lights to see him by, I was struggling. When I reached out to bring up a light, he reached out to stop me. I was surprised, because Micah, although he often hovered around me, rarely if ever touched. "Is it the storm?" I asked. "Are you afraid?" I saw his response as a crack of thunder seemed to shake us. Yes, he was afraid. I smiled. "It's okay, Micah. It can't harm us. We're safe in here." I wondered why he hadn't gone to Faith as he usually did. Perhaps he was growing up, I thought, and didn't want to look childish in front of her. "Try and get some sleep, huh?" I smiled encouragingly at him. He settled down with difficulty, shuffling until he was comfortable. I felt him shiver with each crash of thunder, because his head rested next to my thigh.

I was surprised to be shaken awake by Faith bearing a fiendishly strong mug of coffee. If she was surprised to see my companion, she gave no sign.

"The storm's eased," she whispered. "Trinity says there're no external signs of damage. Everything's secure."

"Thanks."

With great care, I freed myself from Micah's grip – his fist was gripping my top – and wriggled my way through into the back. "How old is Micah?" I asked as Faith joined me.

"I'd guess around fourteen or so," she replied. "Why?"

"Oh, just curious."

"Something familiar?" she suggested with a smile.

I shrugged. "Maybe; only at his age, it wasn't storms I feared."

Faith's features became reflective. "I guess not. Sometimes we express our fears in strange ways, though. I know he looks up to you."

"Me?"

She laughed. "Why should that seem strange? He could have a worse role model."

"He could have a better one," I replied wryly.

She gave me a strange look. "Why so? Haven't young boys always had adventurers as heroes?" She grinned. "You rescued him, after all."

I winced. "I don't want to be anyone's hero, Faith."

"Too bad," she shrugged. "I don't know what you dreamed when you were captive... of how you might escape. Perhaps you dreamed you would be rescued. Perhaps you had no illusions."

In the silence of the pause she left, I reflected. "No, I had no illusions. My worst imaginings came true, you see." Images flashed, unwilled, into my mind. Things I'd been glad that Dante hadn't been able to see. It must have shown on my face, because I felt Faith's hand touch mine. I tried not to flinch away, given what was in my mind.

"He wasn't captive long enough for that to happen, and I thank God, if God exists, for that mercy. He's at the age where hormones are kicking in. Don't... don't be surprised if you catch him spying." Her cheeks were flushed, and I was trying not to laugh. It wouldn't help, I knew, particularly if she didn't know he already had!

"I get the idea," I said as casually as I could, particularly as Dante had just appeared behind her with Trinity at his shoulder.

"You want me to drive awhile?" asked Trinity when I smiled and blew a kiss in her direction.

"You might have to shuffle Micah over first," I said, receiving a funny look from her. "He fell asleep."

"Okay." She didn't ask any questions, for which I was grateful.

Dante joined me at the table carefully and we chatted for a while as Trinity drove. Faith joined her up front some time later – I assumed that Micah remained with them; he certainly didn't come back past us – and I was grateful for that because I had a crick in my neck that Dante was more than willing to take care of for me.

I was just servicing my weaponry when Trinity's voice called me up front. "Strange glow on the horizon," she said as my head appeared through the door.

"Keep driving, but keep your eyes open. Make sure all the scanners are on," I said, going back for my crossbow. I don't know why I picked that as opposed to a gun, but I did.

Dante picked up my quiver and followed behind, a hand on my arm for support or perhaps reassurance. I wasn't looking at Dante; I was looking out of the window. Fire, I thought, it had to be fire.

"Tool-up time, folks," I said, "Trin, you want me to take over?"

"No, I'm okay," she replied. I accepted her word. If necessary, I could soon replace her if I needed to.

"Anyone comes at you, run 'em down." Her grin of response was savage.

I had a bad feeling in my gut as we closed on the station, or rather what remained of it. It had been a dawn attack, I suspected, although I did wonder whether the fire had been deliberate or accidental. If deliberate, it had probably been to hide what had been done. I didn't think they'd linger. It turned out I was wrong. I should have restrained my curiosity, I thought, as I calculated whether I could make it back to the rig, because I had Dante with me and the terrain was rough. If it had been smooth I'd have had no worries, but I couldn't steer Dante at speed over rough ground. I shouldn't have gone to check for survivors, I told myself. But if there'd been any chance, I'd have probably taken it, as I had with Faith and Micah. Call me a romantic, if you wish. Or a fool.

I knew Trinity would be armed by now, and possibly Faith. I had my new crossbow, and Dante had my old one over his shoulder. He could use it if he had to. Whether he could hit anything with it I wasn't sure. But then, they couldn't know either. If anything made a noise, Dante could probably hit it. I could feel him pressed against me, using me as a locator.

"Four machines," I said. "Count two on each. Damn, I wish I'd brought a gun!"

"And I wish I could see the whites of their eyes," muttered Dante. "Seems like we're both out of luck."

I gave a soft laugh and squeezed his hand. "Give me room, they're stopping."

I felt him move away and felt strangely bereft. Then the adrenalin kicked in. I raised my bow to my shoulder and waited. If I wanted a killing shot, I'd have to gauge it just right. I didn't know what this weapon could do to a human, but I knew that the crossbow had once been regarded as one of the deadliest of weapons, and although I'd never used one on a man before, the prospect didn't trouble me. I hoped Trinity and Faith would remain inside. If they thought we were alone they might take more risks. I'd have back-up then.

"Well, what we got 'ere?" came a voice in the stillness. One of the men dismounted and removed his helmet. "If yer after spoils, yer too late." I didn't reply. I watched. Waited. "Yer outnumbered, fella. Lower yer weapon."

"Not a chance."

I heard the sound of a weapon being readied. "I don't like ter repeat myself."

"Neither do I," I admitted. "Be ready to drop or run." The latter was for Dante's ears. I saw Dante's head turn and the crossbow come up. Like mine, it was loaded. Unlike mine, it had a single bolt. I didn't wait, simply readied my body and fired. "Drop!" I screamed as I let fly. I heard Dante's weapon release and him drop, and the sound of firing from the rig. In the silence that followed, I drew myself to my feet and pulled Dante to his. Without turning my back on the carnage, I raised my hand in salute to Trinity. Reloading, I held my weapon ready as I walked forward. I didn't know what it would do if fired so close. I hadn't been sure what it would do at a distance. I was, however, grateful for Dante grabbing at and restraining Trinity as she ran to follow, because it wasn't a pretty sight. I'd have vomited if I'd been alone. Having company kept my stomach's contents in – don't want to ruin my image, do I? One of my shots had hit the shoulder, but the other had made his head. It was a sight that would haunt my sleep for a while, I thought, as I kicked through the remains, searching, none too gently, for signs of life. One of them was moaning, but he wouldn't live long even without my intervention. I knelt, took the knife from my boot and cut his throat – something I hoped no one could see. I didn't regret it; he'd have done the same to me. Or maybe he wouldn't. Maybe the fact that I didn't leave him for the hot sun was all that made us different. I didn't care. The vultures would deal with their remains.

"Salvage anything of use," I said to Trinity. "Dante, help her." Dante gave me a look of concern, but obeyed without question. I didn't expect much: a few weapons maybe. It was a diversionary tactic to keep her away from the man I'd mangled and whom I was searching. I had no compunction about taking what they in turn had taken; it wouldn't do them any good, and there were no survivors. It may seem callous to profit in such a way, but it wasn't the first time and it probably wouldn't be the last. Besides, I wanted my bolts back and it wasn't going to be a pretty sight. I came very close to spilling my guts then. The sight wasn't one I'd care to repeat, although, given time, it wasn't impossible that I would.

I didn't speak as we made our way back to the rig, or even after for some time. I needed to wash myself. Repeatedly. I ignored their concerned glances and locked myself in the bathroom until I felt fit to leave. Then I went and poured myself a very stiff drink.

Chapter 17

Trinity took it on herself to drive, and I was glad of it. Only when we were well away from the area did she stop.

"He's lying on his bed," I heard Dante say through the partially open door. "He'll join us when he's ready."

"He had no choice," she said.

"He knows that. He's only ever shot animals with one before, as far as I know. On a human it has quite an effect."

"How do you know?"

I heard Dante chuckle. "I have a vivid imagination. Brains all over the place, most likely. I could hear his guts churning."

Charming, I thought!

"Never thought of Angel as squeamish." Trinity's voice was part anxious, part amused. "Must've been a mess. Should we take his mind off it?"

I was tempted to let them know I was listening, but suspected at least one of them already knew.

"No. Let's give him time. If he wants us, he knows where we are."

"Should I drive on?"

Dante didn't respond for a few moments. "Find somewhere to make camp – set up a secure perimeter. How's that sound?"

Trinity laughed. "Efficient."

Dante would be smiling, I thought. I heard a rustle and almost opened my eyes. Stillness. He would be looking towards the bed, sensing whether I was asleep or awake. Perhaps he knew I wasn't and chose to pretend that he thought I was. Then I heard the sound of music as Dante began to play. He didn't sing, but the simple act of playing soothed me into genuine sleep.

When I awoke, I made my way into the small kitchen/seating area, where I found Dante's guitar discarded but close to hand. Faith and Trinity were laughing together by the work surface; Micah was sitting at the table next to Dante. They stopped talking as they became aware of my presence. Well, I should say Dante stopped talking. I was puzzled at what seemed to be a one-sided conversation until I realised that Micah's hand was on Dante's. Instinctively, Dante understood my puzzlement and smiled his bewitching smile.

"Micah can talk, Angel."

"And what has Micah to say?" I asked, sitting down on Dante's other side.

"He was asking me if I could teach him to play," he replied.

That, I thought, would be interesting to watch. It might not, however, be interesting to hear, and Dante must have felt my silent laughter because he dug me none too gently in the ribs. I remembered listening to him trying to learn, and he knew why I was laughing. He'd been terrible!

"I said I might try, if I could find earplugs for everyone else." His lips twitched as he smiled at Micah.

Micah's expression was strange. I wondered if he was angry with me for interrupting a private conversation, but I wasn't sure. He hesitated for a moment then slipped out of his seat to join Trinity and Faith, occasionally glancing over his shoulder. I interlaced my fingers with Dante's below the table, grimacing as my stomach rumbled loudly. Dante laughed and placed his free hand on my belly as if to silence it. I wanted to kiss him so badly it hurt, and I was surprised at the intensity of that desire. Perhaps if Trinity had been close it would have been the same with her. It was probably adrenalin or something. I was grateful at least for the fact that I was wearing more than I had been when Micah had inadvertently caught us. I wasn't going to give in to my impulse, I decided. I was going to store it away until we were behind closed – and probably locked! – doors. I had a feeling Dante understood my mind, as he often seemed to, because I felt his fingers shake. I was, I'll admit, rather pleased about that, but the mood was broken by an announcement of food. It was probably just as well.

Somehow, we managed to keep the mood light. I'm not sure how. I was even able to push the images from my mind for a while. I wasn't expecting trouble, but I checked the perimeter anyway.

When I returned, Micah had retired and Faith followed shortly after. Trinity snuggled up to me and slipped her arms around me from behind, whispering, "Come to bed," in my ear. I wasn't sure about that. Closing my eyes, unless I was exhausted, didn't appeal for some reason. I wonder why!

I saw Dante grin and wondered whether they'd been cooking something up between them. But bed wasn't a bad idea. Better than a public place, I guess. Raising my hands in surrender, I wriggled free and headed for the bedroom. There isn't a lot of room, to put it simply. Even when you're the only one there, it's sore shin time. Having both of them in there with me made it interesting.

I was struggling with my boots, mostly because they're not easy to get off, partly because Trinity was trying to separate me from my clothes. I was trying not to laugh, trying not to make too much noise, and not doing too well at either. I swear they were trying to drive me insane, or wear me out. I'd settle for being worn out, I decided.

I awoke suddenly, fighting a scream. Hands restrained me, soft voices reassured me, but it took some time for the memories to go away.

I wasn't sure, in truth, why the sight had affected me so. After all, he hadn't been the first man I'd killed. He'd been the first I'd killed so messily, perhaps.

As I lay in the darkness pretending to sleep, listening to the breathing of my companions, I began to wonder at the changes in my circumstances. Perhaps it had been that which had caused the response. After all, I was used to having only myself to answer to, having no witnesses, perhaps, to things I might do. Was it simply that I didn't like having to justify myself *to* myself or to my lovers? I wasn't used to such responsibility, such complications, I reasoned, as I felt limbs stir, hands reaching out to hold, to caress in sleep. Neither, I supposed, were they. It had been a long time since I'd been in either of their lives for any length of time. I'd changed, and so had they. We were in a learning curve, I thought, amused at my sudden burst of intellect, although I wasn't absolutely sure what it meant.

"I can hear your mind working," said Dante sleepily, turning to face me.

"Go back to sleep."

"I can't. You're thinking too loud."

I chuckled at his complaint. I felt his fingers seek out my face, his thumb run along my mouth followed by his kiss. His mouth was soft with sleep, and I didn't suppress the moan that rose unbidden as I drew him closer.

"Leave some for me." Trinity's voice at my ear almost caused me to jump, and I'd have probably responded had I been able to at the time. I was a little distracted.

I was grateful when morning came and I could find an excuse to drive. Not that my resolve didn't almost weaken as I paused to look back at the bed, but driving fast and hard was an acceptable outlet for my frustrations given the treacherous terrain.

These were known as the Burning Sands for many reasons, primarily because there was barely a scrap of vegetation for miles, and what little grew there was prone to spontaneous combustion. Then there were the sandstorms, dust devils, magnetic storms, the cracks in the ground that took some negotiating or traversing.

I wondered why anyone of sound mind would want to settle in this godforsaken land. But someone evidently had. As we came in sight of the perimeter fence, that much was more than evident. According to my systems, the area positively prickled with electronics. Unusual, because the mag-storms played hell with most systems. If theirs were fully functional, I'd be interested to know how; more than interested, in fact.

"Glenn Creek, this is Angelus, out of Vesta. Over."

It was some moments before I heard a voice respond, "This is Glenn Creek. What brings you out here? Over."

"I am the Messenger. Dan Truman asked me to call in if I was passing." That gave them pause, I thought. No one *ever* passed Glenn Creek. I heard a chuckle.

"Then pass this way, Angelus."

The gates opened for us and I drove through. They closed straight after, I noted, and saw the system come immediately on line. There must be something dodgy in these parts, I thought, hoping it wasn't wolves. I'd had my fill of wolves. I drove down the long road with a crowded cab, all eyes on the growing evidence of civilisation.

Only when I came to a halt did a door open and a man emerge. He was small, white-haired and wearing a lab coat that had once been white. "Angelus. I've heard your name on the airwaves." He offered his hand. "Jon Fevre. Welcome to Glenn Creek."

I accepted his hand and smiled. "Thanks... I think. We'll unload, if that's okay. I'd rather get it indoors—"

"We?"

"My crew."

"I'd heard you travel alone."

"Not this time. They wouldn't let me," I chuckled, turning to offer my hand to Trinity. "This is Trinity, Faith, Micah. Micah doesn't talk. And last but not least, Dante." I didn't need to explain Dante's problem, which was self-evident as he sought my hand and jumped down carefully. "C'mon, you guys. Let's get unloaded before we get hit."

"We have a window of about an hour," said Jon Fevre. "It's a Force 5 from the south, so we'll see it coming."

"Good enough," I replied. "Where do you want it?"

"Anywhere inside the tunnel will do. We'll concentrate on that bit first. I'll round up my people and we'll set up a relay."

I nodded and went to unhitch the trailer so that we could open the rear of the rig. I made sure Dante was included, because I didn't want to discriminate – he'd have been pissed off with me if I had! – and I didn't think there was anything that could be damaged if it were accidentally dropped. Anything marked 'Fragile' I handled myself.

It didn't take us long to unload, given the bodies that suddenly seemed to come out of the woodwork. I left them to put the stuff where they wanted it, because I'd a feeling there were things going on that they didn't want us to see – at least not yet – and I didn't really want to know. Given the rumours about the place, I didn't really want to find out if any of them were true. There'd been all kinds of rumours over the years, mostly along the lines of 'forbidden experiments' and 'genetic engineering' – Frankenstein stuff. I had to admit that given some of the weird and wonderful – well, perhaps not wonderful – genetic cock-ups after Damnation Day, anything was possible. Certainly, Jon Fevre didn't *look* the mad scientist type, but hey, perhaps he changed when there was a full moon.

"We have a few spare rooms," he told me, running his fingers through his wild hair. "If you have any particular preferences..."

I wasn't sure what, if anything, to say. After all, I didn't know the man, any of his people, or any beliefs they may have. "Just show us where you want us, we'll sort ourselves. We don't want to keep you from anything you need to do."

He seemed to hesitate, torn between expediency and politeness. "Well, I do have something cooking, so to speak. If you don't mind moving your rig under shelter before the storm hits – don't want any damage after all. We'll talk later about the other business. I'll introduce you properly to my people. I couldn't help but notice the instrument in your rig. Who's the musician?"

"Dante," I admitted with a smile. A look came over his face that told me they were starved for outside entertainment. "Perhaps I can persuade him to play."

"That would be wonderful!" he exclaimed, clapping his hands. "If you don't mind." He looked almost embarrassed and I couldn't help but chuckle.

"I'm sure I can persuade him," I said lightly. Dante told me he would enjoy being persuaded. Later.

Chapter 18

Sitting listening to Dante play brought back memories, although they were elusive. Something I couldn't quite put my finger on. I was struggling, and must have had a strange expression on my face, because Trinity took hold of my hand.

"Don't fight so; it'll come," she said intuitively. I grimaced. "Hey, we understand."

"You do?" I was confused.

Trinity chuckled and stroked back my hair. "We've all got memories, honey. Things we don't wanna remember, but won't quite go away."

I bent my head to touch hers. "Be patient with me. I'm tryin'."

Trinity chuckled. "Course you are. Bloody trying, ha ha."

"Ha ha," I echoed. "Guess we all have things to get used to. I've been meanin' to ask..." I hesitated.

Trinity's eyes softened. Given our position in the room, we were unlikely to be overheard, particularly given the fact that most people were intently listening to Dante.

"Dante?"

I nodded wordlessly. It had been something of a fait accompli, after all. "I've always known there was part o' yer heart that was still his. No matter what yer said. I remember yer tellin' me once, when you was drunk."

"What did I tell you?" I asked softly, unsure I wanted to know.

"How hard it had been." A bittersweet smile touched her lips. "But hey, I was just a whore, right? Back then. Before..." Before. Before I'd fallen in love for the second time in my life. I sure could pick 'em, I thought; or they could. "I've seen a lot o' stuff, Angel, in my professional capacity." Her lips twitched and I touched her cheek affectionately. "Not my first threesome, shall we say? You never treated me no less cos o' what I was. I always liked you for that. Dante is gentle, kind and he loves you. Can't say I blame him for that." She pulled my head to hers and kissed me. Dante finished playing and I took him a drink.

"You okay?" I asked softly.

"I guess. This place smells strange."

"Strange how?"

"Chemical."

"I think they do research here."

"Oh. Yeah, that would do it. You don't happen to know where the—"

"Sure I do. Come on." I gestured to Trinity where we were going and she grinned. When we returned, we'd only just sat down when Jon Fevre came over to us.

"Thank you. That was more than we hoped for. You have an extraordinary voice, Dante."

Dante smiled. "I have what I was born with," he said, "but an artist always likes to be praised. Would it be discourteous to bid you goodnight? Angel?" Earlier in the evening, I'd promised Jon Fevre a few words, but I doubted it was urgent.

"We'll talk in the morning. I'm sure you're all tired after your long journey. Sleep well."

As we made our way out of there, I wondered where Faith and Micah were. I was puzzled that we hadn't seen them since we'd unloaded, but perhaps they'd fallen asleep. I figured we all needed a good sleep, which might even be possible, because no matter how bad the storm outside, little sound of it penetrated within. Mag-storms made me restless, memories of winds howling around the mines, perhaps. Or memories of other things... screams in the night …

Chapter 19

can't say I was really surprised to see Faith sitting in Jon Fevre's office when I arrived. She did, however, have the grace to look embarrassed as I turned from closing the door to take the vacant seat.

"Coffee?" Fevre asked, grinning, "now that we have some again."

"Thanks," I answered, nodding appreciation as Faith placed a large mug by my hand.

"May I?" she asked him.

"If you wish, my dear." He sat back in his well-worn chair, fingers steepled.

Faith perched herself on his desk, facing me. "I'm sorry I didn't confide in you, Angelus. I should have. But a secret once started..." She gave a sigh and a rueful smile. "Micah is what I told you he was – a fellow captive. I'm here for a purpose. I was trying to reach this place when I was taken..." She paused, looking down at her hands. "My father was – is – leader of the expedition whose tracks you intend to follow. My husband is with him. They had been missing for some time when … you cannot know how grateful I was to find you heading in the direction I wished to go. Forgive me for not trusting you, but if you'd been a profiteer..."

"Oh, I am, my dear, "I replied, "but sometimes I remember what honour is." My words came out more acidic than I'd intended. There'd been no reason she should have trusted me in the beginning. I could've been as bad as those who'd taken her. But later... I was surprised that it hurt.

She must have read it on my face because she asked, "How many times must I apologise?"

I didn't respond, simply turned my eyes to Jon Fevre. "Tell me what you know. If I'm to risk my life and that of my friends, I need all the information you have."

Jon Fevre slipped a map across the table towards me. "This is what we know," he said.

A lot of it was blank. "And?"

He grinned. "This is what we *suspect*."

The second map had me intrigued. Beyond the 'forbidden zone', the 'hot zone' was something I assumed to be a mountain – either that or a building of massive proportions. I sat back. "Are the natives friendly?"

His smile didn't slip. "Well now," he said, "that brings us to the reason you're here, doesn't it?"

I nodded thoughtfully. "When are we leaving? I'd kinda like to give my rig the once over."

"No problem. We need a clear window, and there's a front passing. Lookin' at day after next."

"Sounds good," I admitted, elaborating, "itchy feet."

"Ah... and a remarkable lack of curiosity, if I may say so."

I raised a brow. He was referring, I assumed, to my lack of interest in what they actually did there. "None of my business. If I wanted to know, I'd find out." I didn't care what they did, unless it affected me. My view might change, of course, depending on what happened. "I'll go see to my rig. Don't lock me out."

"Wouldn't think of it," he replied. He might not, I thought, but someone else just might.

When I didn't return after some time, I'm told, Dante began to grow restless. He persuaded Trinity to go out with him, only to change his mind when he felt the air outside, the sand in it. Dante, of course, was unconcerned about the storm because he had no need to see his way. He could completely cover his head and feel his way to where the rig was because his sense of touch was acute. I was found, he told me later, half under my rig. I had, I discovered when I awoke with a massive headache, a large bump on my head – and an enemy in the camp.

Dante had dragged me back – he's stronger than he looks – at least to the entrance to the tunnel, where Trinity waited with Micah. They dragged me back to the room, treated my wounds, bathed me and waited for me to come round.

"There seems to be a serpent in the Garden of Eden," observed Dante as he sensed me waking.

I swore vehemently and heard a chuckle of sympathy. "Somebody thought it fun to loosen the pipes," I said. "Bang, no brakes." I winced and probed my head as I started to rise. "This is getting to be fuckin' habit!"

"Never mind, we'll kiss it better," assured Trinity, laughing.

I grimaced. "Don't I get any sympathy?" I saw Trinity look towards Dante, which struck me as strange, but perhaps they didn't need to exchange glances in the accepted sense of the word.

"What kind of sympathy do you have in mind?" enquired Dante, his voice making my belly tighten in response. He gave a throaty chuckle. "Methinks someone is feeling horny."

"Nothing new there," retorted Trinity, pulling at my hair.

"Hey!" In revenge, I made a grab for hers.

"Help!" she giggled, which prompted Dante to leap onto the bed and join in the fun. I was muttering darkly and being tickled to death when I realised that there was someone else on the bed with us. Among a tangle of limbs, I discovered Micah, grinning like I'd never seen him do before. Out of pure mischief, and mock outrage, I pelted him with a pillow. Mayhem ensued. I wouldn't have thought we could have so much fun with such limited resources, but we all ended up in a heap in the middle, laughing hysterically.

"Can anyone join in?" asked Jon Fevre, amused, from the doorway. "It was open." Micah, I assumed. I saw Faith at Jon Fevre's shoulder and rolled my eyes. We must, I thought, have looked a sight! "I was most alarmed to hear... was it…?" He hesitated.

"Deliberate? Yeah. Very." I replied, tucking my hair behind my ears. We were somewhat dishevelled, and, I admit, not wearing very much. I wondered if we would be providing a bit of juicy gossip in this out-of-the-way place. It wouldn't be the first time and probably not the last.

"Did you see...?"

"No, unfortunately not."

He sighed. "We'll leave you then. To tender mercies." He grinned and closed the door, pushing Faith before him. I was, I admit, a little surprised Micah didn't follow Faith. I didn't realise I was bleeding until Micah reached out to touch my head and it came away red.

I saw his face change and hastily reassured him. "It's okay, kid. No worries." He wasn't convinced, I thought, as I saw him look at his fingers and shake his head. "It's okay. Honest." He raised his eyes to mine and gave a shy smile.

"Come on; let him rest," interjected Dante, drawing Micah's eyes to him. "We all need to rest if we're going to be in any state to get out of here any time soon. Would you find Faith and make sure she's ready?" Micah nodded and then added his strange sort of sign language onto Dante's hand. Dante had a strange look on his face as Micah departed, but he did not speak until the door had closed behind him.

"Go gently with that kid, my Angel. He thinks himself in love with you."

"What?"

He laughed softly. "You're surprised? You shouldn't be. One does not need eyes to see."

Trinity grew thoughtful. "He's right, you know. He does like to be close to you. And you're the only one he really touches."

"That doesn't mean..." I began, but fell silent. "He's too young to be thinking of those things," I offered lamely.

Dante snorted. "We weren't much older than he is, dear heart."

I was surprised by the term of endearment. It wasn't one he'd used for a long time, and never in my memory in company. "That was different."

"How so?" asked Dante quietly. "You rescued him, remember? Hero worship's a strange thing. Gratitude. I remember how that felt. To be afraid and suddenly not afraid any more." He smiled faintly and turned his head to where Trinity sat. "I remember the voices, the sounds of fighting, the smell of blood. I learned to use a blade only because Angelus taught me. And to use my hands and feet. I learned not to be ashamed of what I was, what I felt. And I learned about love, about friendship. Age had nothing to do with it."

"I'm not about to—" I began in something close to anger.

"No one said you were, but pride is a terrible thing. If you discourage him, do it gently."

"If?" I asked. "IF?"

Trinity sighed. "When, if it sounds better." Trinity slipped from the bed and went to pour us drinks. I needed a drink badly, I admitted. It had shaken me. I couldn't believe I'd missed signs that must surely have been obvious if Dante had caught them, and Trinity. Perhaps I simply didn't want to see. "He's unsure, that's all. He's at that age, after all. He admires you and thinks it's love. He'll no doubt grow out of it. It's a crush." She grinned. "I guess I know how he feels, too."

"Huh?"

"When I first met you I figured you for a good time. That maybe you'd be a little rough, but not as bad as some. You wouldn't beat on me, you know? You had a reputation for danger," she chuckled. "Exciting, yeah? Tall, blond... and those eyes of yours..." She had me laughing with her. "A face like an angel and a body made for sin, that's what one of my friends said." I was sure I was blushing. "When yer walked into a room, folks moved out o' the way. I made sure all yer wanted was me. I wasn't 'bout to share yer."

"So all yer wanted was my body?" I asked, pulling her towards me.

"Sure." Her hair tickled as she bent to run a finger over the scar across my ribs. "Better 'n most who came through. Least you was gentle." I waited for her to continue, stroking her hair.

"You never told me how you came to be—"

"A whore?" she offered softly against my chest. "I did once. Maybe you was drunk at the time."

"Tell me again. Please?" A time for confessions, perhaps, before... who knew what.

She lay with her head on my chest, absently running her fingers over my skin. "Old story. Raped by Mom's boyfriend, kicked out pregnant. Lost baby. How else was I to survive back then?" I felt the wet on my skin. Tears. "Who cares 'bout a whore? Beat 'em; they don't have feelings, right? Do what you want to 'em, make 'em do anything to you."

I held her while she wept, and when she stilled, I whispered Dante's name. He joined us on the bed, settling himself so that she lay between us: warm, safe, protected. I was surprised, a little, when he pressed his lips to her shoulder and linked his fingers with mine over her body. I couldn't remember ever seeing him kiss a woman before, even in such a non-sexual fashion, and I was touched – and comforted. A confirmation, I supposed, of the bond existing between the three of us. I had a family, I thought, whether I wanted one or not. Strangely enough, I discovered that I did want one. Whether it would last or not, I don't know. Who does? But I knew I ought to treasure it while it lasted.

Chapter 20

While we made ready to depart, I sat watching Jon Fevre's people as they milled about before deciding it might be a good time for a little target practice. Not only for me, I decided, admitting that Trinity and Dante could use a little as well. Dante, I discovered, was extremely proficient with a knife, although we kept the use of actual blades to a minimum – I'd enough injuries as it was, he said. With my spare bow he wasn't half bad either, if he had something audible to aim at. We took to tossing objects for him to aim at, and his proficiency shocked me – and one or two of those who were surreptitiously watching, I guessed. Trinity was the first to admit she was much better with a gun. She didn't like my crossbow, she said, using the excuse that her boobs got in the way, which had Dante grinning mischievously and suggesting she try strapping herself down like he'd heard of women doing to disguise themselves once long ago to live in the world as men. Trinity had laughed and stood on his foot. Watching them chase each other round was funny – and unnerving given Dante's visual impairment.

When I decided to get in a little practice myself, I found myself trying to take aim with Dante at my back, his delicate fingers stroking the back of my neck, his voice whispering in my ear. Trinity sat watching us. Out of the corner of my eye while Dante tried to distract me, I could see her laughing. He was very good at it, I had to admit, but I was very good at resisting. Dante stroked my arm, blew on my ear, every trick he could decently try in public, although how decent some people would regard it I neither knew nor really cared.

We would be setting off tomorrow, we were told, and it was suggested we have an early night. I wasn't sure, even still, whether Micah ought to accompany us, but Faith didn't want to leave him – and I wasn't, in truth, entirely sure if my unwillingness to have him along was because of the possibility of danger or something else.

Trinity had left the bed to take a shower, and I lay with Dante simply being.

"I think you need a trim," he said after a while, pulling a strand of my hair through his fingers.

"If you think I'm letting you near it with a pair of scissors," I grinned.

Dante laughed softly. "I'll ask Trinity, if you're going to be like that about it." He was pretending to be hurt, and I was pretending to placate him. Any excuse for a kiss, I thought, a caress or two. I'd had a long meeting with Jon Fevre, and I was itching to be under way. I wouldn't sleep, no matter how much either of them tried to tire me out, so it was as good a way as any to pass the time. Trinity came out of the bathroom wrapped in a sheet and stood for a moment or two simply looking as us. "Angel thinks he needs a trim," said Dante, stretching. "What do you think?"

"I'm trying to imagine him with short hair," she admitted, her head cocked to one side.

"I'm not going that far!"

"Don't think I've ever seen you with it shorter than the bottom of your shoulder blade," she smiled. "Might be kinda cool."

"I'd feel naked."

"Honey," she responded dryly, "you are." Well, that was true enough. I rolled my eyes in response. "You look good together, you know?"

"Tell me," whispered Dante, and my breath seemed to catch. "Tell me what you see."

Trinity's eyes met mine, and I saw hers bright with tears. She had, she was thinking, what Dante never had, and unless there was a miracle he never would see my face. "His head is close to yours; he's looking at you. His eyes are pale, the left one is blue, the right one green, his hair is long, straight, almost white—"

"And is he beautiful?" asked Dante softly.

Trinity smiled. "As beautiful as your imaginings, I dare say," she admitted.

"And you?"

"Me?" she asked, startled.

"She's lovely, Dante. Her hair's red, her eyes are green, and she has the most beautiful smile, and an equally beautiful heart," I held her gaze and smiled. "You..." I didn't continue, but reached out to touch his face.

"Turn his insides to mush when you sing," chuckled Trinity. "I never figured our Angel was romantic like, though he once told me you had the voice of an angel. No lie. Now, likes it or not, we need sleep. 'kay?"

"Sure," agreed Dante.

"I'll try," I added, as she settled down with us.

"Hands to yerself, mister!"

I hadn't done anything, I thought. Well, not much, anyway!

Chapter 21

Hitting the road was always welcome: the thrill of the unknown, perhaps even if in unfamiliar company. I would rather have left the Glenn Creek people behind, but I couldn't blame them for wanting to go, although I suspected their reasons. Maybe I'm just the suspicious type, but I just didn't go for the 'mission of mercy' bit.

"I'm truly sorry I didn't tell you," said Faith as she slipped into place next to me as I drove. I saw the proffered mug of coffee, hesitantly held, and the tentative smile on her lips. "But..."

"You didn't quite trust me," I offered in return, taking my eyes briefly from the road. "Fair 'nough. Said I understood, didn't I? So, how long you been wed?"

"Six years."

"And yer let him wander off alone?" I grinned. "Must trust *him*, at least."

She shot me a look of reproach. I told myself I hadn't meant it that way. She had known him longer than she had me, was what I meant.

"Angelus. Look me in the eye and tell me you trusted *me*."

I couldn't help smiling at her return. "Point taken. Did wonder why you were still taggin' along. Coulda gotta lift if yer'd wanted."

She nodded slowly and nudged the mug closer. "Drink your coffee. You know, your accent's a mess."

I laughed. "I know. Comes from wanderin' so much. Pick up things all over."

"Guess you would at that. Can I ask you something, Angelus?"

"Sure."

"How old are you?"

"Not sure. Around thirty, I guess, give or take. Why?"

"Curious, that's all. Do you remember your folks?"

I hesitated, then shook my head. "Can't say I do, not really. I remember faces, but whether they were my folks, I don't know. Been alone long as I remembers... remember," I corrected with a rueful smile.

"How old were you when you were taken?"

I shrugged. "Not sure. No more 'n twelve, fourteen maybe. Why?"

"Just trying to get a picture of what you were like then."

I shook my head. "You don't wanna know. Guess I'd been alone for a while, because I was a vicious little punk. I had my knives, and I used 'em. Cut a few of 'em when they took me. Earned me a beating. More 'n one, truth. I was chained – whipped – till they thought they had me tamed." I smiled coldly as I looked out of the screen. "Only way ter survive, to be on top. To beat the crap out of others weaker 'n you. Did what I had ter; don't apologise for it. Made yer a target for the line bosses, but yer can't have everything." I shrugged. "Then I met Dante. Some o' the others thought him an easy mark. I guess I didn't like 'em beatin' on him on my turf. We became friends. Time passed."

"He saw something good in you."

A smile flickered. "Maybe it was because he couldn't see. He never saw the things I did, though I guess he knew. When finally we were free of the mines, we travelled together until..." I faltered, unsure about how much I was willing to divulge. "We argued. I didn't see him again until… well, you know that much."

"It must've been quite an argument," she mused.

"It was." I wasn't willing to continue and reached out to contact the other rig as a diversion. "This is Angelus. How long are we running? Over."

After a moment there was a crackle. "The doc says about an hour before dusk falls. Over."

"Good enough. Out." I thought for a moment she was going to continue where she'd left off, but she didn't. She left me to my driving and I thought the matter ended. I should have remembered a woman's persistence!

We made camp and I wandered over to Jon Fevre's rig. He had a campfire going already, and his team were, as far as I could tell, checking equipment.

He looked round as I approached and smiled. "Going hunting?" he enquired. I had my crossbow slung over my shoulder out of habit.

"I thought I might. Safe enough?"

"Within reason. Far enough away from the hot zone," he admitted. "Don't know what we'll find out there, though. Wolves, probably."

"I've met wolves before," I shrugged.

"What happened?"

"I came off worst. I think."

He studied me closely. "Yet you still go out there alone?"

"I don't dwell on it."

"You're not taking your shadow with you?"

"My shadow?"

"Dante."

My face must have gone cold, because I saw him flinch. "Dante is not my shadow."

"No offence intended... to you or your lover."

My fingers were itching – I was beginning to dislike Jon Fevre very much indeed. "You gotta problem with that?" I enquired.

"Would it matter if I did?" he returned. He was either very brave or very stupid. I hadn't decided which. I'd killed people for less than that.

"Not a fuck," I replied lazily.

"Angelus." Did he know he was treading on very thin ice indeed, I wondered? "We are an isolated community. Not used to—"

"Loose morals?" I offered helpfully. I saw his cheeks flush and wondered if he were beginning to suspect how close he was to feeling my knife because I saw his eyes flicker to my belt. Inside the belt of my pants and revealed by my half-open coat was one of my knives. "You didn't hire me for my morals, Doc. In fact, I think I was probably hired for my lack of them... about certain matters, anyway. So keep your nose out of my business, and we'll get along fine. In the meantime, I'll bid you goodnight. Sleep well." I contemplated blowing him a kiss just to irritate him, but thought that would be a little childish. Needless to say, when I came back with a couple of small rodents, I didn't share them with him.

I wondered what might have been said in my absence, because I caught shared glances between Dante and Trinity, but thought it wisest not to ask. I might well hear something I didn't want to know. Dante played for us while I prepared my catch for cooking, under Micah's eagle eye. When Trinity wandered over to see if I needed help, I caught the look he gave her. He wasn't much pleased when she drew me to her and gave me a kiss.

"Need any help, my Angel?" she asked, offering a flask of fiery Vargas liquor to my lips. I almost choked as she tipped it too far and spilled some, although she did attempt to put matters right by licking off the excess.

"Minx," I chuckled as she evaded me, which was probably wise, as I did have a knife and two bloody hands. I went back to my cooking with the feeling of eyes boring into the back of my neck. This, I thought, was getting ridiculous! I was about to say something when Trinity caught at my hand and shook her head. She, too, had seen Micah's reaction. She was right, I thought. This was neither the time nor the place.

"Where's Faith?" I asked curiously, realising suddenly she wasn't there.

"She went over to the other rig, but it looks like she's on her way back," replied Trinity, gesturing across the way. "She doesn't look happy."

She didn't. She looked pissed off.

"Hypocritical bastards!" we heard her say as she approached. I threw Trinity a side-glance. Neither of us remembered hearing her swear before. We were even more surprised as she snatched the flask from Trinity's hand and took a long swallow. "Sanctimonious pricks!"

I blinked. "Faith?"

"What?"

I wasn't sure what to say exactly. I looked at her face, at the flask, back over my shoulder. "I hesitate to ask."

"Then don't."

Which, I had to admit, left me a little short of words as she turned for the rig and slammed the door behind her. "Whoa!" Even Micah looked startled.

"Give her space, honey," advised Trinity, catching at my arm. "C'mon, dance with me."

"Huh?"

"You heard, mister. Dance with me. Dante?"

"Yeah?"

"Play something we can dance to. Nice 'n' slow."

Dante grinned. "You got it." I saw his head tilt to one side in contemplation then he began to play.

Trinity grinned and began to sway as she walked towards me. "Hey, mister, you lookin' for a good time?"

Her first words to me, as I recalled. Memory took me back. I'd been young, physically at least. Far from naïve, far from innocent. Blood on my hands, and on my soul, if I had one. She'd seen something good in me, as Dante had, and as much as I might pretend otherwise, I quite liked that. Feeling her in my arms took me back, as she had no doubt intended. I'd walked into the room already more than a little drunk, as I remembered. I think I was with a group of fellow 'runners'. I remember the guys telling me it was the best place in town. I remember the lewd comments, the nudges and winks, something about 'making a boy a man'. She'd come up to me, egged on by the guys, and taken me by the hand to lead me to her room. "I hear you're lookin' for a good time," she said. "Ever been with a woman before?" I'd shaken my head truthfully. "My name's Trinity. What shall I call you?"

"They call me Angelus," I'd said.

"I'll call you Angel," she'd told me as she'd undressed me slowly. "What would you like, Angel?"

"I'd like you to dance with me," I'd said, and she had. I'd felt her in my arms, felt her warmth, and thought for the first time in a long time of Dante. I'd found myself lying in her arms and talking about him, and she'd listened. While she'd listened she'd stroked my hair, spoken softly to me, taught me things about myself I hadn't known, and somewhere along the way I'd fallen in love again. We hadn't stayed together, no more than Dante and I had, because of my wanderlust. But whenever I'd been in town I'd called in on her. I hadn't wanted to be tied down – by anyone, even myself. My life might not be perfect, but I was responsible to no one. But maybe it was getting older that made me wonder if it was time for something else, and while I couldn't see myself settling down to what most people still considered a conventional family life, I had a strange feeling that I'd be a little less nomadic in future.

"Can I cut in?" I jumped, startled, as Faith touched Trinity on the shoulder. "Do you mind?"

"Of course he doesn't," replied Trinity, giving me a smile that might have been intended to convey something. I wasn't sure what, and I didn't particularly care. The music was good, the liquor wasn't bad, and I had a woman in my arms. Life wasn't bad.

"Well, are they lookin'?" I asked after some time.

I felt Faith stiffen, and then relax. "I hope so. Sanctimonious—"

"Yeah. Right." I chuckled. "I get the idea. Guess I've been stuck with a few pins, huh?"

"More or less," she laughed, relaxing. "I know it's not my business, but shit, that bastard's screwing his student!" I didn't ask which 'bastard' she was referring to – I had a pretty good idea.

"Some folks have always been prudish when it comes to what they think should be 'acceptable', and it's often because they've got guilty consciences themselves. Don't sweat it, hon. I don't give a fuck what they think of me. Never have, never will. Just don't make it hard on yourself, huh?"

She sighed and sagged against me. "Angel, I don't expect to find him alive, you know. I need a friend to lean on."

"And you've got one. Three in fact. Trin, Dante and me. We'll see you all right, whatever happens."

"I want to find Tom alive, believe me. My dad, too. But I have a bad feelin'. Tell me the truth, Angel. What chances do *you* think we have of finding them alive?"

I didn't know how to answer. I wanted to tell her that of course we would, but that would be a lie. I was no surer than she was. "Honey, I wish I could give a guarantee, but I can't. I don't know the answer any more than you do, although whether the doc knows, I couldn't say."

"You don't trust him."

"I don't trust the bastard as far as I could throw him," I replied.

"Surely Dan wouldn't have sent you into danger knowing..."

I hesitated, trying to decide how much I could trust her. Still, I thought bitterly, I could always kill her if I had to. It wouldn't be the first time, after all. "No, but he doesn't know everything. Knows a hell of a lot, though."

"He doesn't trust the doc either?"

"Let's just say he's uneasy." She drew back enough to see my face and studied me. Slowly, she nodded. "C'mon. Time to eat."

We all sat down and ate, ignoring the other rig completely. After we'd eaten, we settled down to drink and listen to Dante play again. His fingers must've been sore, I thought sympathetically, but I did so like to hear him play, and to hear him sing.

"Time for bed, I think," Faith, with whom I was dancing at the time, said. I bit my lip. "Alone!"

I laughed aloud and made a game of pretending disappointment. She shook her head. "You're irrepressible."

"I hope so. Goodnight."

"Goodnight," she said, kissing me on the cheek. "Night, Trinity. Dante. C'mon, Micah. Past your bedtime." Micah looked as if he were going to protest, but he didn't.

When we were alone, Dante fell silent. I took a drink to him and sat next to him.

"I wish..." he began.

I understood. Standing, I offered a hand to him. I didn't need music to dance with him, although it would have been nice. Drawing him into my arms, I held him close. In the near darkness we slow danced. The hard planes of his body were so different to the softness of Trinity's, but equally familiar. They'd both been a part of my life for so long.

Chapter 22

After my last encounter with Jon Fevre, I wasn't looking forward to my next. We had made camp by the side of the last waterhole before 'the zone', and although we had sentinels out, I was uneasy. I found him perched on a rock – just watching.

His head turned at my approach. "Not going in?" he asked.

I shrugged. "Wouldn't want to shock anyone," I responded dryly, and saw him wince.

"I'm sorry. I was out of line. None of my business – right?" I inclined my head and watched him closely. "My only excuse is I'd just had some news."

"Good or bad?"

"I'm still trying to decide," he admitted. "Can I talk to you in confidence?"

Oh shit. "Sure. My lips are sealed." I moved closer and perched on the rock.

"At my age – I've just found out I'm going to be a father." His gaze held mine, almost challenging. What the hell did he want me to say?

"How do you feel?"

"Shocked. Sad. Happy. That's it – I don't know!"

I laughed gently. "Sounds 'bout right. Do you love the girl?"

"I... yes, I do." Ah, a spark of defiance. Good.

"And how does she feel?"

"Shocked – happy."

I nodded slowly, thoughtfully, and grinned. "Then I guess it's congratulations, Doc. You gotta reason to get back in one piece. Make sure yer do." I rose slowly, figuring it was over.

"Angelus." I turned my head. "Guess it was just lookin' into a mirror, you know? Not easy – breaking taboos – right?"

I'd figured that one myself: in looking at me thumbing my nose at morality he'd seen himself, him being so much older than her. If he wanted to rationalise it that way, that was cool with me. "Sure."

"Last chance for a dip," he said, nodding towards the water.

"Thought yer wanted ter talk 'bout the zone."

"Can wait," he smiled. "Go on. Chill out... or whatever."

I laughed and waved my hand, wandering over to where the others were. Trinity was in the water with Micah and Faith. Dante was sitting at the edge, listening to the laughter.

"Hey," I said as I hunkered down next to him.

"Hey." He looked up. "You goin' in?"

"Ain't dressed for it."

He reached out to feel what I was wearing. "So strip off," he suggested. He was wearing a thin pair of calf-length pants, which was fine. "What you got under?"

I chuckled. "Boxers."

Dante gave an exaggerated sigh of relief. "Which ones?"

I laughed dryly. "Let's just say they won't leave much to the imagination when they're wet."

Dante bit his lip, but they still managed to twitch with mischief. "Do you care?" I had to admit I didn't, so I tied back my hair and stripped off. "What's it like here?"

"Dusty. Some vegetation... shallow... might be rocky close in."

"I'll hold on to you then." That was what I was afraid of. Well, that and the fact I can't swim. Dante, perversely, could swim like a fish. Getting me *in* the water was an achievement, and it was Dante who led the way, feeling with his toes and guided by the sound of Trinity's voice.

She gave me a kiss of greeting and then kissed Dante on the cheek. "Major achievement, Dante." She grinned at me, referring, of course, to the fact that Dante had got me into the water at all. "It's sandier here on in. If yer want ter swim, Dante, it's safe."

"Thanks." He hesitated.

"Go on. I'm okay." Dante gave a quick grin and a token protest, but succumbed in the end. He was beautiful to watch, I had to admit, and I envied him for it.

"He'd teach you, if you asked," suggested Trinity, glancing my way.

I shook my head. "I have enough nightmares as it is."

"Angel, let him do that for you. He needs to know he's more than just—"

I sealed her mouth with a finger. I knew what she was saying, of course. More than just a pretty face, more than just a beautiful voice: *useful*. Okay, I could do it, I thought. So what if my image took a little battering. I could do it. I'd done worse, after all. "Dante." He trod water at the sound of my voice. I wondered if he anticipated my next question because there was pure joy on his face as I asked, "Can you teach me?" Trinity had been right.

I was glad the water had been tested as safe, because I swallowed rather a lot of it. "You tryin' ter drown me?" I demanded, coughing up half the pond, or so it seemed.

"Sure I am," he replied. "That way I get to give you the kiss of life."

His face was serious, but I sensed his playfulness. Time to get my own back, perhaps? I ventured a glance shoreward. It was almost deserted, except for Trinity and Faith, who seemed deep in conversation. I wasn't sure where Micah was, but I assumed they did. "Well now..." I murmured, taking my courage in both hands and allowing myself to sink. Curious, he followed. I wasn't about to scare him by being too far away – I didn't want him to think he'd lost me, after all.

I simply came up behind him, put my arms around him and turned him into my embrace. When he wrapped his legs around me we came close to drowning each other, but it was worth it. Infinitely more erotic than a shower. By the time we found ourselves in shallower water, I'd completely forgotten any possibility or probability of an audience. By then my hair had come undone and was causing problems, distracting me.

"Are we alone?" asked Dante softly.

I felt a tingle of anticipation. "Can't see anyone," I replied, which was true. I had a gut feeling Micah was around somewhere, but I couldn't see him. Still, I was getting a little tired of having to 'play nice'. Gloves off – let the little prick snoop if he wanted. I really didn't care.

"Wanna get sand in your hair?" he asked, his voice and touch speaking volumes. "Or do you wanna..."

If it were a choice between spending hours trying to get sand out of my hair and staying in the water, I'd take the water. "I wanna." I pulled him tight in answer, felt his groan against my mouth and all the way to my toes.

It was a long time before we returned to the rig, fingers entwined. Faith, to my surprise, came out to meet us. "Have you seen Micah?" she enquired, looking from one to the other of us anxiously.

"Oh fuck!" I'd have to go hunting for the little prick! "Get me a flashlight," I sighed.

"You want me to come?" I felt Dante's fingers on my arm. I hesitated, knowing he was better at hunting in the dark than me but reluctant to drag him along.

"And my crossbow," I called after. Just in case. "Sure. Why not?" I put on my most reassuring face as Faith returned. She looked for a moment as if she were going to speak – but didn't. I had a feeling she suspected why Micah was missing, just as I did. "Come on, Dante." I didn't think he'd gone far. I believed him to be hiding.

It seemed as if we'd been wandering for hours when we finally came upon him. In the shadow of tree roots, almost hidden. I heard him, or rather Dante did. When I listened, I could hear him, too. Sobbing as if his heart would break. I felt Dante's hand on my arm.

"Go gently with him, dear heart," he whispered. "A kiss for luck?" I was only too willing. "Do go gently with him." Touching my face gently, he ran his fingers over my mouth.

With a sigh, I advanced on the place where he was curled up, thinking himself concealed. "Micah? Faith is wondering where you are. Come back with me." I kept my voice low as I crouched down. "Don't cry." I reached out for him and he slapped at my hands, struggling to be free. "Micah, what can I say? What do you want of me?"

"A... A..." The first sound I'd ever heard him make. "A... An... gel." His face, as far as I could see in the flashlight's glow, was a mask of pain. "W... wan... h... he... h... h... has." His voice caught and he turned away from the light, sobbing as if his heart was breaking.

I didn't know what to do, I really didn't. Should I reach out or push him away? I was on shaky ground here. I really didn't know what to say. Dante might know, but I dare not call on him because his presence might make matters worse. Use your heart not your head, I told myself; put yourself in his place. You were once. "Micah, listen to me." I killed the light, sensing he'd be more comfortable in darkness for the moment. "You're young. What yer thinks yer wants now might not be what yer wants as yer grows. No, do me the courtesy of listening. I'm not saying what yer feel isn't real. Maybe it is, maybe it's not. You won't know till yer grow. Let me tell yer a story. Once upon a time..." I felt him move closer and rest his head against my leg. I didn't push him away, though I was tempted. "Once upon a time, there was a young boy, oh, bit older 'n you..." Keeping my voice soft, I told him of my early life, of my uncertainties, of my meeting with Dante and with Trinity, of how it had been for me. I couldn't tell him how it would be for him, because I didn't know. "But don't rush things, kid. I knows how it feels right now, and I guess part of me's flattered. But it's not gonna happen, Micah. I won't let it. Some laws even I won't break, 'kay?" I felt his stillness and the trace of tears on my skin. I was glad of the darkness, because I was beginning to feel like a bit of an idiot in my boxers and a pair of boots! I hadn't planned on this when we'd come back from our swim, and I hadn't troubled to take the time to dress. Maybe I should have, I thought belatedly, but it was too late.

"'K... k... kay."

"Let's go back, huh? Don't know about you, but I'm freezin'." I wasn't – quite – but I was growing cold. It was late, and I wasn't wearing one hell of a lot. Then I heard the sound of footfalls – not human ones. "Fuck!" I was on my feet and loading my crossbow. "Dante?" I called. "Dante!" When he emerged from the darkness, I was relieved. I didn't know about Micah, and didn't care, but Dante was foremost in my mind. "We got company," I murmured.

"Figured."

"Micah, I'm gonna trust yer. Take care of Dante." I was taking a risk, I knew. If Micah was really antagonistic towards Dante, he could lead him into danger instead of out of it. "I'm depending on you, Micah, to care for him. He's everything to me." Shining the flashlight on his face, I saw him straighten and nod as he reached for Dante's hand. "Keep outta my way. I only have two bolts." I didn't much fancy facing wolves even with a full quiver, not after our last encounter, but I would if I had to. "Now get the fuck outta here!" I turned as the first wolf leapt, letting fly. I might have to use my crossbow as a club if the second wolf attacked.

Part of my brain rebelled against the existence of these creatures out here. They just shouldn't be. But that didn't matter. All I had was the strength of my arms and the physical weight of the bow as the second wolf leapt. I rolled, narrowly missing a rock as I tried to reach the body of the fallen wolf in the hope of retrieving my bolts. To my surprise – and shock – the second wolf positioned itself between me and its fallen companion as if trying to keep me from my objective. I watched, fascinated, as it sniffed and turned back to me. With an intelligence I didn't want to acknowledge, it faced me down. Fuck, I thought, this can't be happening. Almost face to face, I looked into its eyes. With a snarl, it lashed out at me. I didn't want to kill it, I realised, but it wasn't going to give me any choice. I don't know why I thought it wanted me to kill it, but it did. Call me crazy if you like. I don't care. That's what I thought. "Don't make me," I said lamely, reaching for the piece of driftwood that probably wasn't going to be of much use but was all I had. It lashed out again and I struck back. I had no choice. I could feel its breath and wondered if it knew how frightened I was. Being afraid in such a position isn't something to be ashamed of; in fact it's entirely logical, so I'm not apologising for it. But adrenalin's a powerful ally. When I heard the sound of an arrow in flight, I wasn't really surprised, but I must admit to more than a little surprise when the damned animal landed on me and knocked the breath out of me. I found myself looking up at Dante, my bow in his hand and Micah at his side and half the Glenn Creek people at his back with torches and guns. "Nice shot," I gasped.

His grin was more than a little smug – deservedly so. "I do my best to please."

Cheeky bastard, I thought. "Can someone get this thing off me?" I asked, and there was a sudden burst of activity. "Micah, get my bolts, will yer?" I didn't think him squeamish, and he wasn't. He retrieved my bolts – and my arrow – before coming back and waving them in triumph. Dante helped me to my feet, puzzled initially when I caught at his hand to prevent him separating me from my boxers, and I saw the flash of his smile as he realised I was holding onto my side not solely because I'd got a nasty scratch there, but because the scratch had resulted in my boxers being ripped in two!

"C'mon. Let's get you seen to," he said, nodding to Micah to pick up my crossbow. Micah's smile was as bright as the sun as he carried his trophy back to the rigs. I was limping a little, and grateful for the injury in that it kept me from having to make explanations I didn't want to give right then. "Okay, let's get you seen to," said Dante, closing the rig door behind us. "Trin, you got the hot water?"

"On the boil," she said in response, glancing at me and grinning. "Inch or two more 'n' you'd be singing soprano," she chuckled. "Get me the kit, Micah. Oh, Faith, pass the kit will yer? I don't want him sick again." She had a point. "Drop 'em." That wasn't hard, I thought, seeing as they were only attached at one side, but I was damned if I was flashing in front of everyone!

"Trin!" I exclaimed plaintively. I saw the laughter in her eyes. The damned woman was doing it deliberately.

I saw Micah point to himself, offering to go. Much as I didn't want Micah rifling through my underwear, I didn't have much choice.

"Thanks." While he was gone, Trinity pulled back the flap and examined the wound. It didn't look too bad, but then neither had the other one at first, and given its position, I had to admit I really was lucky. I swore vehemently as she cleaned the wound and jabbed the needle into me. Only when it was safely dressed did I breathe a sigh of relief. "Thanks, hon."

Micah came forward and extended a hand. "I... th... th... 'kay?" he mumbled, eliciting a response of pure amazement from Trinity and Faith. He was offering me a thong, logical given the fact that I had a dressing on. I winked at him and he blushed.

"They're fine, Micah." It took them a moment to realise I wanted them to turn their backs, which they seemed to find amusing for some reason. Charming, I thought. I needed a drink, which Faith provided after a few pleading looks. If Trinity objected, I really didn't care. I thought I deserved one, and that was that.

I was barely decent when there was a knock on the door. Puzzled, Dante went to open it. In walked Jon Fevre, bearing a bottle and a dish covered by a cloth.

"Greetings, oh mighty wolf slayer," he intoned, eliciting laughter from those who'd followed him. "Tradition demands we bear a trophy for your bravery." With a flourish he pulled off the cloth. I wasn't sure at first what I was looking at, but he must've known what I was thinking because he grinned. "As you nearly lost yours, we figured you might care to have his."

It was a tradition I'd never heard of, so how much of a joke he might be playing I wasn't sure, but I was damned if I was going to throw up in front of him! "Er... thanks. I think. What, might I ask, am I supposed to do with it... them?"

"Why, eat them, of course," he responded guilelessly.

"Balls!"

"Exactly." His eyes twinkled, and I saw him wink at Trinity. "Enjoy." With an over-theatrical flourish, he departed, still laughing.

"What am I supposed to do with that?" enquired Trinity archly.

Faith leaned over her shoulder. "Twenty minutes on a high heat?" she suggested. We all roared with laughter. I accepted the drink, of course. The dish and its contents ended up as far away as we could throw them!

Persuading Micah to go to bed wasn't easy, but he did as I asked. Faith lingered for a few moments, but seemed to sense I wanted to be alone, so she made her excuses.

"I'll be in the bedroom," announced Trinity, glancing at Dante. "Don't keep him up too long," she said before she left us.

Dante edged closer to me, his fingers searching. I watched with amusement as his brow puckered and then as recognition came. "I see what they meant. Before long, you'll be able to join them up." His fingers slid lazily over my hip. "This is Micah's idea of sparing your modesty?"

"Uh-huh."

"I approve." His voice made me shiver. Given where his hand rested, I wasn't sure I trusted myself to speak. "Only time will tell how well Micah listened, but you were honest with him. I hope he's old enough to understand."

"We'll see." I stretched and winced. "Bedtime, I think."

"Oh yeah." Dante was on his feet and pulling me onto mine. "Before I forget..."

"Forget?"

"Yeah." His smile grew teasing. "Must be catching."

"What must?"

"Memory loss."

"Comes from near drowning," I chuckled.

"Ah." Taking me by the hand, he led me to the bedroom. "I think we've had enough excitement for one day, huh?"

"Too right."

"Time for sleep."

"Yeah."

I looked at Trinity lying in bed and had to admit it was cool that I didn't need to undress, which saved a hell of a lot of time. Dante wasn't wearing a whole lot more, which was cool, too. Soon we were wrapped in darkness and in each other's arms, and the world was all right again. Strange, I thought as sleep came, how we'd come to accept our little threesome so easily. Beyond that, I didn't want to rationalise.

Chapter 23

As time passed and we drew nearer the hot zone, we all became aware of a growing instability of the weather. The temperature difference between night and day became more extreme, and dust hung heavily in the air when the wind wasn't blowing at full force. We'd been lucky – it had mostly been light dust storms and sand devils, but when noon brought Jon Fevre's voice, I went to re-check the screens.

"Angelus? Over," I heard as I arrived back up front.

"Just a second, he's... oh, he's on line now, Jon. Over." Trinity handed the mike over to me.

"Jon, Angelus here. Over."

"You okay? Over."

I laughed. "Just had to take a leak, Jon. What's wrong?" I added hastily. "Over."

"My screens tell me there's a bad one building. What've you got? Over."

I slipped onto the front bench and ran my fingers over the console. "I got it. Coming in at speed. Gonna be a bitch. You want to run or anchor? Over."

There was a pause and the hiss of static. "Go for a run; let's see how it pans out. If need be, anchor down and hold. Out."

I bit my lip. "You wanna drive, honey, or you want me to?"

Trinity hesitated. "I guess I should, in case I ever need to – you know."

I nodded and smiled. With my run of luck recently, nothing would surprise me. "If you're cool with it, it's fine by me. I'll be up back. Just yell." I was getting a stiff neck from driving, and a spell away from the wheel would do me good. Besides, Trinity had a point. She needed to know her limits.

I went back to the table and studied the maps I'd laid out there. Not that we had much in the way of data, but what we did have didn't look good if we got caught 'between a rock and a hard place'. We were heading into gorge country, which might work in our favour from the aspect of providing shelter, but conversely, it could act as a funnel and make matters worse. I was staring into space and telling myself I was doing some work when I felt it slam into us. As I picked myself up, I heard Trinity screaming – at the rig, not at me – calling her a bitch and several other things I'd never heard Trinity call anything, let alone an inanimate object!

"What's wrong, honey?" I asked, hanging on to the back of the seat. She was about to reply when another gust hit. I saw her muscles tighten as she struggled to keep on the 'road', her mouth in a tight line. "Easy, Trin. You'll do yerself a mischief. Relax. Let the old girl ride; she's stable," I soothed, my fingers massaging the back of her neck. She'd locked down the screens and we were navigating by systems, which was apt to give you a headache. Something I've done many times, but Trinity hadn't, not with a storm this bad. "Jon, this is Angelus. We're anchoring. Out."

"Copy. Out."

"Hit the brakes, honey," I urged, as she fought with the wheel. Once locked down, we were vulnerable to a side-sweep, but there'd never been anything that we couldn't ride out. In a calm voice, I talked her through the routine. I was uneasy, and I wasn't sure why. It wasn't the storm, and it wasn't the rig. I just felt jittery.

There was something out there in the storm, waiting.

As there wasn't much else to do, I set about cleaning our weaponry. I had a feeling I was going to need it. That *we* were going to need it. I reminded myself I wasn't a one-man army. Glancing up, I saw Dante by the door watching me. Although I knew he couldn't see me, I never thought of him as doing anything else. So what if he was watching with his ears? As if sensing my awareness, he moved carefully forward and reached out to locate the edge of the table, the seat and me, in that order. As his fingers moved lightly down my arm, I held my position.

"Ah," he said, discovering what I was doing. "That's a beautiful weapon, if a weapon can be called so. Have you given it a name?"

I looked at him, startled. "Er... no. Why?"

"I seem to remember it used to be traditional. A harp might have a name, often a woman's name. A sword might have a name like... oh, Slayer, I suppose."

"Oh. Well, they say yer learn somethin' new every day." As I watched his skilful fingers examine my crossbow, I felt my heart break as I often did when I remembered that those beautiful eyes of his were sightless, and as he often did, Dante knew.

"It's okay, dear heart. I don't know anything else."

"But don't you—" I began, breaking off.

A poignant smile touched Dante's lips and his fingers fell away from the weapon. "Don't I what?"

"Regret..."

"My only regret is that I've never seen your face," he replied wistfully, turning his head towards me as he reached up to place his fingers on my mouth. As I took his fingers from their position to kiss his palm, we heard a soft movement. Micah, of course.

I grimaced. "Can't you learn to cough or something?" I complained lightly. He gave a shy smile.

"Tr-try."

Dante relaxed against my side. "Can't you sleep, little one?" he asked gently.

"Do-don't... like." He was getting better. Before long we'd be telling him to shut up!

"Come on and sit down," suggested Dante without stirring. Micah hesitated, but moved towards us. As he settled with his head against Dante's thigh, Dante smiled at me and began to sing as he stroked Micah's head. It was a somewhat bizarre scene I had to admit as I went back to cleaning the weapons, an opinion Faith clearly shared given her expression as she wandered into the galley. "He couldn't sleep," Dante offered softly by way of explanation.

Faith stood looking down at Micah for a moment, her features softening. "I was having a little trouble myself."

"Angel's got a vacant spot," he replied deadpan.

Faith grimaced. "Trin'd probably have my guts. 'Sides, you'd get oil in my hair."

"I'd wipe my hands, promise," I grinned. "See?" I pushed the cleaning equipment across the table.

"It's not his hands yer need to worry about, honey – it's his mind!" I glanced over my shoulder and saw Trinity, who was wearing an old shirt. Faith chuckled. "On second thoughts, maybe yer were right the first time," she added as an afterthought. "Can I make anyone a hot drink?"

We settled on hot chocolate, even Micah, who must have smelled the aroma because he woke just in time. With the winds howling outside, none of us were inclined towards sleep – or indeed anything else – and we remained awake, playing cards for the rest of the night. Morning brought a minor lessening of the fury, but it was still unsafe to go outside. We kept radio silence because I didn't want anyone out there to pick up on us if they hit on our frequency – the only exception would be a full emergency, as Jon Fevre well knew.

When the storm had abated enough, we hit the road again. I didn't want to stay fixed for any longer than I had to, because my guts were still telling me we had company.

Risking a shower, I allowed myself to be 'diverted' by Trinity, but even she couldn't lighten my mood. I was antsy as all hell, especially as I was taking point and had sand swirls on my port side.

"Contact," came Trinity's voice, taut with a mixture of fear and excitement. "Incoming, or whatever."

I grinned savagely and hit the warning. Whoever was out there knew where we were as surely as we knew where they were, so there was no point in playing games, unless we played hide and go seek, I mused, wondering how manoeuvrable the old girl would be among the canyons. If the raiders were herding us towards an ambush, we'd have to do our best. I didn't want a firefight, but I wasn't going to run from one, although I knew that we had to prevent them following us through the zone. Hanging on for the other rig was a bitch, but we had no alternative. We were better armed, and we knew how to use our weapons. They only thought they did.

When the raiders came in, they came in fast and hard. I perched up in the 'turret' with what Trinity called my 'cannon', while she manned the other gun, with Faith acting as 'eyes'. Micah and Dante kept us supplied with ammo, although I'd given Micah instructions to keep Dante out of the way. Trinity had also suggested to Dante to keep Micah out of the way, so it made for an interesting situation. The battle seemed to last for an eternity, but in reality scarcely any time at all had passed.

Only the silence that followed tempted us to leave cover. We needed to inspect the rigs and to check for survivors. I don't think Jon Fevre liked that part too much, particularly when I refused to have any of his people accompany me. I didn't want witnesses, not because I intended any cruelty, but because I didn't want to be hampered by anyone who was squeamish. I didn't see what happened back at the rig. Must've been a lone sniper, Faith suggested, tears running down her face.

I panicked. I admit it. My first thought was Dante, my second Trinity. I found Trinity sitting on the step of the rig with a bloody cloth held to her head. Micah was bravely trying to persuade her to let him clean it, but she wouldn't have it until she saw me coming towards her with a pale-faced Jon Fevre at my heels.

"Angel...Dante..." she choked, reaching for me.

"Where?"

"Inside."

Much as I wanted to hold her, I needed to get to Dante. I wondered what he'd been doing, how badly he was hurt. Given Trinity's distress, I feared the worst.

"Micah, see to her. Sit on her if yer have to. Hear?"

"Sir." He'd never called me 'sir' before, and it gave me pause. I met his eyes, held his gaze in what I hoped was a reassuring fashion and hit the steps. Inside, I found what I feared – Dante covered with blood and Faith in tears.

"What happened?" I asked, hardly recognising my own voice.

"Someone must've thought he was dangerous. He had your bow in his hand. He was... he was half outta the turret. Took one in the shoulder... so much blood."

I closed my eyes, took a deep breath and ran my eyes over him. He was breathing, I told myself, and that had to be hopeful. He hadn't taken a head shot – probably struck his head when he'd dropped – but he'd cut his head, and it was a mess. Something, however, didn't smell right.

"S'pose you tell me what really happened?" I wasn't sure knowing would help, but I had a feeling she was hiding something and I don't like secrets, unless they're mine, of course.

Tears were running down her face as she raised her head. "Micah was all for going after you. He was scrambling out and Dante was reaching out to grab him, pull him back, when he was shot. Please, don't make it worse. He's so scared you're gonna be mad at him." I wasn't feeling mad; I was feeling... what was I feeling? Numb. I needed something to get me moving.

"I'll get to him later," I muttered. "Meantime, get me a kit, water. Get your ass in gear, woman!" I snapped. It was what she needed, because her eyes flashed and she was herself again.

"You got it."

"Anything I can do?" asked Jon Fevre from the doorway.

I turned my head and snapped, "Yeah. Get the fuck outta here!" I didn't want him there, but I didn't have time to see if he went because Faith was back. "Start on his head," I told her, reaching out for a knife to cut away the rest of his tunic. I didn't want the wound any more contaminated than it already was. I wondered if this was how he'd felt when he'd tended to me, although that must have been a hundred times worse because he couldn't see the damage. Still, seeing might be worse, I acknowledged as I cleaned. He moaned, but didn't give any other signs that he knew I was there. The bullet was still in him, I decided, instructing my hand not to shake. It looked awfully close to his heart, but I couldn't allow that to affect me. It had to come out, no ifs, no buts, no maybes.

Faith had finished cleaning, disinfecting and binding his head and hovered at my side, waiting for me to move so that she could disinfect his shoulder. "Angel." I raised my eyes slowly. "You can do it."

I hesitated, gave a weak smile and said, "Okay, nurse, do your bit."

She grinned at me and began to clean while I tried to remember anything I'd ever read and dug into his flesh. It had gone pretty deep and he'd lost a lot of blood, but I got it out. I had to pray there'd been no internal damage to anything major, but I didn't think it'd gone near any internal organs. All I could do was patch him up and wait – and pray to a god that I didn't believe in that he'd pull through. It wasn't the shot alone that was the danger, I knew; it was infection, and we were limited as to what we could do on that score.

I sat with him, leaving him only when nature called, as I knew he'd once waited with me. When I did leave his side, it was to do a little 'cleansing' outside.

I burned their bodies, of course: built a pyre and set them alight. I told myself it was to prevent contamination so near the hot zone, but if I was honest, it was a modicum of revenge. Did it help? No. It didn't.

I didn't want to move him, but I had no choice. We couldn't linger. I spent my waking hours tending to his wound – dosing it with powder, obsessively checking, sitting with him every moment I wasn't at the wheel. Even the exhaustion of driving didn't bring sleep. I must've looked like hell, because everyone kept their distance, even Trinity.

"They used to call him the Black Crow," I heard her say to Faith one morning. They were sitting on the steps of the rig watching the sunrise. I'd been trying to improve matters by washing my face. It hadn't helped: I looked worse than Dante did. "In that black coat of his 'n' all."

"The one he's wearing now?"

"Uh-huh. Because he often brought bad news and... other things."

"He's taking it bad."

A pause as Trinity reflected. "Bad memories, I guess. Now he knows how Dante felt, and the truth of how *he* feels."

Was that it? The reason I seemed to be feeling lost?

"Do you mind?" asked Faith.

I gripped the wall, not sure I wanted to hear but unable to move. "A little. I guess I wish his heart was all mine, but we're all a product of our past and he... he's come face to face with his."

She was right, but hearing it didn't help. I was about to make my presence known when Faith spoke again. "Why don't you... you know... wear him out? Then the rest of us can relax."

I held my breath. Was I so bad? I heard Trinity's musical laughter. "I would if I could get him into bed."

"Who mentioned a bed?"

I imagined Trinity's smile. "Getting him alone *anywhere* is..." Probably a shrug, I thought. "He's wired. Sprung so tight." Did she think I'd hurt her, I wondered. Was I so close to crazy? "Truth is, only thing he'd do is crash. It's not just sleep deprivation; it's all the rest. All we can do is catch him when he falls."

I opened and closed a door to let them know I was there, poured myself a strong black coffee and hoped I looked half alive.

"Mornin', ladies," I said brightly.

"You look like hell," was Trinity's laconic greeting. I knew I looked a mess – I felt a mess – but a guy likes to be flattered just as much as a woman does. Vanity, vanity, all is vanity, right?

"Thanks, babe." I bent to kiss her cheek and she grinned up at me.

"Yer won't do him no good if yer knackered, yer knows." She stretched and rose to her feet. "I'll drive. You sleep." In truth, I didn't think I *could* drive. Not without going off the road at least – if there'd been one. She stroked my cheek gently, her eyes warm. "We'll wake yer if he does." I hesitated, tempted. I didn't know when I'd last slept. How many days – or nights. Or how long since I'd eaten properly. Logic told me I was being a prick, but I was almost past logic. "Dammit, Angel. Lie down on the floor if yer have to be near him. If you don't trust us to watch him." Her words stung, but there was truth in them.

"I'm sorry," I apologised, looking down at my feet. Trinity caught at my hand as I swayed. I remember opening the door and checking Dante – again! I don't remember hitting the floor. But seeing as I woke up there...

I groaned as my body made its protest. I don't know how long I'd slept because the room was in darkness except for a small light. Raking back my hair, I ventured a glance towards the bed, half-convinced I'd lost him while I slept. Seeing his eyes open didn't necessarily mean he was awake, and his steady breathing was no indication either. I tidied his hair and ran my fingers over his jaw, trying to decide whether he needed a shave.

"Don't you like the rugged look?" The sound of his voice, little more than a whisper, was a shock. I couldn't speak. "Don't weep, dear heart."

"I'm not," I told him. I'd lied, and he knew it.

His smile was tender as he touched my face, damp with tears as I kissed his palm. "Must I beg for a kiss, love?" he asked. I hadn't dared, to be honest. "I won't break."

Just a kiss, I told myself severely. No more, no less. As I brushed his lips lightly with mine the last thing I expected was his fist in my hair, his mouth as hungry as a vampire's.

"Easy," I protested, gasping for air. I heard soft laughter in the doorway.

"Methinks he doth protest too much," was the quote I vaguely heard before the door closed again.

Dante pouted a little when I drew away, laughing as he touched my mouth. "I never thought I'd do that again," he offered by way of apology. "I guess I went a little crazy."

"I've been a little that way myself," I confessed. "How d'you feel?"

"Weak," he grinned. "Lay next to me; it'll make me feel stronger," he cajoled, his fingers tracing a line on my collarbone. When he raised his head, I could have sworn he could see me. "If you do, I promise to be good."

I groaned. That was the problem, I thought. Some time later there was a discreet knock on the door. "You two decent in there?"

I felt Dante's chuckle against my shoulder.

"Yeah. Come in." I was lying on the bed wearing my pants; Dante was under the covers wearing not a hell of a lot. I guessed that made us 'decent'. If not, tough.

Jon Fevre entered, his smile widening as he did so. "Thank God for that," he said. "Maybe we can crash the zone now. We didn't want to make the last push without you at the wheel, Angelus. Nice to see you back with us, Dante. We've missed your voice."

He smiled and bent his head in acknowledgement. "You'll have to wait awhile before I play. Guess it'll be stiff for a while."

"Probably not the only thing," quipped the doctor, his eyes sparkling.

I tried not to laugh. Given the fact that Dante was pressed against my back, his chin on my shoulder. I was trying not to react when I felt his breath on my neck. This was Jon Fevre, I reminded myself, who'd once been so offended by the thought of Dante and me.

"What changed?" I asked, curious.

He met my gaze evenly. "Perhaps I realised that love takes many forms and that you're not about to try to..." As his voice trailed away, he caught my amusement and grinned. I was trying to keep a straight face because Dante had his lips on my neck, having pushed my hair to one side. He was, of course, teasing Jon Fevre, who I had a feeling was enjoying my discomfort! "Although I'm not sure how far I want to test my theory right now."

I laughed. Not a good idea, in the circumstances. "Dante!"

Chapter 24

had to admit that the 'barrier' was one hell of a sight. Light shimmered and flowed – light being a loose term, of course; it was more likely to be magnetic fields at play – and it was truly awesome.

"Once we approach, we'll be running blind until we hit the other side, assuming there is one," I added as an afterthought. "So when we hit the barrier, keep on the course you've chosen until you can see where the hell you're going." Tam Owen, the other rig's driver, nodded. "And good luck."

It had seemed simple then. Now, the actuality of it had us breathless. This was the 'hot zone', according to all the maps the 'no go' zone that had been sufficient to keep most people away. That and the rumours of marauding bands who obviously risked the vagaries of the atmospheric anomalies. Part of me wondered, I had to admit, how the band we'd encountered had found us. Maybe they'd just fallen lucky or maybe they'd had help. Which brought me back to the crack on the head I'd received before we'd departed. Food for thought while I drove.

The temptation was to drive with the screens down and trust to luck when the instruments cut out, assuming they did, but I wasn't feeling particularly suicidal. Leaving the driver's screen up, I decided to trust to eye shields and navigate myself. Dante had offered to drive, with the elaboration that as he was already driving blind, he'd have the advantage. I didn't take him up on it. I had Trinity up front with me, having refused Micah's pleading. Dante had accused me of neglecting Trinity, and he had a point. But his idea of 'quality time' with her – i.e. this mad drive – had me puzzled. I'd thanked both Trinity and Faith for their patience and care and even Micah, who was still speaking little but was slowly opening up. We were a unit again, and I had to admit I kind of liked that.

"You okay with this?" I asked, not for the first time.

"Too late to back out now, ain't it?" she returned, patting my hand. "Just put your foot down, darlin'."

"How about a kiss for luck?"

Trinity grinned. "Any time, any time." She gave me a quick kiss.

"That all I get?" I asked, and was rewarded by her laughter.

"Why? What do you have in mind?"

I winked at her and she rolled her eyes. "I thought we could play a little." I felt her shiver of anticipation and felt absurdly pleased.

"The three of us?"

I slid my glance her way. "If you wish, or the two of us, if you prefer."

"You'd do that?"

"Of course I would. Nothing's changed. You have a voice in this family of ours."

Trinity slipped her arm through mine and rested her head against my shoulder, snuggling up. "Family. I like the sound of that."

I felt a little guilty that it had been Dante's suggestion when it should have been mine, but this wasn't the time to confess that. "You ready, honey?"

"I'm always ready," Trinity responded gaily, gripping my thigh and winking at me. "Don't yer know that by now?"

I didn't reply verbally, simply gunned the engine. "Let's eat dust, honey."

The only way I could think of to break the barrier was to crash through it, simply because even with shades the swirling patterns were making me feel sick. Perhaps that was not a random effect. How better to keep oneself isolated than to think up all sorts of nasty 'surprises' like this? Did I think there was intelligence behind it? Sure I did. There was something about it that didn't shout 'coincidence' at me.

Taking a deep breath, I put my foot down, hoping that everyone who didn't need to be sitting up was lying down. This was likely to get a little rough, especially as I didn't have a clue what was waiting on the other side.

Time seemed to flow slowly as the field enveloped us, and I wished I'd taken Dante up on his offer to drive. "After all, I can't see it, can I?" he'd said. I'd have considered it, crazy as it might sound, if he'd been physically up to it. I'd left him with Faith and Micah, wishing he were by my side but with his other words ringing in my ears: "Don't neglect Trinity, dear heart," he'd warned. "It wouldn't be fair."

Emerging from the veil of light was something of an anticlimax. Beyond looked little different from behind, except that the sky had grown somewhat darker, indicating that time had indeed passed. "You clear, Angelus?" came a familiar voice amidst the excited chatter.

"Yeah. I feel like the White Rabbit on acid," I chuckled. "Plan still holds, over?"

"Put a few miles behind us, then lock down. You take point, over?"

"Affirmative. Out." I glanced at Trinity, who put her hand reassuringly on mine.

"I'll check 'em." While I fretted, she did as she'd promised, returning with coffee. "Faith was vertical, at least." I gave a soft laugh. "Said she'd thrown up twice, though."

I knew how she felt. I had barely held on myself. "Micah okay?"

"Seems. You're gonna have ter talk ter him. He's too young ter be carryin' that much guilt."

"Nobody thinks—"

"He thinks you do," she informed me. "He's scared."

"Of what?"

"You."

"ME?" I almost hit the brakes in surprise. "Why?"

Trinity thought carefully before answering. "He knows what you did... what you can do to someone you hate." She touched my wrist lightly. "I know yer wouldn't, 'n' so does he, but he's all mixed up."

I didn't know what I could do. I'd had enough problems myself, but there'd been no one there for me. Trinity was right. I had to be there for him. Who else did he have? I'd tried to talk to him, but perhaps I'd gone about it wrong. I wasn't used to being a role model after all. I told her I'd talk to him the first chance I got, which seemed to satisfy her.

It wasn't until we'd been camped for some time that I got around to checking Dante's wound, mostly because I'd been distracted by Trinity. It didn't look too bad, I thought. Not as angry, at least.

"Admiring your handiwork?" asked Dante with a smile.

"It's lookin' better," I told him. "Why can't a guy just look?"

"This one can't," he reminded me softly.

I felt my insides lurch: he sounded depressed. "Dante."

"It's okay." He reached up to locate my mouth and rested a finger on it. "I just hate—"

"Ssh." I'd felt this way myself when I'd been wounded, but I wasn't sure he was referring to his wound. If he was referring to his blindness...

"I wish, just once, I could see your face," he said in confirmation, his voice wistful. "For even a moment. I see you in my mind, but it's not the same." I held him and soothed him as best I could. I'd only just succeeded when Micah burst in.

"Will you fucking learn to knock?" I exploded savagely. It wasn't that we'd been doing anything; I'd just reacted. His stricken expression told me I'd fucked up again. I swore as he turned and bolted.

"Go!" urged Dante. "Bring him back."

He was right, of course, but I didn't relish going out into the night. I would, of course, but no one said I had to like it! I found him – eventually. He wasn't trying very hard to hide.

Hunkering down next to him, I didn't look at him but out into the night. "Micah, what do you want me to say? If I knew what yer wanted of me." I tucked my hair behind my ears and half-turned my head, offering a smile I hoped was friendly. "Talk to me, Micah. I'm listening."

He sat with his knees drawn up to his chin. In the faint light of my flashlight his face looked drawn. "How do you... kn–know?"

"Know what, Micah?"

"You know," he lowered his eyes briefly, before looking up at me shyly. "If you... you know!"

How to answer? "Sometimes you just know. Everyone's different."

"How... for... for you?"

"Me?" I smiled.

"I mean... how... how can you love two?"

I sighed and gave a soft laugh. "Beats me. Just lucky, I guess."

He managed to raise a smile, at least. "Do you love them both the same?"

I bit my lip thoughtfully. "No, of course not. You never love two people the same. It's always different. With Trinity it was... maybe it was an experiment at first. To see if I could. With Dante..." How could I explain when I didn't understand myself? "Don't rush into growing up, Micah. Being young might not be much fun sometimes, but growing up sure as hell isn't. We're here for you if you need us. Just learn to knock, huh?"

"You weren't doing anything," he frowned, puzzled. "Well, apart from a little tongue wrestling." I blinked in surprise and tried not to laugh at his choice of phrase.

"But we might have been. Courtesy, huh? Would you like it if someone burst in on you?"

I'm sure I heard him mutter, "Chance'd be a fine thing," under his breath. "G–guess not. S–sorry."

"That's okay. You ready to go back now?"

"Yeah. My butt's g–getting cold." I chuckled and helped him to his feet. He looked at me for a moment then gave a shy smile. "Thanks."

"Welcome."

Slipping my arm companionably around his shoulder, we began our slow walk back.

Chapter 25

Coming up on the rigs from behind, we didn't see them until it was too late. Then everything happened at once. I remember pushing Micah aside and screaming at them that they were hurting Dante, to let him go. I remember a struggle, a blow to my head, thinking 'not again!', and nothing else until I became aware of something soft beneath me, covering me. And panic, because I couldn't see a damned thing!

"Dante? Trinity?" I heard a door open and close, running feet, and felt familiar arms catch at me, holding me.

"It's okay, Angel. I'm here."

"What...?"

"You took a blow to the head. They covered your eyes for safety. Stop wriggling and I'll take it off."

"Who's 'they'?" And whose safety? Mine or theirs?

"They'll explain – just sit still!"

I tried. Honest. "Dante..."

"HE'S FINE. Soon as they realised he was only trying to reach you, that he was hurt... There, how's that?"

I blinked, tears filling my eyes because it was suddenly so bright. "Trin, where is he? When can I—?"

"Ssh. Soon. Relax. I'll get someone." She had a strange look on her face, as if she knew something and wanted to tell me but couldn't.

After some time, the door opened and a woman came in. She was wearing white and was very elegant as she perched on the bed next to me, leaning towards me to examine my eyes. "Mm. Good. No concussion." She examined my head, turning it left and right. "You'll do. I'm Nadia Christof, and you are Angelus, I believe." I nodded. "You'll be wanting to know about your friend, seeing as you were so desperate." She gestured to my head and smiled. "In fact, my guess is you have a hundred questions at least."

"I'll settle for one. How is he?"

"He should be coming round any time soon. When he does, you'll be the first to know."

"Coming round? From what?" Alarm made me reckless. I'd strangle the damned woman in a minute.

"Easy." She pushed me back onto the bed gently. "You'll do yourself a mischief, son."

"I'll do you a mischief—"

"Please, Angel. Trust me. He'll be okay." I looked from the woman to Trinity. Her expression was unreadable, but her eyes were bright with – excitement? Anticipation?

"Need something for your head?" asked Nadia Christof, as if I'd never threatened her.

"I'll be okay."

"Sure?"

"Yeah, I'm sure."

She turned towards where Trinity was perched, her eyebrow arched with amusement. "Seems this one's got more balls than brains."

Trinity gave a bark of laughter and wagged a finger at me. "Gotcha, she has!"

I grinned. "So, do I at least get my pants, Doc?"

"Depends. Want him in bed or out, dear?" She was addressing Trinity, and I suppressed a grin. They might be in for a shock when I came face to face with Dante if they thought...

"Oh, might as well. He's more 'n likely ter walk outta here without 'em."

"Well then, to spare a few blushes I'll have them sent in," she grinned. "May I say you're one of the most incurious people I've ever met, Angelus."

"All things come to he who waits," I quoted. In other words, what I wanted to know I'd find out in good time. I trusted my eyes more than I trusted what any of them said. "So, where am I?"

She looked pleased I'd asked. "The founders of our little enclave called it 'New Eden'," she replied, launching into an explanation of its ethos. It all sounded very noble, but far removed from the world we knew. Isolation had its advantages. Perhaps.

"Wonder if Eden now has its 'serpent'?" speculated Trinity when we were alone.

"Huh?"

"Someone to challenge their 'safe' little world," she smiled, leaning over to kiss me.

Someone came with my pants a few moments later, but at least they knocked before opening. I suppose, in retrospect, I should have asked about Faith and Micah, but my mind was too full of Dante and the last time I'd seen him. But although I didn't trust them – yet – I did trust Trinity. She did her best to take my mind off things, and when they came to take us to Dante, we were laughing. She interlaced her fingers with mine and squeezed my hand encouragingly.

We were escorted to a small room, which was lit only by a single faint light. Nadia Christof came to us and caught hold of my arm. "Don't build his hopes up," she whispered before letting me go.

I saw Dante's head come up at the sound of my footfalls, and felt my heart leap at the joy on his face as he reached out for me. I didn't care who was watching or what they thought, I was going to kiss him and that was the end of it. I'm not sure what was written on my face as I held him close, but no one said a word. Defiance perhaps. Challenge. Trinity said later it was my 'if-you-don't-like-it-you-can-go-fuck-yourself' look! As I cradled him, I felt his tears through the bandages over his eyes.

"What have you done?" I demanded, feeling Dante's fingers moving to touch my face.

"It's cool, Angel. Don't be angry." He told me that they'd tried to 'do something with my eyes', but that it might not work so not to get my hopes up. Get *my* hopes up? I felt as if a knife had gone into my guts. *My* hopes?

"Can I have a word, Angelus?" Nadia Christof whispered softly in my ear.

Reluctantly, I released Dante and went with her to a corner. "He didn't want you to know... before. We don't expect to give him sight in both eyes, though we *hope*, but we may be able to give him sight in one eye. Enough."

"And if it fails?"

"He'll be no worse than he is now."

"And if it fails?" I persisted, very softly.

Her eyes were full of sympathy. "All he wanted – all he asked for – was to see your face just once. Now I know why." She smiled. "He wanted you with him when we took the bandages off. Can you do that for him?"

"I can do anything," I said. Anything but stop loving him, I thought to myself.

"Just make sure he wears shades for a few days, whatever happens, so that he doesn't strain his eyes if we're successful. It'll be exciting... new."

"I'll make sure he behaves," I affirmed with a grin, glancing over my shoulder.

"Be sure you do. Seriously." She held my gaze, now the doctor. I nodded crisply. For that chance, however slim, I'd do just about anything. "Perhaps you'd like to hold his hand or something?" She suggested, and I went to sit next to him. I felt his hand shake as she said, "Turn out the light." As we slipped into darkness, I felt his hand tighten and his nails almost cut into my flesh. I raised his hand to my mouth and pressed my lips to it. "Here we go, Dante. Don't expect much at first. It will be blurred, so don't assume it's failed. Then we'll raise the light, bit by bit."

"Okay." His voice, little more than a whisper, shook. I could see Trinity leaning against a wall for support and gave her what I hoped was a reassuring smile.

The medics with Nadia Christof moved to do her bidding as she slowly unwound the bandages. "Keep your eyes closed for a moment. Do you feel okay?"

"They itch."

"That's normal. Whatever you do, don't scratch. Tilt your head back. I'm going to run some liquid over them. Try to let it flow; don't fight it."

I felt his fear and murmured reassurance in his ear.

"That's fine. Just try to relax. Can someone raise the light a little? That's fine. Now, try to open your eyes. How does that feel?"

"I... " he began. "They feel strange."

"That's normal. What can you see?"

"Shapes. A little blurred." She covered one eye and then the other. "Nothing in the left, just blurred. The right... blurred but clearer towards the middle." His voice sounded strangely dispassionate. I was supporting him from behind and looked up to gauge her reaction. She didn't seem surprised.

"Raise the light a little more. Whoa!" She raised a hand and moved closer to him. "How do you feel now?"

"Scared," he said.

"And your vision?"

"Left... same. Right... a little clearer."

"Dante, I know this is going to be hard, but I need you to promise to wear shades when you're in any light for a day or two. It's important. Don't worry; the signs are good. We'll leave you now. I think you'll want to be alone." She smiled and gestured to her assistants. "Remember, Angelus. A few moments then the lights go out – clear?"

"Yes, ma'am." I said firmly. I caught Trinity's expression. There were tears on her face and she was trying not to laugh with joy. She smiled at me and followed them out. Only when I heard the door close firmly did I turn back to Dante. I wasn't sure what I would see, but for the first time I found myself wondering what *he* saw. I gave a slightly nervous smile as he turned to face me. He was weeping; I could see the tears on his cheeks. I wanted to know, but didn't dare ask. So I waited, feeling my heart thump in my chest. Finally, when I could bear the silence no longer, I ventured, "She said to be patient."

"How patient do I need to be?" he asked, reaching out to touch my face unerringly, pulling my head to meet his. I swear I felt my teeth rattle in my head as the floodgate of emotion broke loose. It was a long time before I was able to gasp, "Let me turn out the light."

"But I want to see you, every inch of you."

"And you won't if you don't listen to me."

"A moment," he pleaded. "Just a moment." I could feel myself weakening and told myself to be firm. When I saw the look on his face when he looked at me, I knew he could see enough to make him happy, and that was enough for me.

"If you let me turn out the light," I said, caressing his face with my fingers, "when it's safe, I'll be at your mercy."

"You will?"

"I will."

"Promise?"

"I promise."

He gave a sigh of contentment and surrender. "Turn out the light." I did as he asked and he settled contentedly in my arms. "At least I know now."

"Know what?" I asked, pressing my lips to the top of his head.

"If you are anything like my imaginings."

I wasn't sure I wanted to ask, but I did. "And?"

I could feel his smile. "I'll tell you... later."

"When?"

"When you fulfil your promise, of course," he replied, his voice full of mischief. I groaned.

When I left him, it was to accept an invitation to join Trinity and the others on a 'tour'. I was glad the first person I ran into was Trinity, because I have to admit my image was shot. When I saw her, I burst into tears while she held me in her arms, my head on her shoulder.

"That's it. Let it out. Look, let me..." She dragged me into my room, made me wash my face and generally make myself presentable. "C'mon, big guy. Let's see what they want to show us."

Arm in arm, we made our way to join our guide. When I found Faith and Micah with him, I couldn't hide my smile. Faith flew into my arms, followed by Micah, much to everyone's amusement.

"I heard the news," she said, hugging me. "Fingers crossed."

"Fingers crossed," I echoed, easing her away. "Watch the image, huh?"

"Oh yeah," she grinned. "The Black Crow. The Dark Angel."

I didn't speak to Micah but gave him a nod of greeting, which he understood. Slipping to my side, he almost swaggered as we began to see – and be seen.

Our guide, whose name was Stefan, talked eagerly about the city. "We'll try and arrange a trip outside when we can. It's quite something, you know. Used to belong to a big company or something. The laboratories were why the founders came here, or so it's told. They took over the building, brought people in, before Damnation Day." He pointed out various people, various facilities – shops, markets, inns, even a school, which didn't appeal to Micah, I felt. It was impressive, but I wondered whether the people who'd come here so long ago had been part of Damnation Day; whether they'd been the cause or whether they'd just been in the right place at the right time. I let Trinity and Faith explore the shops – with a token protest – while I sat at a table in a square that had fountains with running water and trees. Trees!

"So, what do you think?"

"Impressive," I replied. "Stefan, have you ever wondered what was, you know, outside."

"Of course I have," he replied. "But we have all we need here. What could the world outside offer?"

I grimaced. "Mag-storms, dust storms, acid rain." I laughed shortly. "What about Faith's father, her husband. Any traces?"

"Not that I know of, but I'll do all I can to find out. It may be that if he is here, he's out of the city."

"So you do go out."

"Of course, but not beyond the veil. Into the land beyond."

"What's out there?"

"When you're ready to see, you'll be shown," he assured me, smiling as the ladies came into view, laden with packages and accompanied by a young woman who came up to us and kissed Stefan on the cheek.

"This is Taylor; my girl," he explained, smiling at her. Chatting on, he talked about the plans they had. "We'll be wed when we have enough saved."

"Good luck," I said.

"Oh, we'll do it. We have faith that we will." He rose to his feet. "Come, time to go back. Enough for one day, if the ladies have bought enough."

"I think they have," I replied, not giving them a chance to refute my announcement.

"I think the Council wish to honour you with a celebration, when your companion is able to accompany you. It would please them if you would accept."

Did I have a choice, I wondered. "I'm sure we would all be honoured to accept," I responded smoothly. With any luck, they'd forget. Unless it might be a source of information about Faith's family, I reasoned.

Chapter 26

Keeping Dante occupied was not overly difficult. As long as he had an instrument to play, someone to talk to, some way to pass the time, he was okay. But he wanted to get out and about, and I agreed provided he wore the shades. I knew we were being watched, of course – both covertly and overtly – but I wasn't about to court controversy in public. Well, not yet, much as I wanted to. In private, that was something else.

He'd fallen asleep listening to music and I'd gone to take a shower. Coming back into the room, I had a bath sheet wrapped around my waist and damp hair, and was so relaxed from a surplus of hot water that I didn't realise he was awake and looking at me.

"Why don't you just drop the sheet and come over here?" His voice was husky and I couldn't help but smile. "I want to examine your scar."

"Yeah?"

"Yeah." He ran his hand up my thigh, over the scar on my leg that the wolves had made. All the while, he held my eyes with his. "I told you I wanted to see every inch of you," he said, "and I will. An inch at a time. Is the door locked?"

"I think so." I wasn't sure I cared.

"Make sure." I hesitated and then went to do as he asked. "Now drop the sheet," he repeated as I returned. I bit back a laugh and promptly did as he asked...

***

"I think I need another shower," I murmured lazily, stretched out on the bed.

"Why waste time?" he returned, his hand on my belly. "Not when you'll only get all hot and sweaty again."

126

"Will I?"

"Oh yeah."

He was right, too. I remember dozing for a while and awaking to darkness. He'd turned the light out, I realised, which was good. At least *he*'d remembered. I turned onto my side carefully, trying not to wake him. I needn't have worried. He wasn't asleep, as I discovered when his teeth dug into my neck.

"I haven't finished with you yet," he murmured, his lips against my throat. "I know what you look like now, remember."

"So?"

"My Angel, I want to store up memories just in case." I wasn't expecting that, I had to admit, and it shook me a little. "I hope you're not planning on getting any sleep. Anything I wanted, you said."

"And what do you want?" Ever asked a question you shouldn't? I had a feeling I just had. I felt his smile, his breath against my ear. "Dante."

"Yeah?"

"I think I'm about to fall off the bed."

"No, you're not," he murmured, pulling me onto my back.

"I don't know what they pumped you full of, but I'm gonna make a protest," I muttered.

"You complaining?"

"Yeah. No." I laughed and tried to push him away. I suppose I could have, if I'd been serious, but it was kind of flattering. "Am I allowed to play, too?" I asked, surrendering.

"How do you wanna play?" he asked, raising his head. I couldn't free myself of the thought that we were being watched, but I didn't care. If they hadn't had enough already, we might as well give them something to watch. I raised my head and murmured in his ear. I didn't have to see his face to know his response. I could feel it where his body pressed against mine. Submission didn't come easy to me, but I'd made a promise. Dante reached out and brought up the light – just enough to see by. "I want to watch your face," he said softly. "I'm hungry and I want to watch your face while I..."

***

Even a shave, a shower and shades didn't help next morning. I felt as if I'd been up all night. Which I had. Dante had a smug look on his face and wore his shades, so at least I didn't feel too much of an idiot. Trinity gave me a sympathetic grin, but

Micah wasn't so merciful. "Keep you up all night, did he?" he asked cheekily and without the trace of hesitation he'd often had before.

"I tried," replied Dante smoothly.

Trinity rolled her eyes in exasperation, but simply said, "Serves you right, darlin'."

"What does?"

"Making him an offer he couldn't refuse," she replied, and I had to laugh.

"Why don't you join us? Then he'd really be in trouble."

Oh shit, now they were ganging up on me!

Trinity's eyes were dancing with laughter as she inclined her head. "Maybe I'll take you up on that, if you're still willing to share."

"Of course I am," replied Dante, extending a hand to take hers and draw it to his lips. "You know, you're every bit as lovely as he said you were. I'd be honoured. He loves you, too."

"Er – we have company," I reminded them, nodding towards Micah, who looked every bit as if he were enjoying this conversation immensely.

Dante turned his head and looked towards Micah. "I know," he replied. "And if he hasn't learned manners yet, he'll get an education he might not be ready for."

Micah bit his lip, his eyes merry. "If I have my facts right, I'm not much younger than you were, so don't get too cocky." He winked at Trinity. "Unless you're offering, honey."

Trinity, I must say, kept her cool remarkably well. "When you're ready, *honey*, I'll tell you. Now piss off!" Laughing, he actually did as she asked. "Whatever did you say to that young man?" she asked when we were sure Micah was out of earshot.

"At no time did I ask him to join us," I chuckled, "but maybe we'd better check under the bed at regular intervals, just in case."

Chapter 27

Now Dante no longer needed medical supervision, they found us an apartment, but getting them to allow me near my rig was less simple. They simply didn't understand why, as we weren't planning on going anywhere, I should need to. I told them I just wanted to give her a check over. I didn't say I wanted to check that my weapons were still there. I also wanted to check for bugs – not the kind with legs and wings, but the surveillance type – and I certainly *wasn't* about to tell them that. I took Micah with me because I thought it would attract less attention, and he seemed happy to come. I'd told him what I planned, so when he spoke it was loud enough to be heard without microphones.

"You want me to pass you something, Angel?" he asked. "How about coffee?"

"I'd love some." I replied. "Think I'll put some stuff away at the same time." An excuse for banging a few doors.

"That'll be a first. Wait till I tell Trinity."

"Don't you dare."

We kept the banter light while I checked that everything was where it should be and contemplated whether I could get my crossbow inside. I felt naked without it. Still, I made sure I had my knives, at least. With any luck, those should go undetected. If not, I'd find out how good their detection systems were.

"Seen anything of Dr Jon?" I asked Micah as casually as I could. Micah shook his head. It puzzled me that there'd been no mention of him, or of Faith's family. I wondered how much I still knew on that score. It still didn't ring true. If I were in her position and my father and husband were missing, I'd be going crazy trying to find them. If, say, Dante or Trinity were missing, I'd be creating all sorts of mayhem. I'd been wondering for some time if there weren't more to this than met the eye. Perhaps she was some sort of 'agent' of Dan Truman's, or an equivalent elsewhere.

The circumstances of our meeting were genuine enough; I didn't dispute that. But the rest – the more I thought about it, the less I liked it. I was looking forward to doing some gentle probing at this celebration they had planned. It came to me, though, that it was Faith I wanted to talk to more than anyone. I was growing more certain by the minute that I was being kept in the dark about something.

If I were less than happy about 'being on display', it was nothing to the mayhem that ensued as we dressed for the occasion. Trinity was struggling with a dress, much to our amusement. I hadn't realised that getting into a dress could be so entertaining. She'd ask me for assistance, but all I could do was sit there and laugh.

"Useless. Absolutely useless!" she complained as she struggled to pull up the zipper that ran down the back of the tight-fitting dress. I couldn't tell her I was enjoying the view; she'd have kneed me one. In the end, it was Dante who went to her aid. I don't know what he said to her, but I caught her looking my way and muttering a response to him. The sight of Trinity in a tight-fitting dress did little to calm my libido. The contrast of the conservative 'work' dress these people wore and the somewhat exotic – or erotic – leisurewear puzzled me. Both Dante and I wore close-fitting pants, over which was a sort of long, black, form-fitting coat. Trinity's dress was white and tight in all the right places.

Dante's hair needed a trim, I thought... or maybe not. It had grown somewhat from his old style and had taken on a more jaw-length wild style, which I thought suited him. I discovered later that Trinity had been working on it for him. Mine hung loose past my shoulder blades, a stark contrast to my clothing as ever, but because of the almost severe, close-fitting collar, we looked more like olden-day priests, or, as Dante put it, two saints and a sinner.

"You two? Saints?" chuckled Trinity. "I don't think so."

I pulled her to me, settling my hands on her butt. "You could at least try and tempt me."

"You don't need tempting," she retorted, removing my hands. "Behave yourself."

"Me?"

"Who else?"

"Dante?"

She gave Dante a side-glance. "True, but you'll be the one everyone's watching." She had a point. Whether or not I caused a stir would depend on whether or not doing so would gain me some kind of advantage.

It appeared, and we were told by our guide Stefan, that half of New Eden's 'elite' was present. I spotted Faith at the same instant she spotted us, and we met part way across the floor.

"You look lovely," I told her as I kissed her cheek.

"You don't look so bad yourself," she murmured in my ear.

"I want a word. Later?"

She withdrew slightly and then nodded. "Agreed. Now, where's that brat got to?" It took me a moment to realise she meant Micah, whom we located after some moments talking to a couple of young people. "Looks like he's okay. You seen Jon Fevre?"

"No. Is he here?"

"If I knew, would I be asking?" she retorted, and then sighed. "Sorry. You're right – we do need to talk. Your place later."

"Fine by me."

The meal was amusing, if only for the fact that I had only a marginally better idea which item of cutlery to use than Dante had. Trinity simply told me to start at the outside and work in, which seemed to help. The wine, which I was informed proudly was grown in their hydroponics farm, was light and refreshing. Most important in my mind was the fact that whenever I steered the conversation to our 'fellow travellers', it was skilfully steered away again.

I was itching to rattle their complacency, but before I did so I wanted a little more 'ammunition'.

***

When Faith arrived at our door, it was Trinity who admitted her. "Love the dress," I heard Faith say to Trinity as she closed the door. "How're their lordships?"

"Dante's sight's improving, which is a blessing, though I'm not sure whether Angel would agree." There was amusement in her voice, and I heard Faith's soft laughter.

"Keeping him busy, is he?"

"You could put it that way. Go on through. Angel's in the lounge."

I was stretched out on the couch, my coat flung open. Faith hesitated in the doorway, looking at me. Dante came in from the bathroom and seemed to break the seal on her inaction, because she smiled and went to him, kissing his cheek. "You can't know how pleased I am," she said, running a finger next to his eye. He smiled.

"Believe me, you can't be half as pleased as I am," he responded, taking a seat. I'd expected him to perch on the arm of the couch, which he often did. I wondered why he hadn't. It wasn't as if Faith were a stranger. Perhaps it was because if he'd been close, he'd be distracting me. Idiot, I thought. Proximity wasn't the only factor.

"Any news of that husband of yours?"

She shook her head. "It's as if he's vanished into thin air."

"Or never existed?" I enquired lazily. She hesitated, uncertain how I'd meant the question to be taken. I decided to take the chance. "C'mon, Faith. Don't we merit the truth by now?"

"Truth?"

"You don't have a husband, do you?"

It took a long time for her to reply. I held her gaze without blinking. If she didn't trust me by now, I reasoned, she never would. I was weary of games, my own included. When she reached into her purse and pulled out a small box, I knew I was on the right track. I knew what it was, and her smile told me she knew that I knew. "I said that it was a bad idea, keeping you in the dark. Dan, in his wisdom, insisted. He asked me to give you this." She handed me a letter.

> *Wheels within wheels, my old friend... sorry I didn't tell you, but that's the way the game works, as you well know. You can trust Faith. I thought I'd lost her – would have, if not for you – which is why I kept her secret, and yours. In case you're wondering, her name's no more 'Faith' than yours is 'Angelus'. But as you have your reasons, so does she. Take care, 'Dark Angel'.*

I raised my eyes slowly and folded the notepaper. "So, 'Faith', do you know what it says?"

She shook her head so I passed it to her. "I had a husband once. He was killed by raiders. That's when I started working for the Wayfarers." I knew who the Wayfarers were, of course. I should: I worked for them myself. Freelance because I travelled, but the fact that I travelled so much kept me from the suspicion of being allied to any particular group. The Wayfarers had been formed after Damnation Day as a sort of intelligence service, keeping an eye on the groups that formed, who allied to whom, who the bad guys were; tracked gun runners, drug dealers, slave traffickers, that sort of thing. Some time ago there'd been rumours of this place, this New Eden, that if they hadn't started the whole damned game, they'd profited from it. "The Council had heard rumours that someone was trafficking between Glenn Creek and New Eden, so Dan arranged that I accompany you under the pretext of looking for my husband and father. He didn't tell me that you were a Wayfarer, just that you could be trusted. As, of course, he didn't tell you about me. What you don't know can't be used against you, right?" She gave a rueful smile. "The factor we weren't sure of was Jon Fevre. Whether he was part of the ring or not. Any ideas?"

I bit my lip thoughtfully. "Naïve, perhaps, but I don't have him pegged as a ringleader. Unless he's a very good actor, of course. I think it's my friend with the blunt instrument. His contacts here will take some tracing. We've got an uphill struggle, unless we're lucky."

"And you're the lucky man, aren't you, Angelus?"

I shrugged. "Sometimes." I didn't know what the deal was between Glenn Creek and New Eden, but we had to keep up the pretence of looking for her husband and father. "You did have a father, I suppose?"

"Ha ha. Although as I've never seen him, I'd be very much surprised if I did find him." She relaxed in her chair. "I'm glad that's over."

"Why?"

"You can be pretty intimidating, you know."

"Me?" I must have sounded strange, because I heard Dante's bark of laughter and shot him an annoyed glare. It didn't cow him in the slightest; he just laughed all the harder.

"He puts his pants on one leg at a time like anyone else," Dante assured her between bouts of laughter.

"Yeah?" She allowed her gaze to pass from one to the other of us. "I'll take your word for that. And if you're planning on taking him out of them, I'll take my leave."

"You might learn something," he offered, his eyes full of laughter.

"After travelling with you these long miles, I've learned all I wish to, thanks."

I turned my head slowly towards where Dante was sitting, lingering on Trinity for a moment. "If I'd known yer were listening," I drawled, my accent slipping again, "I'd have made it more interesting."

"Believe me, it was quite interesting enough," Faith rejoined, rising. "And don't tell me you cared if you had an audience."

"I wasn't about to," I replied, rising also. Kissing her cheek, I opened the door for her. Only when she was gone did I realise she'd left the bug detector on the table. Deliberately, I guessed. I'd have to conceal it, or put it somewhere it wasn't immediately obvious.

We had a strategy to plan, I knew, but I wasn't up to planning. As it was, I knew I was going to have to pay for keeping a secret from Trinity and Dante, although I had to admit they'd concealed their surprise well. If it had been a surprise, I thought. I'd probably talked in my sleep or something. Not that it was going to be much of a problem in the immediate future. I had a feeling I wasn't going to be getting much sleep.

***

"So..." Trinity, who was laying on my left, hitched herself up so that her breasts dug into my chest, "when were you gonna come clean?"

I hesitated and then decided to be honest. "I wasn't, unless I had to. Safer for all of us. Lots o' people I deal with wouldn't take it well." I shifted, trying to get myself comfortable. That's the problem with three in a bed: you lose out on room to spread. "Honey, would yer mind? Yer elbow's digging in."

"Sorry," she apologised, shuffling. "That better?"

"I don't think it's your elbow that's digging in him now, Trin," came Dante's lazy voice from my other side.

"Huh?" She looked down and giggled. "Oh. Shall I...?" I think the arm holding her close convinced her that I didn't mind at all. "You haven't said what you think of Dante's new hairstyle."

"Fishing for compliments?" I asked, grinning.

"A girl likes to receive 'em as well as give 'em," she said, winking at Dante. "Don't think he needs to say, d'you? Hardly taken his eyes off yer."

Was I so obvious, I wondered? Yeah, probably. Dante's hair was wilder than it had been, and the fact that I thought he looked as sexy as hell was more than obvious. He also looked more than a little smug, damn him. That was the point I discovered that long hair could be a considerable disadvantage, because when I tried to move, Trinity, who was not being the slightest bit secretive about the fact that the pair of them were colluding, impeded my movement.

"Call the shots too often, you do," murmured Dante against my throat, raising his eyes briefly. "Time for us to play."

"Unfair!" I made a concerted effort to disentangle myself. "I do not—"

"Ssh!" I felt his lips brush my ear and felt his breath as he murmured, "Case you hadn't noticed, it's flashing." It took me a moment to realise he was referring to the gadget Faith had left behind. Trinity, of course, was close enough to hear. "Showtime?" Let's just say their response wasn't verbal and leave it at that.

I don't know at what point it stopped flashing, but I know we gave them a damned good 'show'!

Chapter 28

wasn't surprised when I received an invitation to meet with people who called themselves 'Logistics', although I was a little surprised to see that one of the people there was one of the Glenn Creek people.

"Take a seat, Mr Angelus," the guy I took to be the man in charge suggested as the door closed.

"Just Angelus," I said, allowing my eyes to scan the room. He hadn't given his name, I noted, as my eyes lingered on the only face I recognised. I wondered if he was my 'friend with the blunt instrument'.

"You must be wondering why we invited you to join us."

I pulled my eyes back onto him. "It crossed my mind," I shrugged, allowing my posture to relax and stretching my legs out in front of me. He seemed to be waiting for me to continue, but I didn't.

After a few moments, he chuckled. "I'd been told you don't ask too many questions. I see that's true. My friends and I have some business you might be interested in."

"Always interested in a proposal," I replied carefully. "Legal or illegal?"

"Would it matter?"

"Not much if the price is right," I responded truthfully.

He glanced at his companions. "I've been told you're prepared to take risks, Angelus. We're always on the lookout for runners."

"What do yer have in mind?" I asked.

His eyes seemed to bore right through me, which confirmed my belief that whatever we were talking about here, it wasn't in the least bit legal.

"If we tell you, we need to know you're 'in'. That you'll keep your mouth shut. Do you know where Starburst is?"

I could feel the tension now, and that I had to be careful. I wasn't sure what they knew about me, but I couldn't take any chances. "I've heard of it," I replied non-committally. Sure, I'd heard of it. So had Dante. I'd thought it blown to hell and back. Seems I was wrong. Still, there was always a chance I could amend that, wasn't there? "You're running slaves."

"People come here as shouldn't. What else can we do with them?" he responded smoothly. "You gotta problem with that?"

"No," I shrugged, knowing that if I showed the slightest revulsion they'd be on me like a shot. "What's the deal?"

"Would you leave us, gentlemen?" he asked, waiting for them to do so before he continued. "Call me Alex," he said when the door had closed. "Can I offer you a drink?"

I shrugged. "Sure." Watching him carefully, I looked around the room. "Nice set-up you got here."

"Not bad," he admitted, placing the dark liquor in front of me. "I don't figure you as the talkative type, Angelus. Your reputation don't come over that way. If you were, guess you'd be dead," he added thoughtfully with a laugh I wasn't sure I liked. "So I figured, what'd buy you?" He seemed to be talking more to himself than to me, so I let him. "And keep you bought." I wasn't about to offer a suggestion, but I felt cold inside. "Just so we know we can trust you. One trip; out 'n' back. Your friends stay here."

"Go on."

"Can you handle it alone?"

I shrugged. "I've been alone a long time."

"I meant without your 'playmates'." I didn't respond, although he seemed to expect me to. "Your business. I thought, what would keep Angelus in line, bring him back and keep him?" He had a shark's smile, and it was all I could do to stop myself planting my fist in his face. "Suppose I told you I could give you the one thing you want most?"

"And what might that be?"

"Dante's sight." Quietly spoken, it had the required impact of course, at least as far as he was concerned. He wasn't looking beyond what he expected to see. Of course, I knew one thing he didn't: that Dante already had his sight. He didn't move in the right circles to know, and it wasn't yet public knowledge.

Keeping my voice as neutral as I could, I asked, "On what terms?"

"What I said. You do this run solo. After – well, maybe they can accompany you. One, maybe both when we trust you. You're good, Angelus. Some say you're the best. You willin' to prove it?"

No point in asking if I could talk it over with them; not only would it put the others at risk, it would make me look suspicious. Reputations don't always work to your advantage, I thought. "What guarantees do I have that they'll be safe?"

"I could say 'my word' – but why should you trust that? You can have anyone you name with them all the time, even one of mine as a 'guarantee', if you like. We can discuss terms once I know you're in."

"And if I say 'not good enough'? Out of curiosity."

"As I said, we can discuss terms. C'mon, Angelus. A chance to run against the law, to prove you're the best. You gonna refuse?" He had a point. Angelus the runner wouldn't. Angelus the Wayfarer couldn't.

I shrugged nonchalantly and said levelly, "You know, of course, that if one hair of their heads is harmed I'll make you eat your balls."

He grinned. "I know you'll try."

My smile was cold, even arrogant. "I won't 'try'," I assured him. For a second I saw the flash of uncertainty in his eyes. Even fear. Good. "I guess I've nothing better to do." He offered his hand and, after a moment, I took it... and wondered how the fuck I was going to explain this one and to whom.

In the end, it was Faith I chose to come clean to. 'Come clean' being almost literal and not entirely metaphorical, as I was in the bathroom at the time, to all intents and purposes in the shower.

"I do one run, there and back, alone," I informed her. I told her about Alex, my meeting, and what I wanted her to do while I was gone. I also told her what to do in case I didn't come back. She wasn't pleased, but she understood. Then I told her where I was 'running' to.

She went pale, her eyes anxious as she said, "You can't—"

"I can. I can do anything – remember?" I returned bitterly. "Just don't tell them where I've gone. If I don't come back..."

"Angel, what're you planning to do?"

I smiled coldly. "I thought that place should be sent to hell. I intend to make sure it is." Which wouldn't please them, I thought, if word got back here before I did. I wondered how fast the old girl was, if I could do a little tinkering. I told her that if I wasn't back by a certain date, to go to Jon Fevre and trust in him, to get his rig and get the hell out of there, to head for Vesta, that sooner or later I'd turn up there. I don't think she believed me. If it went that badly wrong I wouldn't be coming back. "No matter what, look after Dante and Trinity for me. Do whatever you have to, but keep them safe. That's the only thing that matters to me."

"Suppose you make it back. What then?"

"Then we get the fuck out of here."

"You'd renege on your contract?"

I laughed coldly. "Damn right I would. I don't condone slavery, nor should you, given where you were bound."

"I don't. I just know that if you break your contract with these people—"

"I can deal with that side of things. After all, they're hardly likely to try and enforce it, are they? Without blowing it all wide open. I know what I'm doing, honey. Trust me."

Faith regarded me with an expression that told me she thought I'd lost my marbles. She was probably right. "I was always told never to trust a guy who said 'trust me'," she replied, "but you're the exception. Keep your back covered, you bastard." Then she gave me a quick kiss and bolted, leaving me standing open-mouthed.

Telling Dante and Trinity that I was leaving alone wasn't easy, even when I told them that it would be worth it. It was a 'jaunt' with a hefty paycheck, I told them. I was lying through my teeth, and I think they knew it. I told Trinity to watch over Dante and to get out of there if there was any hint of a threat and that Faith was going to act as back-up. I told Dante about the deal I'd made for the run, and asked him to pretend, if it worked, to be more incapacitated than he was. I told both of them that I loved them and would move heaven and earth to get back to them.

I asked Micah to make certain he was with Dante if either Faith or Trinity weren't, and gave him one of my knives and a small gun. He told me his friends had told him about ways to get around the city without being caught, and that he'd use them to move about and to watch goings-on. I had a feeling his 'friends' weren't exactly model citizens. I had visions of having a band of teenagers on board when we left. I was beginning to feel like – what was the name of the guy in that old book, the guy who had all those kids picking pockets? – Fagin. That was it. Fagin.

Saying goodbye to Dante and Trinity was harder than anything I'd ever done, because although I hadn't lied to them, I'd been somewhat economical with the truth. For a reason, but whether that would save my nuts when they found out! Driving away, I dared not look back. I wasn't the only rig on the run, and I had a reputation to uphold. But that wasn't the reason. I knew that if I looked back I'd turn back and take the consequences. But I couldn't ask Trinity and Dante to pay with me. I kept my trusty crossbow on the seat next to me – just in case.

Chapter 29

Faith would have told Trinity the truth as soon as I was safely on my way – when it was too late or too difficult for them to follow. The air, I imagine, would have turned blue. I hope Micah covered his ears but I don't suppose he did. Dante would be more introverted, his expression unreadable; he certainly wouldn't be happy.

I can imagine Micah trying to reassure him, the exchange along the lines of, 'Don't worry. He'll be okay. Isn't he always?'

'It's not that simple, Micah,' Dante'd say as he ruffled his hair. 'Not given where he's bound. You don't know…'

'So tell me. I'm not a child, Dante! You need to talk. I–I know I'm not *him*, but please?'

Dante's face would soften and then he would say that he wouldn't need to tell me, but that I didn't know everything. He would agree to spill the beans if he received Micah's promise to forgive him. Micah would tell himself afterwards that Dante had needed to talk to someone, as he'd said things no one else was meant to hear. But when all was said and done, Micah would feel that he understood a little better the bond between Dante and me. I hoped Micah would have time to examine his feelings for me and admit to himself that there was a degree of hero worship there. I had saved his life, after all. But he could also admit that there was a little bit of a crush there, too. I think he thought that I didn't realise the impact I had when I entered a room, and sometimes he thought that I knew very well and played it to the hilt. There's a sense of danger about me, I guess. You don't always know quite where you stand with me or what I'm thinking. Except when I'm looking at Dante or Trinity, of course. Dante's been part of my life for so long that even my composure is sometimes shaken by the strength of feeling that still existed between us.

Micah had seen me with my crossbow in my hand and death in my eyes, and he'd seen me when I looked at Dante. I guess my feelings are complicated, but there's little about my life that isn't, given that I'm saddled with the rest of them. And I was likely to be saddled with a whole lot more people, if only for a short while: a bit like the Pied Piper, I guess, if I managed to bring this off. Who I shack up with is no one's business but mine when it comes down to it, and I don't need Micah complicating my life. But if he needed advice, he'd some good friends he could call on even if I wasn't around.

Alone too much with my thoughts, I began to wonder if I was biting off more than I could chew this time. I was anxious about Dante; about leaving him and Trinity behind; about a great many things that I hadn't allowed to concern me before. Perhaps because when I'd left them before I'd left them among friends. This time I was leaving them in uncertainty if not actual danger, and although I knew that they were not entirely helpless, it was hard to keep my mind on what I was supposed to be doing.

Chapter 30

hadn't made any contact with my cargo, because if I did and I saw them as human beings, I was bound to empathise and blow my cover. But my conscience pricked. Every time we halted and I heard the other drivers laughing among themselves I had to grit my teeth, particularly as I suspected I was being shadowed by my friend of the blunt instrument, Dex, I think his name was. But as we came closer to Starburst, I knew I had to take a chance – a big chance, if any of my cargo were ringers – so when it was time to feed and water them, I took it on myself.

Closing the doors behind me, I kept my weapon in clear sight as I looked around. It hurt. It hurt like hell – the hopelessness. As I looked at them, I felt memory rush back.

It must have shown on my face, because one of the men gave a soft laugh. "Been here, ain't yer?" I didn't reply, but I couldn't look away. "I knows yer. Heard yer name, I has. You's the one they call the Black Crow."

"And you are?"

"Zak. Zak Reeves. What you doin'…?"

I glanced over my shoulder towards the door and lowered my voice. "I need yer ter trust me, all o' yer. I won't sell yer out. If I tell yer, scream fer all yer worth, hear? Yer life on it... and mine." He held my gaze. "I've been there, as yer say. In Starburst. Knows it well, I does." I should, I thought. I'd spent enough time there. The trouble was, I didn't know if anyone there would recognise me. I could be in deep shit if they did, seeing as I'd tried to blow it up when I left! "They probably still got a 'wanted' poster with my face on it," I added recklessly. "Yer want to help me finish what I started? I won't leave yer behind, any o' yer." I looked around at their faces, knowing I was pushing my luck with time.

As I heard the door begin to open, Zak said, "Hit me."

"What?"

"Pistol-whip me. Now."

Cursing under my breath, I did as he asked, just as the doors opened. I whirled, glaring at the interruption, ready to strike out again as Dex jumped in.

"Trouble?" he asked.

"Nothin' I can't handle," I said, looking down at Zak, who was wiping the blood from his lip and glaring back at me. "Yer wantin' somethin'?"

"Just wondered what was takin' yer so long. Boss'll be pleased ter hear yer keen on discipline."

I longed to wipe the sneer from his face, and when he kicked out a booted foot it was all I could do not to smash his head in. Calm yourself, I told myself sternly. Grit your teeth and take it. Do something about it when you can. So I locked the doors and curled up in the front, away from the laughter, cursing Dan Truman for getting me into this – and my own arrogance.

I fell asleep, dreaming of Dante as he'd been when we'd been young, when Starburst had been all that we knew and all we'd had to rely on was each other. I'd sworn then to destroy the damned place. I thought I'd succeeded. Seemed that the greed of those who profited from the place had opened it up again. I'd have to make doubly certain this time, I told myself. More than that, I'd do my damnedest to bring as many out alive as I could. I owed it to myself and to Dante, as well as to the poor souls who hadn't made it out.

How the hell I was going to do it I didn't have the faintest idea.

The closer I came to Starburst, the more I questioned my sanity. I must've been crazy to take this on, and if I came out of it in one piece, I'd probably have a word or two to say to Dan Truman on the subject, in private. He had to have known where the trail would lead and what I'd do when I got there. Not that I minded being 'used' to throw out the trash, but hey, he could've asked, right? I had to admire the bastard, though. He was almost as ruthless as me. My only fear was that someone there would recognise me. Unlikely, I hoped, but far from impossible. With a bit of luck I could bluff my way out of any confrontation – I'd changed a bit since then, after all – but the feeling in my gut was that this was a set-up. That if they didn't know already who I was, they soon would. Although I didn't know why they considered it worthwhile going to all this trouble.

Chapter 31

got word when I could to Zak Reeves and those I'd brought with me, mostly when I went to 'torment' them. I hoped my performance was convincing, but I was by no means convinced I was that good an actor, particularly when I felt the memories flooding back. I slipped them weapons when I could, and explosives, knowing all the while that I was on borrowed time.

When I saw him, I knew that I would be looking death in the face when he put a name to the face he was looking at. I could see it in his eyes: the trace of memory. It was there, just a thought away. He knew me. Not the name yet, or at least he hadn't yet connected the name I had now with the one I'd had then. We were talking almost fifteen years ago, after all, and he'd probably seen a lot of faces since then. As I laughed with my fellow 'runners', as I played out my game, I kept my voice out of his range in the vain hope of buying a little time.

I'm not sure about the exact moment hell broke loose, or even who started it. I'd cautioned against trying to take on the guards directly, but I guess the taste of freedom goes to the head, or at least the promise of it. I'd offered that hope, and now I'd have to 'reap the whirlwind'. I don't know who 'set fire to the powder keg', but in the end it didn't matter. I had my crossbow, of course, but I knew I hadn't made a killing shot when I heard someone shout, "Break the bastard's arms!" I told myself I should never have given them the explosives so soon or even at all, but shit, I'm not a one-man army. Angry as I was at Dan Truman for sending me in, I understood his reasons. Being freelance I was not going to be sanctioned for going too far. At least I hoped not!

Knowing Dex had set me up made having him in my sights feel good, and I waited an instant too long before firing. The bolts flew wild, but struck home, as I heard screams attest, as I saw stars. I went for my knives as I hit the floor, knowing that I was in for a world of pain as I looked up into his face.

"You should'na come back," he told me as his boot crashed into my ribs. "Still, nice 'o yer ter give us a second crack."

I wasn't going to make it easy, because I knew what they'd do to me given half a chance. My only chance would be to piss them off enough to make it quick. Some hope, I thought, as I felt bones crack and tasted copper. They enjoyed their work too much. I'm told I went a little crazy then, but it eased the pain I couldn't allow to incapacitate me. Among the explosions and the screams it was Zak Reeves who found me. He told me later that I'd looked more demon than angel, my hair more red than white, my clothing ripped. He told me he'd taken one look at me and vomited. I don't remember that or the flight; don't even have the satisfaction of having watched Starburst implode, although I know it did. I was on a stretcher being dragged out of there to my rig, to the convoy of stolen vehicles.

I have a vague memory of waking to find a crowd of faces around me, but I can't say I remember anything clearly until I regained consciousness in a bed, in what I discovered to be Dan Truman's house, with strapped ribs, both arms encased in plaster and splints. What little I could see of myself was a mass of scrapes, scratches and bruises of varying hues. I felt like shit and probably looked it, but mostly I was pretty much out of things for a long time.

When I opened my eyes again I wasn't alone, but the last person I expected to see sitting in the chair opposite me was Dom Truman.

He grinned when he saw my eyes flutter open. "You look like shit!" he proclaimed gleefully.

"Thanks a lot!" I ran my eyes over him. "You look..." I didn't know what to say.

"A day at a time," he smiled, "thanks to you. A lot of people are grateful to you, seems to me." I wondered what he knew. "Case you're wonderin', you're a bit bent." I raised a brow and he chuckled. "Bones 'n' such."

I laughed. "Figured. What do I have to do to get a drink?"

"Oh. Sorry. Hang on." He reached out for his crutches and I watched, both proudly and agonisingly as he struggled to his feet and came towards me. That he was mobile at all was something of a miracle in my eyes. If there was one thing I was proud of in my sorry life it was that. "Sorry if I get you wet, but I'm not much good at this," he apologised. It hurt to laugh, but it was impossible not to as he tried to raise my head and give me a drink without choking or drowning me. "Least you won't need a bed bath later."

I lay back, gasping. "True. Where's yer dad?"

"Sorting out the mess you dropped in his lap... still. Why?"

"Cos I need ter take a leak," I pointed out.

"Oh. Right. I can handle that."

"Er – I'd rather you didn't." I replied uneasily as he grabbed for a bottle.

"Trust me. I know how. They showed me."

"Who? Faith and Trinity?"

"Doc Christof, actually. But they're here. Had quite an adventure themselves, as I'm sure they can't wait to tell you."

Why did I get the impression that he was hoping I was going to take the bait and let him off the hook? I might have if the little prick didn't have a smug expression on his face, as if he knew something I didn't, which, in all probability, he did.

"Where's Dante?" He went still then, which set alarm bells ringing. "Maybe you'd better fill me in," I suggested, but he knew from the tone in my voice that I wouldn't accept anything less than the truth, the whole truth, and nothing but.

"I thought you were desperate to take a leak." A last vain effort to escape, for which I couldn't blame him, as I was getting steadily more irritable by the minute.

"Not that desperate."

"Oh... fuck!"

I listened to Dom's report, all thoughts of a full bladder forgotten as he told me what had happened in my absence – about Micah's involvement with a small but determined 'underground' who were dissatisfied with how things were run and suspicious of what lay behind their 'perfect' society – I guess I'd planted the seeds. I just hoped they didn't know where to get hold of any explosives! No point in worrying about that, I told myself, at least not while I'd enough problems of my own – how Micah had kept his promise to look after Dante, about Nadia Christof's latest efforts on Dante's behalf. I owed her – big time, it seemed. I owed them all, I reminded myself.

Dom watched me silently as I absorbed what he'd told me. I imagined Micah refusing to leave Dante's side after the operation because of promises made, wondering if he had reassured Dante that it was going to be okay and if Dante had in turn sought to reassure Micah of the same. What was I supposed to do when I saw Dante, I wondered. Pretend I didn't know how the 'miracle' had come about?

"So where *is* Dante?"

"That's for him to tell. Look, you want me to do this or you want to lie in a puddle?" He demanded, exasperated.

Time to swallow my pride, I thought. "No. I mean yes," I replied humbly.

When Dan Truman came in some time later, he was greeted by the sight of his jubilant son waving his 'trophy'! He rolled his eyes at me and shooed his son out before pulling up a chair. He didn't speak for some time, simply sat looking down at his hands. "I never intended... this," he began, gesturing.

"But you knew it could happen if anyone recognised me."

He winced. "I do what I have to, I guess. In my position you have to be ruthless. You knew that when you signed on."

"I'm not bonded, that's why. Because while I'm freelance, I have back-up and freedom to do your dirty jobs for you." There was no recrimination in my voice, simply a statement of facts. "So we both win... or lose; I'm not sure which. How many got out?"

"Before you and your 'band of brothers' brought the place down around their ears? Seventy, give or take." I closed my eyes and sighed. "For those who wanted to go home we've arranged it... with compensation. The others we'll relocate with time, when they're ready. We have Faith's collection, too, but that's another story. Good work, Angelus."

I'd learn the rest bit by bit. "Faith? Trinity?"

"Let them tell you themselves later. Give 'em that."

I closed my eyes for a moment and gathered my thoughts. Pain washed over me and I found it hard to focus. "What did I bust?" I asked.

"Your arms, of course. They made pretty sure you wouldn't use your crossbow again." I closed my eyes and swallowed. I'd pretty much assumed that.

"We'll see," I replied softly.

He smiled weakly. "Your ribs, of course. Got a crack to your skull, broken nose, two black eyes..." The catalogue seemed to go on forever. "You need to sleep, or are you hungry?"

I hesitated. "I guess I'm hungry."

"Good. I'll see what I can arrange," he promised with a quick grin. "I'll sort out some pain killers, too, okay?" His eyes told me that if I wanted to be macho and tough it out, he'd likely ram them down my throat himself, or stick the needle in *hard*.

I was pleased to see that my next visitor was Faith, and that she was carrying a tray of food. "There you go. Let's get you comfy," she said, putting down the tray. She propped me up with pillows mainly by manhandling them – and me – with a lot of laughter. "Nearly had to cut your hair," she informed me as she cut up the food. "Open wide."

"You're enjoying this," I accused and she chuckled.

"Course I am. Not often a girl gets her hands on a prime piece o' meat." Her irreverent teasing helped ease the touch of depression I'd begun to feel. "I'll give you a shave later, if you like. Get you nice for when Dante—"

"When Dante...?" I prompted. She bit her lip. Something she shouldn't have told me, perhaps.

"Gone shopping with Micah, that's all. Been with you, him 'n' Trin. Needed a break. Sorry."

I rolled my eyes. "Yer excused."

Faith grinned. "How you feel now?" She brushed back my hair and wiped my face. "Least I didn't choke you."

"For which I'm eternally grateful," I replied.

"So, you want me to stick a needle in your butt, or will you swallow like a good boy?"

"You keep your hands off my butt," I chuckled. "I'll swallow."

Faith pouted. "Spoilsport."

I laughed. "Not fair if you get to play and I don't."

Grinning at me impishly, she said, "You ain't got no secrets from me, honey. Not that you ever were one for keeping your light under a bush. Open up and swallow. I don't want you to choke." Meekly, I obeyed. My ribs wouldn't stand any rough stuff if that happened. "There you go. Now, if you're a good boy and go to sleep, I'll let you have visitors later."

"Do I get a bedtime story?" I asked hopefully.

Faith hesitated. "Kind of story you probably like would keep you awake! You settle for some music?"

I sighed. "Guess I'll have to." Smiling, she brushed back my hair and bent to kiss my brow.

"Sleep well, Angel."

Time passed in sleep. I have a vague memory of waking and seeing Nadia Christof bending over me, but that could have been a dream. When I awoke again I didn't know how much time had passed because the storm shields were down and the room was lit by candles.

As if on cue, the bathroom door opened and Trinity came into the room, Her clothing appeared new, her make-up was immaculate and she looked wonderful.

Her smile when she saw me was radiant. "You look good," she said as she bent to kiss me.

"Yeah, I bet I do," I chuckled dryly.

"You always look good to me, love." She smiled, giving me a gentle kiss. "Even when..." Her composure cracked. She'd have hugged me, if she could, or I her, but it'd be a while before I could even think of... well, I could think, I amended, but there was damned little I could do about it! I couldn't even move a finger to comfort her, I thought, cursing silently as her bowed head and shoulders shook.

"Hey, babe, don't cry. You'll wet the sheets!"

This time the shaking was with laughter as she raised her head. "It was when we bathed you. Between us, we 'bout soaked yer."

"Us?"

"Me and Faith, usually. Weren't very good. Didn't want ter hurt yer, but Nadia said you wouldn't feel a thing."

I wanted to ask who else had been in on that little scene, but I wasn't sure I wanted to hear. "Nadia... Tell me..."

"She decided to stick around. Dan offered her a job, seein' as yer seemed to need patchin' up so often." I chuckled. "Later, the whole story, I promise. Try to sleep."

"I've slept enough!" I snapped and immediately regretted it because I saw her face change. "Oh babe, I'm sorry. Please. I'm just so damned frustrated."

She bit her lip and raised her eyes. "Might be somethin' I can do 'bout that, darlin'," she drawled. Oh, but it was a tempting offer! "Maybe later, if you're a good boy. When those creaky old bones of yours have healed a bit more."

"Aw, that's not fair. Leadin' a guy on."

"Don't pout. It doesn't become you." She ran a finger over my jaw. "Patience is a virtue."

There was, I decided, precious little I could do about it. "How long do I have to be patient for?" I sighed.

Trinity laughed musically. "Next time the doc pays a house call, why don't yer ask her?"

"I will." I'd have to, I thought, because I wanted to find out what I had to do to get my arms back into working order. I wouldn't settle for anything less, which meant my thoughts when Starburst had been coming down were right. I was in for a world of pain.

So what was new? Gritting my teeth, I told myself to flex my fingers. One finger at a time would do, I instructed my digits. That wasn't too much to ask, was it?

***

Inactivity bored me, and the moment I could persuade Nadia to allow me out of bed, I was. With Dom for company, I went through a painful regime of exercises. He bullied me unmercifully, because he couldn't wait to thrash me at chess, he said, and moving the pieces for me just wasn't the same.

Dan Truman watched the process with bemusement, seeing a side of his son he hadn't seen before. I saw quiet pride on his face, though, and knew what was in his thoughts: that it wasn't that long ago he hadn't expected his son to be alive right now.

I waited for Dante to return, trying not to ask where he was.

I'd discovered gradually the details of the flight from New Eden: that Micah and his friends had been instrumental in blowing the shield generator; that he'd given them the opportunity to allow the 'forces of good' in to clean up the pyramidic city from base to apex and to take over the running of the city until a new council could be elected to place it in safer, less corrupt hands. I'd learned how Faith and Trinity, along with Jon Fevre, had brought the convoy out carrying anyone who wanted to leave and escorted the forces of law and order back in.

During all this I'd hovered between life and death. This time, Trinity told me, it really had been touch and go. She'd suggested Dante 'go shopping', she admitted with almost brutal honesty, simply because she didn't want him to watch me die.

I didn't know what to say. She tried to get me to talk about Starburst, but I found it hard. I didn't know what to say about that either.

"You have a visitor," Micah informed me late one afternoon. I was sitting up in a chair by the window of the room that was my world, wearing a large, soft robe. My arms were now free of their splints but still heavily bound, my ribs only lightly. I could move, in theory, but the look on Micah's face froze me to the spot.

"You want me to leave?" he enquired unnecessarily. I was speechless, believe it or not, as I watched my visitor make the long walk across the room towards me on long, black-clad legs, boots clicking on the stone floor. For a long time we gazed at each other. I liked his coat, I thought. It was in considerably better repair than mine was – had been, I amended, as it was long gone now along with most of my favourite gear. Long and black, it fitted his slender frame like a glove. I wondered, as I allowed my eyes to return to his face, what I should say. Something clever, perhaps. But my mouth was dry. I licked my lips and watched his widen into a smile in response, but I couldn't see his eyes. As if reading my mind, he reached up and removed his shades. His eyes were brimming with tears, his irises pulsing as he crouched and leaned towards me. His kiss was surprisingly gentle, even hesitant, as if he was unsure of his greeting. Drawing away, he looked at me, tears spilling from his eyes. Only that freed me from the spell, as I croaked, "Where the hell have you been?"

With a choking sob, he buried his head in my lap. All I could think of to say was, "Hey, don't soak me. They'll think I've had an accident!"

He raised his head sharply, eyes wide, a quick familiar grin on his lips. "Guess that's been a problem, huh?"

"I've had plenty of help," I replied wryly.

"I just bet you have." Holding his gaze, I watched his eyes as his hand slipped beneath my robe. I gritted my teeth as my body began to respond to his touch. "Do you know how badly I've wanted to watch your face?" he whispered, leaning towards me. I ached to hold him, and the fact that I couldn't made me groan with frustration. "Ssh!" he murmured, tenderly running his fingers over my jaw.

"So, where the hell *have* you been?" I asked eventually.

"Shopping," he replied enigmatically.

Hell, I thought with amusement. This was going to be like pulling teeth! "Took you so long, did it?"

"Uh-huh."

"Dante!"

He sat back on his heels and grinned mischievously at me. "You lost most of your favourite clothes, so I went to have some more made. Simple." I could feel his excitement. "Want to see?"

"Want to show me?" I returned. Jumping to his feet, he hurried into the adjoining room, returning a few moments later with a pile of boxes. He seemed to have come back with a complete new wardrobe, I concluded as I watched him open them. I loved the long leather coat, which I estimated would almost reach the ground and which matched the one he'd tossed so casually on the bed. But it was the unopened boxes that held my attention. He'd deliberately left them until last, I assumed.

Slowly, he opened the smaller box and brought its contents to me. "You lost most of your knives, so I had Kaz make you a new set," he offered, raising his eyes after laying them on my lap. They were beautiful, with delicately tooled handles and engraved sheaths. "I also asked him to replace something else," he said softly, returning to open the last box. I held my breath as he carried towards me the most beautiful crossbow I'd ever seen. "Guess you don't want it, huh?" he teased.

Moving my arms to cradle it clumsily, I shook my head in wonder. "It's beautiful seems inadequate."

"That's what took me so long. He wanted it to be perfect."

"It is. Oh, it is!"

Gently, he took it from me and returned it and the knives to their boxes. "Don't worry, you can play with them later," he assured me.

"When can I play with you?" I asked, a tremor in my voice.

His smile changed. "Not yet awhile," he sighed and rose to his feet. "But where there's a will... C'mon, let me put you to bed." Something told me that for once it was going to be fun.

Chapter 32

"So how long before I can have this off?" I asked when Nadia Christof paid me her next house call.

She raised a brow and grinned. "Frustrating, is it?"

"Kind of," I admitted, "although not as bad as those splints. At least I can wiggle my fingers. Sort of." I demonstrated proudly and she laughed.

"Keeps you out of mischief, I guess." Her eyes rose briefly from her examination.

"No it doesn't," I replied cheekily and she rolled her eyes. "So, how am I doing?"

"Well, you've certainly been the most challenging patient I've had in a while," she replied wryly.

"But I'm cute," I offered, deadpan.

Nadia Christof looked a little startled, then shook her head and raised her eyes to the ceiling in exasperation before looking once more at me. "Modest, too. Lie still."

"Sure you want me to?" I batted my eyelashes.

"Behave."

"Sure you want me to?" I repeated.

She stood back, hands on hips, and glared at me. "Want me to do this or not?"

Okay, I cautioned myself sternly. Enough was enough. Behave yourself, fool. "Sorry, Doc."

"That's better." She eyed me curiously. "Don't want any more scars to your collection, do you?"

"No, Doc," I replied meekly. She was going to cut the stuff off my arms and replace it with supportive strapping. At least, that was the idea.

"Scared?"

"Sure I am," I admitted.

"Thought so. Relax. Close your eyes, if it helps."

It didn't. "Talking of eyes... Dante…"

She smiled. "He still has to be careful – eyeshields when it's bright, drops, that sort of thing – but hey, I do good work."

"I know yer do. Hear you gotta new job."

"The Mayor seemed to think it was a good idea, seeing as you keep coming back in bits."

I laughed. "Guess I'm getting too old for this shit, huh?"

"Well, much as I love my job, I don't mind not doing it for a while, okay?"

"Sure thing, Doc."

By the time she'd finished filling me in on the latest arrivals and departures, my arms were free. The relief was immense. And itchy. Very itchy, I decided, wanting to scratch. She could see it on my face and began to massage my arms for me. I looked at the scars, pushing them from my mind as unimportant. Just a few more to the collection, I told myself. They didn't matter.

"I'll give you a programme of exercises to build up your arms," she said, pre-empting my questions. "See that you follow them. And keep away from that crossbow!"

"Yes, ma'am."

"Now, keep still while I put the supports on."

"Do you have to? Please, just a little while," I wheedled. "I'll be good, honest." Hesitating, she pursed her lips. "I guess Trinity or Dante could put them on for you, but if you endanger them, it's back in plaster – get it? If you're lucky." She regarded me seriously and perched on the edge of the bed. "You do know that there's no guarantee you'll ever use that crossbow, don't you? You were pretty badly smashed up. It took everything I know to put you back together. Don't make me have to try again – I might not be able to next time."

I understood. "Gotcha, Doc," I responded soberly. But of course, at the same time my private resolve was that one day I would do justice to the craftsmanship that had created it. In the meantime, I would hang it wherever I was as a reminder of what I was aiming for. After all, I admitted, I could still use a gun, couldn't I? "Doc, I'm goin' stir crazy. Any chance I can take a wander around the house?"

She smiled. "Sure. Do you good, in fact. In fact..." She looked around. "Where'd you hide your boots?"

I chuckled. "Ask Dante or Trinity, or Micah, or..." I shrugged. "Between them they 'bout burned everything."

"Must be something somewhere." She hunted around and returned triumphant. "Okay, this is a novelty for you, right?"

"What?"

"Someone dressing you?"

I saw her eyes sparkle with laughter. "Ha ha." I had difficulty bending and putting on boots so tended to walk around barefoot, but if she was willing, I wasn't going to protest.

"Easy does it." She took the weight of me, easing me gently to my feet. "Think we can get something on you? Don't want the ladies fainting, do we?" I wasn't sure I was up to this, but that she was easy enough to play games was good. I'd had the doc figured for the shy type, given the society she'd come from 'n' all.

"Wouldn't want to shock anyone's sensibilities, Doc."

She snorted derisively. "Yeah. Right." I grinned. My arms were stiff and raising them wasn't comfortable, so she found me a top that zipped up the front, which was fine with me. "So it's not the height of fashion, but hey..."

I laughed. I wasn't laughing when we came to the stairs, though. I'd forgotten the stairs. She slipped her arm about my waist and took the weight and we took it slow. One step at a time. By the time we reached the bottom I was soaked. She smiled at me encouragingly and murmured the soft words doctors are so good at, intermingled with a healthy amount of cursing. I was more used to being called a stubborn son of a bitch, so that was cool. "Number o' times I've been this way o' late, yer'd think I was used to it."

She gave me an encouraging hug. "C'mon, big guy. You're about to make your grand entrance. Showtime?"

With a soft groan, I straightened and tried to stand tall. Well, I tried to stand straight. My muscles didn't like it a whole lot. "Don't go too far away, honey. I'm likely to fall on my butt." She laughed and gave me a gentle push.

"You may've lost weight, *honey*, but you've still got enough padding on your butt to take it. Now go!"

I reached out and slowly opened the door. The tableau that greeted me was comic: to a man – and woman – they froze, mouths open, drinks halfway to mouths, the works. No one moved as I shuffled slowly into the room. It was Nadia Christof who hovered at my side, because no one else seemed able to move. Weird, I thought, as I eased myself onto the high-backed chair simply for expediency: if I sat down on that invitingly comfortable couch I'd never get out of it again. "Am I allowed a drink, Doc?"

"I guess one won't harm. I've got a couple of calls to make. Can someone steer this guy upstairs if I'm not back?"

More than one volunteer, I noted smugly. "Gotta date, Doc?"

"I wish. Baby on the way."

"Ah." I smiled with gratitude as Faith placed a drink in my hand. "Good luck, then, and let me know the outcome? Good news deserves a little something."

"My pleasure, Angelus. Goodnight, everyone. See you later." Everyone said their goodbyes, and I found myself wishing I'd stayed in bed. It would've saved my ears a whole load of grief!

By the time I made it back upstairs, I really *was* wishing I'd stayed in bed. It'd get easier, as I knew full well, but given the amount of sympathy I was offered, I was probably going to play it for all I was worth!

Chapter 33

The time came, however, when itchy feet began to trouble me, so I went to Dan Truman's office. I found Tomas among a pile of paperwork, and by the expression on his face, my arrival must have come as something of a relief.

"Good to see you on your feet, Angelus," he said, rising to his feet and offering his hand in greeting. "Would you like to see the Mayor?"

"If it doesn't take you away from your duties," I said with a smile. He gave me a wry grin.

"Actually, that's the idea. And I don't think the Mayor'll mind a little diversion, between you and me." I grinned and followed Tomas. He knocked once on the door and opened it a short way. "Angelus to see you, Mayor," he announced in his best official tone. "Shall I bring coffee?"

"Please." He settled back in his chair and stretched as Tomas admitted me. "Take a seat. If I don't finish this damned report now I never will." He gave a grimace and a brief chuckle. "I promised Dom a drive out as soon as I was through."

"Pain in the ass?"

"Dom?" he raised a brow.

"Well..."

"I meant the report, and you know it, although he can be. A pain in the ass, the neck..." He sighed. "Actually, this is your fault."

"Still sorting out Starburst?"

"And New Eden."

"I thought that was the idea. New Eden." I frowned.

He glared up at me. "Okay, it was. I just didn't expect you to stick me with Starburst as well!"

I shrugged. "Serves you right. You know I always deliver a little extra."

"So you do." He continued to scan the report until Tomas returned with coffee. As soon as he was through he sat back with a sigh of relief. "Don't tell me – you're bored."

"I haven't been off the road this long in years."

"Your leg."

I shook my head. "No comparison."

"No, I guess not, unless you count the fact that you've been close to checking out on both occasions."

"Not my fault."

"Never said it was."

"You implied it," I retorted belligerently.

Suddenly, Dan Truman laughed. "Are we having a 'domestic'?" he asked. I must have looked confused, because he continued. "You know, you're living in my house, and though we're not exactly married..."

"Oh. Gotcha." I grinned. "So... *honey*... what are you gonna do 'bout it?"

"The fact you're bored? I could set my son on you, I guess. Or I could suggest you take a ride with us. I promised I'd take him out to one of the ranches not far out of town – change of scenery," he wheedled. "Then at least Dom can talk the ears off someone else 'sides me."

I wasn't sure how good an idea that was, but at that point I'd have pretty much agreed to anything. "Should I pack my toothbrush?"

He rolled his eyes. "Lord, I hope not. Much as I love my son, he's starting to drive me up the wall. Guess it's a reaction to being immobile for so long. Not that I'm complaining. I owe you one for that run – and the stuff the doc brought through from New Eden."

I shrugged and tried to dissemble. "It was nothing." But that wasn't true, and he knew it. "All I did was talk to her once while Dante was under her care. Mentioned Dom's problem. She said she'd think about it. Guess she remembered."

"Guess she did. Brought a hell of a lot of stuff out with her, so I gather. Why don't you grab your coat and meet me downstairs?" I gave a crisp nod and went to comply. I didn't expect to be gone long, although Dan hadn't said how far we were going, or indeed where. I figured one of the ranches fairly close. Probably a new settler. He liked to do that when he could. Sort of official unofficial welcoming committee.

Dan drove, which was a novelty, so Dom spread out on the back seat, leaving me to ride up front, which was some relief. Or would have been if he hadn't insisted on leaning over my shoulder every couple of minutes and firing questions at me; occasionally at his father, but usually at me.

"Guess it's a long time since you've been out in the big wide world," I said, if only to try and turn his mind away from his questions.

"Yeah. Can't say it's changed much. Or maybe it has. Sky looks different."

"Depends on the time o' year, I guess. And if there's a storm in the offing. We clear, Dan?"

"As far as they can tell. Seems settled right now."

I turned my head to look out of the window. It looked much like many other places I'd been. Dry, little vegetation – arid, I think they used to call it. "You ever see it any other way?" I asked.

"No, but I've seen places where it is," replied Dan Truman. "They claim they can irrigate, bring life out here. Dig wells 'n' such, deep ones. Down to the water table. You think that's worth a try?"

I thought about it a while. "Guess it maybe. One or two places have deep wells to water their crops. Might work. Gotta, I guess. You thinking expansion, Dan?"

"I'm thinking much more than that. You up for a challenge, Angel? A real challenge."

I shifted my weight to look at him. "Such as?"

"Something you've never tried before. You think you might be able to control those itchy feet o' yours?"

"It depends."

"I'm waiting for Morgan to come back with some info, then I'll tell you more. I need you, Angel." He had me interested, and he knew it. It was likely to involve staying around a while, so it had to be something political. I didn't like politics, didn't know shit about it, except where it got in the way of my business from time to time. So maybe he needed a little muscle. A little law enforcement.

"It's nice ter be needed," I replied ambiguously, and settled back to close my eyes. With any luck, Dom would be quiet for a while.

As it turned out, he was quiet until we came to a halt.

"One of our new settlers," said Dan, slipping out as the group emerged from the building to greet us: a man, a woman, two youngsters and a babe in arms. He turned to me and smiled. "You won't recognise them, but they wanted to meet with you."

The woman came forward, followed a pace later by the man. "Maybe it means nothin' ter you, but if not fer you, this little'un wouldn't be here. You don't remember, do yer?" I shook my head. "Guess we'd be surprised if yer did. Yer was a little crazy at the time."

The man slipped an arm protectively about her waist. "We was in Starburst. She was 'bout to pop an' some o' the guards was about ter..." He glanced back to where the children stood and didn't conclude, but I read 'rape' in his eyes. "They'd o' gutted her if yer hadn't come by. Yer was like somert outta hell, but yer was the finest thing I's ever seen. Didna expect ter see yer alive, but I wanna shake yer hand." He stuck out his hand, and I side-glanced to see Dan Truman grinning with something that shouted conspiracy. He was expecting me to make a fool o' myself, I thought.

"Guess it turned out okay," I said, smiling at the woman. "Boy or girl?"

"Girl," she grinned. "Wanted a girl, bein' surrounded by menfolk." Her man and two sons grinned, obviously used to hearing this. "You're an angel," she announced, and I refused to look at Dan Truman or his damned son!

"I'm Angelus," I corrected.

"You'll always be an angel to us, and welcome, if ever yer passin'. We thought to call her Angelina, if yer don't mind?" She was offering the baby to me to hold, and I didn't know what to do with it. I haven't held a baby since... I wasn't going to think of that. Couldn't.

So I plastered my best smile on my face and figured that if I held the head upwards it'd be a good idea. As if on cue, the baby opened her eyes, gurgled and almost scalped me. Well, okay, she took a fistful o' my hair and pulled with surprising strength. "Hey, little one, go easy," I said softly. "A beautiful baby, ma'am. And maybe yer'd best take her 'fore I drop her."

"I thinks she's safe in yer hands, but..." She took her daughter from me. "Yer'll take a drink with us, won't yer, Mr Mayor? Come in outta the sun. Jamie, Felix, will yer find somert soft fer the Mayor's son?"

"Sure, Mam. Come right this way," the eldest of the two invited, and Dom went happily with the two boys. As mother followed, I remained with Dan and the man.

"How's yer arms, Angelus?" The man nodded his head towards them. "Sure looked smashed up."

"They were," I replied, flexing my fingers. "Getting there. Taken time."

He nodded. "Guess it would. You take care, yer hear?" I smiled and took his hand. "So, come on in, 'fore my lady gives *me* hell."

***

As we drove back, I stared out of the window. Dan Truman had a grin on his face that he removed whenever he thought I was looking at him. Whatever path he was thinking to have me take, this had been part of it, I was sure of that. Making me 'play nice' with those people had something to do with it. It was what politicians did. Oh shit, he wasn't, was he? I gave him a look of alarm, which he must have anticipated because he grinned broadly.

"No, I'm not thinking of retiring." I gave an undisguised sigh of relief. "But sometimes it'd be nice to have a little help. Chill out, Angel. You passed the test."

"What test?"

"You'll see."

He wouldn't say another word, damn him, and he was grinning like an idiot the whole way back. He knew something I didn't, and he liked the fact. I sighed, stretched out and closed my eyes. I didn't have to look at the grin to know it was there, but what he was grinning at, I didn't have a clue.

As it happened, I didn't have to wait too long to find out. It was very late when we got back and I went straight up to bed. I was beginning to ache and I needed to get horizontal because I didn't want to push myself too far. I wasn't surprised to find Faith in the room along with Micah. Dante was perched on a stool playing and Trinity was sitting on the couch with her knees curled up beneath her.

"Good trip?" she asked, getting up and coming to me, giving me a kiss of greeting and grabbing at my coat.

"Interesting," I replied, wriggling as she pulled off my coat. "To what do I owe this?"

"You'll find out," grinned Faith. "C'mon, Micah. Night, Angel. Trinity, Dante. Good luck."

I turned to look first at Trinity then at Dante. As the door closed, Dante put down the instrument he'd been playing and rose to join Trinity. I wasn't sure which of us Faith had been wishing good luck to, I realised as I observed the subtleties of body language. "You gonna tell me what's goin' on?" I enquired, looking from one to the other.

"You wanna tell him?" suggested Dante.

Trinity hesitated, then gave a soft laugh. "No, you can."

"But—"

"Will one of you *please*..." I began, growing increasingly puzzled as Dante took one of my hands and one of Trinity's, and she took the other of mine.

"I don't know how ter say this or how you're goin' to react," she said, "but you're goin' to be... we're goin' ter have a baby."

"What?"

"Trinity's pregnant," Dante offered uneasily.

"I kinda figured that," I mumbled. "How? I mean when?"

"Guess while not all o' yer was workin', the little fellas were fit 'n' well," she bit her lip. "I never thought... it's never happened... I didn't think I could." She was shaking and I wondered what she was scared of. The fact she was pregnant or me?

"Hey, mind if we sit down? I'm feelin' a little shaky myself." I drew her to a seat. "How d'yer feel?"

"Mornin' sickness... how do yer think I feel?" she retorted.

I laughed. "That wasn't what I meant. I meant about—"

"How do *you* feel?" she returned hesitantly.

"I guess I feel stunned. Happy. Surprised. Not surprised. Dan Truman knew, the bastard. He's been dropping hints all day. You told him before you told *me*?" I felt almost insulted.

"I didn't know how to tell yer," she half sobbed. "Thought yer'd be mad."

I swore, and Dante rested his hand on my knee. "Gently, dear heart. We didn't want to drive you back on the road. Away from us."

"Yer think I'd run out on my responsibilities?" I *was* insulted now!

"Dear heart, please!"

I took a deep breath. "Sorry. How do *you* feel?"

"It'll be different, you have to admit," he chuckled. "No shortage of babysitters. Be pleased, Angel. We are. If you still want all of us."

Oh shit! "Of course I do. How can I not? Whatever you think I am, I love you both. That hasn't changed, and I hope never will. Never thought to be a dad, though. Wow!" I collapsed against the couch back, one against one shoulder, the other on the other. "Ain't this gonna raise a few eyebrows?"

"C'mon, Daddy. Bedtime. It's not yer eyebrows we want to raise," announced Trinity cheekily.

I tried to look scandalised. "That's no way for a mom-ter-be ter talk!"

"It's the way this 'ns gonna talk, till she's too big to play." The announcement didn't surprise me. "You need the bathroom, guys?"

"No, you go ahead," replied Dante. She was leaving us alone, I thought. "Hey."

"Hey," I replied, as he kissed me. "You sure you're okay with this?"

"Sure," he answered. "Took a while. Little jealous, you know? After all, it's one thing I can't give you." There wasn't much I could say to that, I thought, but sometimes words aren't necessary.

***

Long after they were asleep, I lay awake thinking. My life had taken another turn, as strange as any other it'd ever taken. A father... me? I couldn't believe it. I wondered what she'd have done if I'd have suggested she got rid of it. Probably killed me. I thought she might feel that having a kid of her own would be a break with her former life, a new start. I could go with that. Although whether I could be considered respectable or not, I thought not. I tried to imagine Trinity as she was going to be in a few short months, and wondered how she was going to react. Whether she'd have cravings, or whatever expectant moms were supposed to have. Whether Dante or I would find ourselves going out into the dark in search of ice cream and pickle, which made me wonder what Dante was really feeling. I admit I'd been surprised how well they got on, how much they seemed to like each other. I'd wondered at first if it was staged for my benefit, but I was sure it wasn't. Guess they'd gone through some stuff together, not least of all over me, but I couldn't help but wonder what he was going to feel as we watched Trinity's belly begin to swell. I'd never seen him jealous and wouldn't have thought he had a jealous bone in his body. But like he'd said, it was the one thing he couldn't give me. It'd be up to me to deal with any complications if they arose.

It wasn't only Trinity who'd changed. Dante had changed since he'd got his eyes. He was a hell of a lot more confident, although he hadn't exactly been a shrinking violet before. He didn't need me – or anyone – to guide him, although he'd done pretty well on his own, and I could foresee changes to come. I'd a feeling he'd become an even more active partner than he'd been of late, because something sure as hell was brewing and I'd a feeling it wouldn't be long before I found out what.

Chapter 34

was a little surprised to be invited to Dan's office a couple of days later with the postscript 'be presentable'. Should've made me suspicious, I guess. 'Presentable' meant having a shave and cleaning my boots, more or less, so when I was admitted to the 'holy of holies' by Tomas, I wasn't suspicious. Until I saw the array of expectant faces and Dan Truman in his official persona, trying hard not to smile.

"Ah, Angelus. Good of you to come at such short notice. Gentlemen, ma'am, you all know or know of Angelus." He paused for the brief buzz of conversation, and I allowed my eyes to wander. I did recognise a few faces, most of which were studiously appearing neutral. I wondered what stunt he was going to pull. "A few of you might even know that for several years Angelus has been instrumental in several successful operations. I'm speaking of the Wayfarers, of course. I have a confession to make, gentlemen and ma'am." He flickered his amused eyes my way but would not hold mine. "I brought Angelus here under not exactly false pretences. I simply neglected to tell him why." Again, the buzz of conversation rose and fell. "It's been on my mind for a long time that I need to review the running of the Wayfarers. The organisation runs well enough, but it could be better, and who better to run it than one who's been part of its operations. We're asking – I'm asking now – that Angelus consider that post along with its co-position as my deputy." His grin was positively evil! "Angelus?"

I knew he could lip-read because I saw the flash of his teeth as I muttered every slur on his ancestry I could think of. "It's a little sudden, Mayor." I dissembled.

"Feel free to take time to consider our request. You will need information, of course. If you come to my office later, I'll tell you all you need to know."

"You can be assured of that," I informed him evenly, but inside I was fuming.

I couldn't get out of there quick enough, but I'd be back. Dante and Trinity kept their heads low as I fumed, but neither of them seemed surprised. I wonder why?

"Deputy Mayor," grinned Trinity. "I like the sound o' that. Take the fun out of corrupting politicians," she sighed dramatically. "Or maybe not. Might be fun trying to... what do they call it? Lobby?"

"Sounds dirty," chuckled Dante. "So, you gonna bite the bullet or tell him to screw himself?"

"I don't know," I admitted truthfully. "It's flatterin', but I'm no desk jockey."

"You don't have to be, do you? Lead from the field or whatever. You can always find an excuse, can't you?"

I could. "I'll listen to him," I promised. "No more. No promises."

***

I was sitting in my office before I realised it, wondering just what I thought I was doing. I hated paperwork, although the tactical side of ops was cool. Dan insisted on showing me the ropes with a smug expression on his face, dragging me everywhere, introducing me to things I'd never thought of as part of his sphere of influence. Dan Truman was a busy man.

Come autumn, I was out Eden way with Dante and some of my team when I heard something I'd never expected to hear again. "Michelangelo!" I went white and the laughter died on Dante's lips as he realised it was directed at me. "Michelangelo?" I found myself almost knocked off my feet as a young woman threw herself into my arms, weeping.

"Someone you know?" he enquired, amused.

"I think she's my sister," I replied hoarsely, incredulous. Finally, I was able to free myself and set her down. As we were using my old rig as transport, I elected to free myself from curious eyes and, over a stiff drink, to find out if she was who she seemed to be. We looked alike, I guess, given a few years and a change of sex.

"I thought you was dead," she was sobbing over and over. "I thought I was alone. When Aunt Lucia and Uncle Ben died..." She swallowed her drink, which Dante courteously refilled before perching himself once more on the edge of the couch close to me. "No reason fer me to stay. Heard... heard there was a new frontier out here. Thought maybe I could find a job. Oh, merciful heaven, I thought yer was dead, Michelangelo!"

"My name is Angelus," I announced quietly. "Your brother died in the mine, Lucy; my name is Angelus."

Dante was looking at me curiously and with a little alarm. Probably wondering why I wasn't welcoming her with open arms, I suspected, but when it came down to it, she was a stranger to me who happened to claim to be my sister, although she probably was. My little sister Lucia had survived because she'd been staying with our aunt and uncle when the raiders had come. She'd been the baby sister who'd followed me around and whom I barely remembered as anything more than a pest. I couldn't claim a sudden rush of familial affection, however much either of them seemed to expect it.

"Angelus. Suits yer, I guess."

"Dante, seems this is my baby sister, Lucia... Lucy." I offered by way of introduction. I didn't like the expression on her face; I wasn't sure what it meant. "Let's find you somewhere to stay, hmm? We'll talk later."

"Why not now?"

"Because I've work to do," I informed her, rising to my feet and gesturing towards the door. We didn't speak much on the short walk.

"Theo! Theo!" I called out, and after a mutter and a thud, one of my rookies appeared from within the tent.

"Sir?"

"Find somewhere for this here lady to lay her head, will yer? Take good care o' her for me; she's kin."

His grin widened. "Will do, sir. This way, ma'am."

I gave her a polite nod and passed her into his care, and then promptly fled back to my rig. When the door closed behind me, I collapsed against it with a sigh of relief. When I opened my eyes, I saw Dante watching me with a strange expression on his face.

"Why did you never mention a sister?" he asked softly as I pushed myself away from the door.

"Because I thought her dead, or if she wasn't, she wouldn't want to know me. I wasn't very nice ter know back then, remember?"

"I remember," he replied, shuffling over to give me room as I sat down. "Do you remember her?"

"Not much," I admitted. "She was oh, three, maybe four. I was goin' on fourteen, I guess. Not sure. Not certain, least. Our aunt and uncle were the religious type, as I remember; lots o' people were back then. Didn't think she'd approve."

"Don't think that's changed," observed Dante with a glance at me. "Do you care?"

"Not a fuck," I replied. "We'll soon as hell find out."

"What makes you say that?"

I shrugged and grinned. "Theo ain't too tight-lipped; he's gonna talk."

Dante nodded thoughtfully. "You gonna finish up? I'll cook." That was an offer I wasn't going to refuse. Dante had become quite a good cook of late, which was just as well. I'd never really taken the time to learn. I enjoyed helping him, of course – or hindering; I'm not sure which.

I'd finish the last report in record time, I resolved, which I duly did. Time to chill out, which I told myself I deserved. I wasn't fond of meetings and I'd had more than my share. While I liked the sound of this 'brave new world' that Dan Truman and the other mayors envisioned, I hadn't expected quite as large a part in it. I was just an enforcer, I'd told myself, not a damned politician. But I was fast finding myself becoming more of the latter and less of the former, and I wasn't sure I liked that.

Lying in bed with Dante, I began to wonder what life might have been like had I never been taken to the mine. That I might never have met him, or indeed Trinity, seemed strange to me now. I wondered, as I held him close, whether I'd change the past even if I could. For all the bad, there'd been a hell of a lot of good.

We were awoken by loud knocking on the rig's side door. Muttering darkly, I grabbed for my pants, slipped them on and went to find out what the commotion was. Before I could speak I was pushed aside and my sister had invited herself in. Given the fact that the bedroom door was wide open, her reaction was more than predictable.

"So it's true," she exploded. "You... you..."

I gritted my teeth and pushed her away from the door. I heard Dante curse as his shin, I assumed, made contact with a hard object as he searched for his pants.

"Get the fuck out of here," I responded, grabbing her arm. "How dare you!"

She struggled free of my hand and I let her go. We were alike in that, I thought abstractedly: we both had a temper when we let fly.

"A whore, a freak and a—"

"Queer?" offered Dante from the doorway behind me.

I glanced over my shoulder and couldn't help but smile. He looked dishevelled, a little worse for wear, and the innocent expression on his face didn't fool me for a moment. He knew what he looked like. Quite deliberately, he'd left his pants half zipped and was standing with his arms on either side of the door in what was undoubtedly intended to be a provocative pose.

I tore my eyes away from him with difficulty and let them fall on hers. "You want to know what they did to us, in that mine? To me? I'll fill you in, if yer like, *little sister*. While you was livin' nice 'n' cosy..." By the time my anger was gone, tears were rolling down her face. I'd been brutally graphic, and I'd gone further than I'd intended. But with my spleen vented, and hopefully hers, I could respond to the eyes burning a hole in the back of my neck.

"Let it go, love," I heard Dante murmur in my ear as he slipped his arms around my waist from behind.

"One person was there for me in that hell and I've loved him longer than I ever loved you, so don't you EVER tell me I shouldn't love him... or Trinity, come to that, because she was there for me when I needed a friend, too."

Lucy shook her head slowly from side to side and tried to speak, but I didn't want to listen to her. I could feel Dante pressed against my back and wondered whether to apply a little shock therapy.

"Angelus," she began, "I can't help... I'll try... just don't push me away. You're all I have."

"I neither want nor need your approval, little sister," I responded softly. "I think you'd better leave before we both say something we'll regret. Come back when you've cooled down."

"Angelus."

"Close the door after you, will you?" I asked, turning as Dante's arms released me. In the doorway, I paused and looked over my shoulder before following Dante back into the bedroom. I vaguely remember hearing the door close, but whether it was her leaving or not I didn't care. He was smiling at me in a playful manner as he retreated as far as he could. When he came into contact with the bed, I pushed him back and followed him with a grin. Dante was stronger than he looked and our wrestling session made an even worse mess of the bed than it'd already been in.

I was late to work, needless to say, and more than grateful for the pile on my desk that kept me from thinking too much. Mo, one of my top men, wandered in late morning and we had a brief meeting where I briefed him on a little operation I wanted carried out, and I was just settling back with the expectation of the imminent arrival of coffee when the door opened and Lucia was admitted. Mo looked a little uneasy, as if I was going to bite his head off, but I wasn't going to make a scene in front of him. I even waited until coffee arrived before breaking the uneasy silence hanging between us.

"You're not gonna make this easy, are yer?" she asked eventually.

I shrugged. "What would yer want me ter make easy?"

"All... everything."

"I'm not sure what you mean," I replied blandly. "What would you want me to do?"

"Welcome me?"

"You are welcome."

"Am I?" she returned, rocking in her chair from side to side. "Perhaps I will be... soon. I want to apologise. You were right. I had no right to judge. I guess I'm a product o' my life as you are o' yours. I'd like ter start afresh, Mich— Angelus. Please?" She bit her lip and offered a hand to me. "My name is Lucy."

I took her hand after a brief hesitation. Dante had predicted this would be what she'd do. While I wasn't prepared to go all lovey-dovey, I didn't want another enemy. I'd probably got enough of those hanging around as it was one way or another.

"We're goin' back to Vesta tonight. Why don't yer hitch a ride? Yer can taste the bright lights and do some thinkin' while I..." I shrugged. Did whatever I had to, I supposed. Depending on what my boss had in mind. I just hoped it wasn't going to take me too far away. I'd got a baby on the way, after all. I wondered what my sister was going to make of that little titbit!

Well, at the back of my mind I'd been thinking life was lacking a little excitement of late. Too late to remember the old saying 'be careful what you ask for, you might just get it'.

Chapter 35

wasn't sure if I was looking forward to arriving back in Vesta or not. With the uneasy truce between my sister and me, I really wasn't looking forward to her coming face to face with Trinity. I had a feeling that Trinity wouldn't be quite as understanding as Dante had been.

It would be good to get home, though, I admitted to myself, and we actually had one now. Dan had found us a small property close to his official residence, which was close enough so Micah and Dom could hang out together but far enough away so as not to be in his back pocket, as they say. It wasn't a novelty quite so much for Trinity, although she rather liked having a place that didn't have any lingering memories of business. But for Dante, in part, and me it was a novelty, as neither of us had had a home before. Well, at least not for a hell of a long time, and not one we'd 'owned'.

When we'd left, Trinity had been in a fury of decorating with Faith's assistance and Doc Christof's supervision, so I wasn't sure what to expect as I drew the rig to a halt inside the courtyard. My back ached and I stretched as my feet hit the dirt. As Trinity emerged through the front door I figured that I wasn't the only one with backache. "Hey," I said, kissing her and resting a hand on her swollen belly. "You're not covered in paint."

She laughed. "Heard you were on your way so I thought I'd best make myself decent. She in there?"

"Yeah. You okay, Trin? Shouldn't you be resting?"

Trinity snorted. "Seems I'm full o' energy, which is normal at this point. You're lookin' good."

"Me? I've been drivin' fer hours and I stink."

"Who told you that?" she giggled.

"Dante."

Trinity made a game of sniffing, grinning as Dante appeared in the doorway. "Hi Dante. So he stinks, does he?"

"Well..." he dissembled, shrugging his shoulders. "Lookin' good, Trin."

"I'm the size of a small whale."

"How big's a small whale?" he enquired.

It was Trinity's turn to shrug. "Don't know. Just seemed the right thing to say. Come here, man!" Dante obeyed, only to be enfolded in Trinity's arms and a clumsy hug. "Damned lump; never know what to do with it," she muttered with a laugh. "Well? You leavin' her sweatin' in there?" My expression must have told her that I'd be happy to do so because she wagged her finger at me in warning. "Don't yer dare. Don't be a bastard, Angel. Bring her in, please."

I didn't want to be sociable, but belligerency wasn't something Trinity would stand for. "All right, all right."

I went to find Lucy while Trinity went back inside to make certain everything was okay. I'd primed her on Lucy's existence, of course, and the rest of it. Trinity's idea was to have Lucy stay until she could find her feet and she had decided we would have a 'welcome' dinner, which meant, I supposed, that I'd have to wash up. She'd have my balls if I didn't make the effort, or Dante would, and I wouldn't like it. Surrender might be preferable, I decided, heading for the shower.

By the time I emerged, Dante was sitting on a stool strumming away and looking very cool and comfortable. Trinity was stunning in a dress I didn't know but which really suited her. And me? I was in my usual black. My life might have been turned on its head, but that hadn't changed. Dante looked up and smiled, his fingers pausing only briefly mid-tune as I closed the bedroom door. Trinity, who was rearranging the vase of flowers for the nth time, gave me a critical once over before announcing, "Not bad. Only one thing wrong."

"What's that?" I asked. She came over to me and pulled out my hair, which I'd tied back.

"Makes you look too respectable," she chuckled in response to my raised eyebrow. I laughed and kissed her. Dante lay down his instrument and went to open the door when there was a knock. Without a word, he admitted Lucia and closed the door behind her. She looked younger, I thought, as she stood there uncertainly. I suppose I ought to be ashamed that it was Trinity who crossed to join her, to welcome her and bring her into the 'circle'.

"You must be Lucia. Welcome to our home." Lucy hesitated and then took the offered hand with an uncertain smile. "Angel, drinks?" Trinity prompted. I wondered if I were being deliberately stubborn. I could give her a chance, couldn't I?

"Sure. What's everyone want?" By the time everyone had decided, I was thoroughly confused. "C'mon, guys, play fair. Make yer minds up!" My ineptness, I think, eased the tension.

"Is the service here usually this bad?" asked my sister, causing me to turn my head sharply, but it wasn't criticism in her voice, merely the beginnings of laughter.

"He does his best," responded Trinity wryly, smiling at me.

"So, when's the baby due?" I heard Lucy enquire.

"Any time, according to the doc." She wasn't as blasé as she sounded, I knew. She'd admitted that she was more than a little nervous, and I'd promised I'd be there if I could. Not for the first time, I regarded the swell of her belly with a mixture of anxiety and awe. I wondered how it felt to have a life growing inside you. I caught her eye and smiled.

As the evening drew on, I could see that she was growing tired and I despatched her to bed. After a while, Dante chose to follow her, leaving me alone with Lucia.

"She's lovely," said Lucia, smiling. "I hope all goes well for her. What do you hope for?"

"A baby would be nice," I responded lightly.

Lucia sighed. "Can't you let it drop for once? I'm not asking for your love, just your acceptance."

I gave a harsh bark of laughter. "I thought I was the one seeking that."

"Are you?"

"No," I admitted after a moment. "I don't want or need your acceptance or your approval, any more than I would expect you to seek mine. My life is not open to discussion."

"What you see is what you get?"

"Maybe." I smiled. "Tell me about your life, Lucy. What happened to you? You know my life, how was yours?"

Lucy looked down at her empty glass, which I refilled. "Not half as eventful as yours, I guess. Maybe cos I was named after her, Aunt Lucia tried to make me like her. Guess more rubbed off than I realised." She bit her lip. "They became more religious after... you and Mom. Maybe they thought that it was some punishment from God. I dunno. I stayed until Uncle Ben died. That was, oh, four years ago, I guess. Aunt Lucia had died a couple o' years afore. Worn out, I figure. It was never easy; the land wasn't good and the storms were getting worse. Didn't know what ter do with myself. Couldn't do much 'cept clean. Got a job keepin' house fer a farmin' family. Never learned, huh?" I smiled. "When he had to sell up, he went to seek work and... well... the rest yer know. When I saw yer I thought I'd lost my mind. Yer hadn't changed that much, just grown taller." I grinned. "And developed a few muscles yer didn't have afore. And a few scars, I guess."

I sat studying her for a moment or two. "Scars take many forms, Lucy. Some don't show." She nodded thoughtfully. "I make no apologies for the way I live my life, however. If you don't like it—"

"Tough?"

I grinned. "Yeah."

"I'm curious," she continued, "as to how you ended up Deputy Mayor."

I laughed, genuinely amused. "So am I, to tell yer the truth. I'm a runner, a Wayfarer by proxy, an' somehow I end up—"

"On the side o' the angels?" she joked.

I gave a soft bark of laughter. "Sort of."

"Whatever name yer took, yer no angel, I thinks." She regarded me shrewdly. "Yer chafin' at the bit, Angelus. Yer not the domestic type. Yer'll be outta here first chance yer get, kid or no. Even in the wilds, we'd heard o' yer. Of Angelus the messenger, the Black Crow, the Dark Angel, that yer took risks no one else'd take, that yer'd go anywhere, do anything. I looks at yer and wonders if that's changed. It's not just the babe, 'n' it can't be Trinity or Dante – they've been in yer life too long – so tell me. I'm curious. What makes yer think yer've changed?"

I didn't respond immediately, pouring myself another drink before I took a sip. While the fiery liquor slid down my throat I took stock. "An interesting question," I admitted. "The answer? Maybe I've grown up at last." Lucy looked at me as if I'd lost my mind. Perhaps I had. I didn't have an answer, in truth, or didn't want to look for one. I didn't want to delve too closely into the question. Her assessment had been too close to the truth, perhaps. But something had changed, that was sure as hell true. Maybe I'd grown up. Maybe I'd run far enough. Shit, it was too late at night for self-analysis. "Maybe I just want to go to bed."

"Not such a bad idea, big brother," she agreed, rising slowly. "Can we talk again?"

"Bound to," I replied, escorting her to the door. "Good night, little sister. Sleep well."

"You, too." She hesitated and reached up to plant a kiss on my cheek.

I didn't figure I'd get much sleep, not if Trinity had ought to do with it. Or rather the babe. Seemed to have developed a habit of kicking me, of late. Getting me prepared for sleepless nights to come, Trinity had giggled. My response had been that she'd be the one with most of those, as I wasn't equipped for feeding and such. Her response was that there was other stuff I could do so best not get cocky.

All I could do was wait, I thought, but it was nothing compared to the waiting Trinity had been doing these long weeks. I went to bed expecting to be awoken by a demand for hot water.

Chapter 36

When the time came I was actually fully awake. Well, more or less – I was in a Council meeting trying to look interested. I was almost grateful when Tomas slipped into the chamber with a note for me.

"Now?" I asked stupidly.

"Yes, sir."

"Right now?"

Tomas almost smiled. "Yes, sir. Right now."

I swallowed and tried to look cool, aware of all the eyes on me as I rose slowly to my feet. "My apologies, Mr Mayor, members of the Council. I have to... if you will excuse me?"

"Will you let us know?" asked Dan Truman, a grin on his face.

"I... er... yeah. Of course I will." Don't panic, I instructed myself sternly. Doc Christof would be with her, and probably Dante. She'd be fine until I got there. I didn't much care what they thought as I bolted out of the chamber and along the corridor as fast as my long legs would carry me. I don't remember much of the path I took down the stairs and across the square, but I was glad that the front door was open because I don't think I remember stopping to open it.

"What kept you?" asked Dante dryly as I crashed into the bedroom.

"Not much," I replied, throwing my coat in the general direction of the couch. "Hey, babe," I said, perching on the bed next to her. "Did I miss anything?" Trinity's response turned the air blue. I shook my head as I damped hers with a cloth. "Is that a way for yer to talk?"

"It ain't you havin' yer guts torn out," she hissed through gritted teeth. I looked up at Nadia Christof, who was standing close by.

"It'll be a while."

"That's okay," I said, taking up position behind Trinity, supporting her.

"Dante?" Trinity gasped, reaching out for Dante's hand. There was no hesitation: Dante moved to her other side and took her other hand. If she was squeezing his hand half as hard as she was squeezing mine, he wasn't going to be playing any of his instruments for a while. Together we held her, supported her while she alternately panted and cursed. I'd been warned she was likely to call me every name under the sun and that castration was likely to be the least she was going to threaten me with, but I have to admit she was certainly inventive, and very vocal. Some births, Nadia had told me, were easy; some weren't. Some were short; others long; and still others needed surgical intervention. Fortunately, that wasn't necessary, but it was going to be a long time before my bones – and my ears! – recovered.

Finally, after several very long hours, a red-faced, irate little being made its way into the world. Trinity was alternately, and sometimes simultaneously, laughing and crying as the squalling bundle was laid on her belly.

"Congratulations; you have a daughter," said Nadia Christof with a broad grin on her face. "You want to cut the cord, Angelus?" I guess my jaw dropped as I looked at the knife.

"Er..." I wondered if I looked a little green, because she chuckled.

"It's tied off, and it doesn't hurt. Some people keep it as a memento."

I thought they must be weird, but took the knife and looked uncertainly at Trinity. She looked knackered, but I could almost say she was glowing. "Sure. No problem." I bit my lip. "Am I supposed to say something?"

"Don't be a chicken," muttered Trinity. "Nadia wants to wash her, and it's a bit hard when she's still attached. She'd bounce back when she let go." I looked at my lady as if she'd lost her head. Maybe she was a little light-headed, I thought as I saw her laugh. "There. That wasn't hard, was it?"

As Nadia took the babe and went to bathe it – her – I kissed Trinity. "Thank you," I said. "She's beautiful."

"Like her mother," offered Dante, kissing her on the brow. "Should we leave or something? Make the announcement? Dan'll want to know. I'll go do that. You stay here, Angel. Get acquainted."

"Dante, calm down," grinned Trinity, settling back wearily. "Let's have some time together first, the three of us. Four of us," she amended. "You'll need to know a few things first."

"Right. Bound to get asked. Weight... they always ask that, don't they? Length. Sex we know. Name. What name did you decide?" I shook my head with bemusement. This wasn't like Dante, to be almost giddy. Guess everyone reacts differently.

"Nia, we thought... Nia Raffaella."

Nadia returned with the bundle. When she placed her in Trinity's arms, I admit I felt more than a little choked up. I met Dante's eyes and grinned.

"I suggest you two gentlemen leave Mom and baby to get acquainted and cleaned up," Nadia said. "Go wet the baby's head or something. Shoo!"

We took the hint, kissed mother and baby and departed. We needed to collect the gifts we'd bought, after all, and pass on the good news. When we returned, we'd had more than a little bit to drink, but Trinity didn't seem to mind. She looked wonderful. A little tired, but as she placed our daughter in my arms, she said, "You feed the end that screams and change the other."

I rolled my eyes. "I'd figured that bit already." I knew the baby couldn't focus and that the smile was probably wind, but I didn't care. "One's your department, the other seems necessary."

"Good time to practise, then," observed Dante, pulling up a chair and placing our gifts on the bed next to Trinity. I gave him a sour look and tried to remember what Nadia had shown us. It had been easier on the doll: that hadn't wriggled and threatened to kick me on the nose. And hadn't smelled quite as much!

"Is this normal?" I asked, eying the contents of the diaper suspiciously.

"Something to do with birth hormones," replied Trinity with a grin.

It looked foul, but hey, I'd dressed more than my share of poisoned wounds, hadn't I? I could do this.

The fact that my daughter seemed to be intent on pulling my hair out at the same time didn't help, but I made it in the end and the clean diaper didn't drop off as I lifted her to my shoulder, which had to be good, right?

"Here, you try," I said, placing her in Dante's arms as she began to cry. Dante smiled sweetly and muttered, but didn't object. He began to sing softly something I took to be a lullaby. It seemed to work like magic. Trinity had tears in her eyes, I realised, as I perched on the edge of the bed. "Well go on, open them!"

"Oh. Right." She pulled at the wrappers, trying to make her fingers work. In the end, I helped.

"Didn't know what to get, so we settled for a bear. The woman at the shop said it was what you do when you don't know if it's gonna be a boy or a girl. When we knew, we got this." It was a fancy dress. "Bit stupid, I guess, cos she's probably gonna puke all over it, but..." I didn't know if Trinity was religious, whether she wanted some sort of ceremony or something. "But you usually have some sort of party, so I thought... That's for you. From Dante and me."

Trinity burst into tears as she opened the red-lined box. I gave her a tissue and put it down to hormones. "It's beautiful!" 'It' was a necklace from which hung three intertwined hearts; jewel encrusted, delicate, but we'd thought it exquisite. I was glad to see she thought the same.

"Hey, you'll make me think you don't like it," I said, holding her close.

"Of course I bloody like it!" she retorted. "Do you think I'm mad? It's gorgeous. Will you put it on for me?"

"Sure." I was doing so as there was a knock on the door and Nadia popped her head round.

"I have a horde of visitors, if Mom doesn't mind," she said, studying the tableau to see if everything was 'suitable' and that Mom wasn't going to object.

"How many is a horde?" asked Trinity cautiously. But it was too late. Nadia found herself pushed aside as the room filled. Dan and Dom were at the forefront, followed closely by Lucy, Rom, Morgan and several of the Council – all bearing gifts. Even one or two of the refugees pushed their way in. Micah and Faith elbowed their way through on Morgan's heels.

"Glad ter see yer good for somert, yer little prick," Morgan grinned, thrusting a box at me. "Sorry fer't' language, ma'am."

Trinity tried not to laugh. "'S'okay."

"So, where's the little lady?" he enquired, almost knocking Dante off his feet. It was kind of funny to see Morgan so clumsy. "Ain't she pretty? Not sure which o' yer she takes after, though."

Neither was I, given the fact that according to Nadia, babies' eyes change colour and when they lose their baby hair, sometimes that's different, too. At the moment it was a sort of red-blonde, which I guess was something of the two of us. I didn't care. She was healthy, and she was about to prove what a healthy pair of lungs she had! Even so, it took some time to clear the room. Dante and my sister, along with Faith, succeeded in bullying everyone out of the room, leaving Trinity to feed the baby in peace. I put the presents on the table for her to open later and sat watching the baby suckle. Trinity looked up and smiled.

"How d'you feel?" I asked.

"Too hyped to sleep," she replied. "Faith promised to hang about tonight."

"Sure yer don't want me to stay?"

"Sometimes a girl needs another girl around, yer know?"

I stroked her hair back and smiled. "If yer want Dante ter sing yer to sleep..."

"I'll call," she promised.

We'd discussed what would happen when the baby came, of course, if it proved necessary for me to take the team out before we deemed it wise for Trinity to accompany us. I didn't often lead myself, but once in a while I liked to get out in the field, and once in a while Dan would suggest that I show my face, not just as Deputy but as Commander of the Wayfarers. It was Dan's intention to bring the Wayfarers 'out of the shadows' – although they would still retain their covert units – to function as what he called 'a proper police force', which Morgan had suggested as a case of 'set a thief to catch a thief'. I guess he had a point.

Chapter 37

If people thought it strange to see Vesta's Deputy Mayor and Chief of Police wandering around with a crossbow strapped to his back, no one said. Well, not to my face, anyway. Habit still kept my knives in their concealed sheaths, although at times I kept a pistol strapped to my thigh, just in case.

I'd accompanied Morgan on a trip out to one of the new settlements with a view to setting up a supply depot for Wayfarer operations when a caravan came into town. Usually, that wouldn't have caused much of a disturbance except for the fact that they were in dire need of medical attention. It was Mo who burst into the meeting, mumbling a half-hearted apology.

"Trouble, Commander. Need yer below, urgent-like."

"Er, 'scuse me, gentlemen. I'll be back soon as I can." I grabbed for my coat and slipped it on, picking up my crossbow in passing. I'd given them a heart attack, almost, by walking into a Council meeting with my weaponry. I'd forgotten I wasn't back in Vesta. Dan wouldn't have batted an eye.

I followed Mo out, meeting Dante at the foot of the hall stairs. He'd already begun getting the seriously injured medical attention, so I concentrated on those with flesh wounds. I needed information, and I needed it fast.

I hunkered down in front of one of the men. He was nursing a head wound and was holding a compress against it. "Sir?" I waited for his eyes to fall on me. "Can you tell me what happened?"

"Raiders. Outside town a-ways." He shuddered and looked about him. "Why us? We wasn't worth their trouble."

"Ready to roll, Commander," said Mo, appearing at my shoulder.

"Which direction?" I asked him. "How far?"

"About ten miles south, south-south-east."

Too near town, I thought. "Dante?"

"Yup?"

"You wanna drive?" I rose to my feet and glanced over my shoulder in time to see his grin of delight. We'd got these new toys, you see; off-road vehicles – fast, light and armed to the teeth.

"Oh yeah."

"You're the Angel," the man murmured as I turned back to him. "I wanna come with yer. I can help. I wanna get the bastards."

I gave him the once over. "Leave it to us, please. It's our job."

"And my family they did this to. I can show yer the exact spot. Save yer trackers time."

"He has a point," Dante observed logically.

"He rides with Mo and the squad," I said crisply. "MO!"

"Commander?"

"Keep this 'n safe, right? He can show yer where to start."

"Right, boss. This way, fella. You sure yer okay?"

I turned back to talk to Dante, only to find him already seated at the controls of the vehicle, waiting with the engine running. With a sigh, I slipped into the passenger seat and tucked in my coat, strapping myself in. Dante hadn't been driving long, of course, and sometimes had a manic style highly suited to the fast little buggies.

"Hang on to your hair," he ordered, but gave me little time to tie it back.

By the time we reached the designated spot, it didn't matter. They were long gone, but they had left enough tracks to follow.

"Storm coming, boss," came the voice of Mo's radio op.

I cursed, but we couldn't fight a storm. We had to turn and run, scarcely making it back to town before the shields went up.

"We'll find them," I promised the man before I sent him off to his people. "Soon as the storm abates, we'll go out again."

"Too late. Tracks'll be gone." He sighed. "Yer tried, but yer ain't God. Not even you can fight the storm."

I gave a bitter smile. He was right, and he was wrong. "Think o' me as the devil's son, mister, if yer like, cos I'll find 'em if anyone can. We'll keep lookin' and yeah, we'll pray no one else gets hurt 'fore we do. Go to yer folks; try ter rest."

He gave a faint smile. "Thanks fer trying. I'll pray fer yer."

I inclined my head, ignoring the amusement I saw on Dante's lips out of the corner of my eye.

"What's so funny?" I enquired when we were alone.

"Oh, just that I wouldn't have thought God'd much care about us."

I shrugged. "Maybe yer right, but yer never know when yer might need divine intervention."

He gave a laugh. "If you say so. C'mon, let's hit the shower."

We headed for the rig, intent on washing the sand out of our hair. I let Dante have first crack at the shower, shaking off my coat and cleaning my crossbow. A long shower helped ease the frustrations of a failed mission as well as the dust from my skin. Dante left me alone, knowing I needed time to get my act together.

By the time I emerged he'd begun cooking. He was barefoot and bare-chested, and as much as I appreciated the sight, I was tempted to remind him – not for the first time – that he'd do himself a mischief one of these days. He turned and smiled briefly as I pulled up a stool and began combing through my hair. It was getting too long.

"Feel better?" he asked.

"Much."

"Food'll be a while. You want me to give you a trim?"

"Will yer?"

"Sure." He grinned. "Anything to get my hands on you, you know that." I laughed and turned for him. "How much you want off?"

I was tempted to give a light reply, but settled for the face-value response to his question. "Couple of inches, I guess. Whatever you think."

Dante took his time, but then he always did. I'd probably have cut my hair short a long time ago were it not for Dante. In my line of work, it might have proved a hazard – sometimes it did – but Trinity liked it, as did Dante, and, I guess, most of the time I did, too. I closed my eyes and tilted back my head, feeling his fingers on my scalp, his lips on my forehead. I smiled in anticipation of his lips on mine.

A feather-light brush left me disappointed, but not for long. The kiss that followed was slow and everything I needed. To see the glow in his eyes when I opened mine was something I still couldn't get over, and to see that look in his eyes was a turn-on that I wasn't going to fight, unless he wanted me to, of course.

"That's just a promise," he said, easing himself away. "Patience is a virtue." I told him I wasn't feeling particularly virtuous and he gave me an urchin grin. "I do hope not, but if you think I'm gonna slave over a hot stove and let it go cold." I made a token protest, as he expected me to. "We're gonna have a proper sit-down meal," he announced firmly. "Just the two of us."

"You aimin' ter seduce me?" I enquired. "Just so I know."

"Well now," he murmured, running his thumb lightly over my mouth. "That would be telling."

I wasn't sure how long I was going to let him play his game, but it'd be fun for a while. Consuming too much alcohol wasn't a good idea in the middle of an operation, but we didn't need alcohol, and an early start was excuse enough to drive us from galley to bed, although washing up was fun.

Lying in each other's arms, we could pretend that the world outside didn't exist, that the little world in that room was the only one that mattered. For a while it was even true, but with the coming of morning, the real world came rushing back, and with it the knowledge that nothing had changed. We still had a job to do and this, too, we could share. I wasn't sure what that meant in the grand scheme of things. Only time would tell.

But I'd meant what I said about going after the raiders. It was our job to clean up the trash, and it was past the time that this particular item was filed away. Dante was passenger this time; Mo and Calvin took the second buggy and the rest of the squad travelled in the second, smaller rig, which served as our operations unit. We kept the buggies in case a rapid response was needed.

Tight-fitting shades kept the sand out of our eyes, and under our outer clothing we wore body armour. Mo had the remnants of an old cigar clamped between his teeth and resembled a pirate more than he did the law, but then he had always had a somewhat disreputable appearance. As I've said before, set a thief to catch a thief, right?

"You on, boss?"

I triggered my throat mike. "I'm on line, Mo. What yer need?"

"Gotta tracin' south-south-east."

"I copy. Are yer feelin' lucky?" I sensed his feral grin.

"Let's go huntin', boss."

I flashed a grin in Dante's direction and gunned the engine. "Rock 'n' roll, guys," I signalled before pulling the mask on. Better than swallowing a whole lot of sand, but not much.

Hurtling over the sand was a heady experience, and one I'd come to love. I could understand Dante's pleasure in it, but it was my turn to play this time. It didn't take us long to reach an intercept location. They didn't realise we were coming until we shot over the dunes, which gave us a slight advantage and proved our equipment was superior to theirs at least in tracking capability. They tried to run, of course, but they weren't as fast as we were, and they were amateurs as raiders went. If they'd been pros they wouldn't have tried to fight. Not against odds that were way superior.

I signalled Dante to take the wheel as we closed, positioning myself astride, and braced, my crossbow in my hand. I was aiming to take out the tyres of the lead vehicle, if I could, because I didn't think they'd stop if I asked, and they were using soft tyres on sand, making them vulnerable – at least in theory – to my bolts. I'd never tried this before, so I expected to end up on my arse, or on top of Dante if he braked too hard. While that might be fun at other times, this wasn't one of them. Dante had a light touch with the speeding buggy, but I still expected to end up undignified, most likely going arse over elbow if he had to brake suddenly. At my signal, a handbrake turn brought me round and into position. I let both bolts fly, grabbing for the roll bar as Dante swung us out of range of the careering vehicle.

"Go, go, go!" I screamed, and the team sprang into action.

It didn't take long in the end. They might have been amateurs, but they weren't stupid. Firing on us had been a bad idea, because we wouldn't be firing wide. Firing on us made them fair game, and I let the guys have their fun – if that's not in bad taste – hanging onto the roll bar because I'd given my ribs a thump. They were still fragile enough to object to rough treatment, and I was going to need more than a hot shower, I guessed.

Slinging my crossbow over my shoulder, I dismounted and walked over to where Mo was questioning one of the raiders, if the poor guy could talk given the fact that Mo's massive hand was at his throat. With difficulty, I clambered into the back of their rig. Inside, a couple of the guys were sifting through the contraband. I had little doubt we'd be able to trace it to our guest and his people back in town, although whether it would give them any satisfaction or pleasure I didn't know.

"You want me to wrap up, boss?" asked Mo, his keen eyes observing me wince.

I hesitated. "Appreciate it, Mo. They won't give much trouble shackled."

"You know it," he grinned wolfishly. "You okay, boss? You crack yer ribs pullin' that stunt?"

"Guess so. Forgets sometimes. Doc warned me to take it easy. Thought it'd been long enough."

"Guess yer never can tell, boss. You get yerself checked out, huh? Don't wanna lose yer. Taken us long 'nough to train yer." He spoke deadpan, but his eyes were twinkling.

"If thinkin' that makes yer happy..." I shrugged in response to his laughter. I took it easy climbing down again. "Dante, take it slow goin' back, huh?" Dante raised a brow curiously, but nodded. With luck, I'd just bruised myself. It was probably the case, but there was no use pushing my luck.

Unstrapping my arm-guards, I winced. Using my crossbow still caused some discomfort and the arm-guards were as much for support as for protection. My ribs, however, were another matter. When I undressed I could see the bruises already forming, although whether they'd been caused by impact or by my body armour I couldn't be sure. Dante frowned when he saw them and I told him not to worry, but I knew he would. It was nice having someone worry about me, but I didn't plan on being wrapped in cotton wool for evermore.

Chapter 38

guess I shouldn't have been surprised when Morgan turned up in town, or by his greeting of, "Fancy seein' you here, yer little prick!" in his booming voice across the inn. I'd hoped for a quiet drink, but it didn't seem like that was going to happen.

"Morgan, how're you doin', yer old fart?" Might as well give as good as I got, right? He elbowed his way across the room towards me and pulled up a stool.

"Can't complain. Dante playin' tonight?"

I smiled. "What makes yer think that?"

He shrugged, smiled and eyed the jug until I poured him a drink. "You're here, he ain't, 'n' you two's like as not together." He let that hang in favour of liquor, which suited me just fine. Dante didn't play often in public these days, and I wasn't about to let Morgan spoil it. I could feel his eyes on me, although he seemed to be pretending to be watching the performance. I just wasn't sure what his angle was. "None o' my business, kid, but take care, yer hear? Not all folks are as tolerant."

I slid my eyes his way. "Yer right, Morgan, about both. It *is* none o' yer business or anyone else's. Hurting no one."

"I know, kid, but not all folks see it that way. They see a threat."

"To what?"

"Their own manhood, maybe. Jealousy. That yer loved in such ways as they can't understand. Fear, yer knows?"

I could understand what he was saying, I guess, but it seemed to be a strange conversation to be having with him. "Is this goin' anywhere, Morgan?"

"Guess I don't wanna see yer hurt, 'n' there's some rough elements hereabouts. Not you I'm worried 'bout as much as him. Yer got the protection o' yer badge."

I guess Dante had, but not officially. Was that what he was saying? Maybe I should deputise him or something. "I hear yer," I said. If Dante worked alongside me, he deserved the protection of the law, such as it was. More to the point, if he had to defend himself, he wasn't likely to feel the law breathing down his ear. Which, I had to admit, had me amused, given the fact that right now the law was me and breathing down his ear wasn't exactly unlikely, as long as he watched my ribs, that was.

Dante regarded my proposition with a degree of scepticism when I finally got around to making it, although he eventually agreed that it made sense, even if, in his opinion, people probably already assumed it anyway.

"I can almost hear your mind working," he said in the darkness, turning onto his side to face me. "What's wrong?"

"Nothin'," I replied.

"I hear a 'but'," he murmured.

I didn't speak for a few moments. "I guess I'm feelin' guilty."

"About what?"

"This." It was, I had to admit, useless to gesture when he couldn't see me. I slipped my arm about his waist and drew him closer. "Being here with you. It's been a long time since it's just been the two of us, or it seems so, and—"

"Trinity?"

"Yeah. I haven't been thinkin' of her. I should, shouldn't I?"

Dante didn't respond for a while, simply stroked my belly absently. "What do you feel?"

"Like I said: guilty. I should be thinkin' of her, of our baby, but all I can think of is how happy I am right now with you."

"I don't know what to say," he admitted. "Once we're back home, things'll get back to normal."

"But it won't solve the problem, if there is one."

"No," he agreed. "That's up to your conscience, I guess. Maybe something we need to talk over when we're all together and thinking clearly." I felt his lips brush my jaw. "But right now, you need to sleep."

"Right now, I need—"

"Ssh!" I felt his smile. "Sleep. You need to heal, and sleep is more important than your libido!"

"Well do I get a goodnight kiss?" I asked a little petulantly. His smile became a grin.

"As many as you like," he promised. I was going to take him up on that, I thought, digging my fingers into his hair. "As long as I get to breathe once in a while."

"Once in a while," I promised softly, wondering how much sleep I was actually going to get and how much I cared.

Chapter 39

suppose I shouldn't have been surprised when, not long after our return to Vesta, Dante announced he was going on a sort of mini-tour. Watching him leave was strange. Part of me couldn't – or didn't want to – understand his reasons, particularly as we seemed to be working so well together. But Trinity did.

"He wants you to have a chance at a 'normal' family life," she said with a trace of hesitancy in her voice.

I had admitted to feeling guilty, hadn't I? The phrase 'be careful what you wish for' came to mind. While I couldn't deny Dante's need to pursue his own interests, I missed him at my side. We'd worked well together and I'd forgotten that he'd been a musician first. I tried to make it work, and for a while it did. Until I had to go away again and discovered that Trinity wasn't at all pleased.

"So come with me," I suggested.

"I don't want to leave Nia."

"Do you have to?"

"You're suggesting I take a baby on a raid?" she asked, incredulous.

I gave a brief smile. "You were all for it once."

"I can't believe you suggested it."

"I didn't – you did. First," I retorted.

She controlled her temper with difficulty. "I could leave her with Lucy, I guess. She's offered."

I bet she had. I could almost imagine my sister's words: "Sure I'll look after her. You go and don't worry. Bit of quality time together, like the old days. I'm sure you can take his mind off other things." Yeah, right.

I went to work, deciding to get out before one or both of us lost our cool, but when I came back early with a thought of talking things out, I wished I hadn't.

They always say that if you listen in on other's conversations you might hear something about yourself you wished you hadn't, and that proved true in this case. I came to a halt outside the part-open door in time to hear Trinity and Lucy in conversation, which surprised me. I hadn't thought them 'cosy'.

"Seems to me that you oughta get that brother o' mine ter make it legal," I heard Lucy say.

"Why?"

"Security for you and the baby, for one thing. Legal rights."

"What do you mean?"

"Respectability, honey, position. As his wife you could set terms. Don't tell me you don't wish Dante wasn't around."

"He isn't around," Trinity pointed out logically. I could almost imagine Lucy smiling.

"But he will be. As long as he's around, as long as he's in the picture, he'll be between you and Angelus. Don't tell me yer couldn't get him ter forget that freak."

"Dante loves Angelus."

"Don't tell me you can't compete. Hell, you gotta baby outta him; he can't be all queer."

"You can't conceive what I am," I said from the doorway, causing Lucy to drop her glass in shock and Trinity to jump and go pale as I sauntered across the room towards them. "I suggest that you keep your nose outta my business, sister dear, and get the hell outta my fucking house!"

Lucy didn't need telling twice. She bolted, slamming the door behind her. I turned back to Trinity, who stood holding Nia tightly in her arms as if she expected me to strike her. "I came back to talk," I said evenly, "but I don't think it's worth it. I'm goin' back ter work. I'll be away a few days." I spun round and fled the house, because I couldn't bear the look in Trinity's eyes. Or the thought that, given half a chance, I'd cheerfully throttle my sister.

When I returned to the house, I found Trinity gone. She'd left a note, which read:

> *My Angel,*
>
> *I think we need a little time to think things out. At least I do. I hope you do, too. I've taken Nia with me, so don't worry about her, but don't follow me. I don't want you to follow me. Give me a little space.*
>
> *I love you.*

Maybe I should have followed her, but I didn't. I did my job. When Dan offered me a run up north, I jumped at it, primarily because it would take me nearer to where I knew Dante was. The fact that I had Micah and Dom with me, with their incessant chatter, helped keep my mind off my domestic difficulties. Perhaps I should have gone after Trinity. Perhaps it was a mistake to believe her when she told me she didn't want me to follow her. Perhaps, looking back, I'd have handled it differently. But that's the trouble with hindsight, right? And this was just a social call, not a prolonged visit. I'd soon be back, soon be able to go after Trinity, have that talk, sort things out. Right?

"I can't believe Dad let me come," said Dom for the hundredth time at least as he leaned over the back of my seat, a grin of delight almost a permanent fixture on his face.

"Maybe he thinks yer'll keep me outta trouble," I offered.

He gave a bark of laughter. "Yeah – right!"

"Look, have I been a bad influence?" I countered merrily, casting a brief glance his way.

"Well, no. But that's only cos you haven't had a chance," he returned cheerfully.

"Wait till he meets up with Dante," inserted Micah, appearing suddenly next to Dom. "Then you'll see what a bad boy our Angel *really* is!"

I shot him a warning look. Micah was unrepentant and grinning from ear to ear. "Micah!"

Micah's grin faded a little. I wasn't quite sure just how aware Dom actually was. He'd led a slightly sheltered life, away from the reality of the street, and, while he knew of my relationship with Dante, I wasn't sure *what* he knew. He was at a romantic age, I suppose, and I wasn't convinced Micah hadn't been telling tales out of school. But I really couldn't remember how much he was aware of and didn't want to be accused of corruption!

Then Dom turned round and completely floored me by saying blithely, "So if you want us to clear out while you two make like rabbits, just tell us, 'kay?"

I must've looked shocked – which I was! – because their delighted laughter rang in my ears for a long time.

I wondered if Micah had primed him. I *hoped* he had. I didn't want to think otherwise. Although I wasn't about to change, I'd have to be more discreet perhaps. Or perhaps it was already too late, if Micah had filled him in, for whatever reasons.

I guessed I'd have to 'come out', although what I was going to say I had no idea. It'd wait until we made camp, I decided, in case I needed room to chase Micah if the brat lived up to his previous impertinence!

As I had the scanners operating along with the audible alarm, I felt reasonably safe building a fire and we had a cookout. Better than setting off the smoke alarms, I reasoned, if I followed my usual habit with such things and overcooked everything.

"Something wrong, Angelus?" asked Micah, crouching down close to the fire.

"Should there be?"

"You seem kinda quiet."

"Now I wonder why that might be." I raised my eyes and saw him wince.

"You're angry."

"Tell me why."

"You think I've been talking outta turn."

"Have you?"

"I don't think so. He ain't blind, Angelus. He ain't deaf either. People talk, yer knows. You don't go overboard ter keep anything secret, do ya?"

"Perhaps I should."

"People will always talk. They like something juicy."

"What did you tell him, Micah? Is this some form of revenge?"

He looked at me, startled, his cheeks flushed. "Angelus..."

"Don't be angry with Micah, Angelus. He didn't tell me anything I didn't already know." I looked up sharply to see Dom hovering a short distance away. When I didn't respond, he ventured closer. "Dad told me."

"What did your dad tell you?"

"About you and Dante."

"And what did he tell you about me and Dante?" I asked as evenly as I could.

"He didn't want me walking in on anything, he said. I thought at first he meant you and Trinity, and then he explained. He told me you were... bisexual?" He hesitated, unsure of the word. I nodded. "And that it wasn't just Trinity I might find you in bed with. Shoulda been obvious, I guess. I saw the way he looked at you, how close you were. Guess I wasn't surprised deep down." He bit his lip. "But I guess my – our – little joke was a little tasteless. Sorry. We didn't mean to hurt you."

"You didn't."

"I can't say I understand."

"What don't you understand?" I asked gently, sitting back. "I won't justify myself, you know. Not to you, not to anyone."

"I'm not asking you to. I guess it's the whole sex thing." I almost choked. "I mean I know the mechanics. I've seen pictures. Okay," he added hastily as I tried not to laugh. "I don't know everything. Dad had some films."

"He did?"

"Don't tell him I was watching 'em, will you?" he begged, anxiously glancing at Micah.

I smothered a grin. "He won't hear it from me," I promised. So Dan Truman had a stock of old porn movies, did he? Hm!

"They was weird. You and Dante..." He let the words hang and I waited. "What I don't understand is how do you know?"

"Know what exactly?"

"That you love someone."

"Guess it's different for everyone. Maybe your heart beats a little faster when you see them. When they go away, part of you goes with them. You'd do anything they asked without thought to the consequences." I smiled. "I've known Dante half my life, Trinity only a little less, but I couldn't explain any of it any more than I could the first time I set eyes on either of them."

He sat down and hugged his knees. "Do you... you know. Mind."

"Mind what?"

"Me asking things." His head bowed a little. "Adults often don't like... you know. Talking about sex."

"I don't mind," I admitted. "What do yer want to know?" Ever asked a question you wish you hadn't? I realised very soon that I just had. I talked myself almost hoarse as they fired question after question at me.

"Bet you're sorry you asked," grinned Dom, bringing me a flask of liquor from the rig.

"Are you?" I countered.

"No, of course not. Why? What did you expect – that I'd run like shit when I knew?"

"Language!"

"Sorry." He wasn't, of course.

"Some people would."

"Some people don't have the sense they were born with," he retorted. "You're honest. You don't pretend to be anything you're not. And even if you hadn't saved my life, I'd still like you." He grinned. "So if you were trying to put me off, you haven't."

"I wasn't. I need all the friends I can get," I shrugged. "I've enemies enough as it is."

His lips twitched. "So I've heard. Was Dante your first lover, then?"

I'd wondered when we'd get around to that. "He was."

"Was that when you were—?"

"In the mine," I concluded for him. Strange, I'd have thought Micah would have told him that, and a glance in Micah's direction confirmed that he knew what I was thinking.

"Not my secret to tell," he said softly.

"Not much of a secret," I shrugged, proceeding to give Dom a brief version, less graphic than I'd used with either my sister or Micah himself. "I don't know about you guys, but I'm hitting the sack. I want to be on the road as early as we can."

"That's his excuse," Micah nudged Dom in the ribs. "He's missing Dante."

I hesitated, but decided to ignore their teasing and leave them to their giggles. They were, after all, quite right.

What I didn't expect was to be awoken in the early hours by banging on my door and Micah's voice shouting my name. I didn't take the time to dress, simply flew out of the door in my underwear to be dragged towards the front of the rig. "Something on the screens," he said. "It looks like a storm, but..."

I understood the fear in his voice. It was unlike any storm I'd seen coming. "Get me some coffee, will yer?" I asked, half turning his way.

"I'll get it," replied Dom. "What do you think it is?"

I shook my head. "I don't know, kid, but I think I'd better get my pants on." I'd seen his eyes on my scars, but that wasn't the reason for my sudden modesty. I really was worried, because my equipment was going crazy. Returning, I found my companions peering out of the windows. "See anything interesting?" I queried, slipping my top on.

"I don't know if it's interesting or not, but it's white," replied Micah. I raised a brow and eased my way between them.

"Hm," I mused, sipping my coffee. "I wonder... " Slipping into the driving seat, I pushed a few buttons. "Buckle up, kids. We're hittin' the road. Fast." I didn't like the look of what was coming if it was what I thought it was. Given the sudden drop in temperature and the white stuff, I wanted to be as far ahead of it as I could.

"What is it?" asked Dom, excitement mingling with fear in his voice.

"I *think* it's called snow." I'd heard of it, of course, but I'd never seen it before. I didn't know how the rig would handle it, and I didn't want to find out unless I had to. I'd heard of people getting lost in blizzards, where the sky turned so white you couldn't see a hand in front of your face. I wondered if it was like the sandstorms I was used to... "Watch the readout," I asked Micah. "Let me know what it says."

"Will do." He sat down and began his litany. With the temperature dropping fast, I didn't want to hang around and drove as fast as I could until conditions began to become treacherous. "Angelus." I ventured a glance in his direction and saw that his face, along with the screen, was white.

"Hang on!" I felt the rig beginning to slide. I wasn't going to be able to outrun this, I reasoned. Time to admit defeat. "Look out for a safe spot, huh?" My arms were aching through fighting with the steering, and it was all I could do to keep it on the road. In the end, fate took it out of my hands – almost literally – as I felt myself lose control and, shortly after, consciousness. I came to, cursing vehemently. Just what I needed; another bump on my head! "You okay, boys?" I called.

"Yeah." I heard a scramble, followed shortly by the two of them appearing at my shoulder. "Let me look at your head." I winced as Micah began prodding my skull, dabbing at it with more than a little enthusiasm. "Not too bad. Not spoiled your looks, in case you're worried."

"Ha ha," I snorted and he chuckled.

We were at a slightly odd angle, but I didn't think we were in too bad a state. I tried to raise the shields, but they wouldn't budge, which had me more than a little worried. I wondered if it meant we were buried in snow. If so... No, I told myself sternly. I wouldn't panic. On reflex, I triggered the rescue beacon and tried the radio, but I'd a feeling the aerial had been snapped off. For whatever reason, no one was answering. Cooking would be risky until I knew whether it was safe, but we'd plenty of food, plenty of liquid. I just hoped we'd plenty of air! None of the sensors were telling me we'd got blocked vents above, so with a bit of luck we might be able to open the roof. If we could do that, one of us could maybe climb out and see what the situation was. I didn't fancy it, but we might not have a choice.

"You okay?" asked Micah at my elbow before I realised he was there.

"I will be when my head stops aching," I replied.

"That's not what I mean and you know it." He studied my face with a maturity I hadn't expected. "I know you sometimes... memories?"

A smile flickered. "Memories – yeah." I wasn't going to elaborate, and he didn't press.

"You figure we're clear above?"

"I hope so."

"We need to find out if we're clear, don't we?"

"We do."

He nodded. "If you hoist me up, we could find out." We didn't want to take too many risks, but we had to know.

I told him how to unfasten the roof vent, and after some hilarity we were able to ease it open enough to discover that the roof, at least, wasn't blocked. I raised him as high as I could, leaving it to Micah to haul himself out.

"Well?" I called after him when he didn't respond. I felt Dom at my side and smiled in what I hoped was a reassuring fashion. After some time we heard the sound of footsteps and Micah's head appeared in the hole.

"We're stuck all right, but the galley side's not too bad. Seems to have built up mostly at the other side, front and back for some reason. We're a little over wheel height at the galley side. Sky looks white, though. May be more on the way. If we want to eat, might be best now, just in case."

"Good idea. Come back in, Micah."

"Comin', ready or not."

I grunted as I took the weight of him, but I don't think I did myself too much damage. We swung into action together, soon having a meal ready.

"Aerial looks a bit bent, though," said Micah. "Might be repairable; I don't know."

"Will... will they come looking for us, do you think?" ventured Dom softly. "When we don't arrive."

"Sure they will," I reassured him. "The rescue beacon's active, and if we can get the aerial repaired... Don't worry. We'll be okay." I hoped.

If someone had to go out and repair the aerial, however, I guessed it was going to be me, although I didn't relish it. Getting out was interesting. The room was precarious and I admit to being afraid that I'd fall, not off the roof, but simply fall, and it was a feeling I didn't like. It was a long time since I'd felt afraid of anything, although I wasn't sure whether that was bravery or stupidity. Fear can give you an edge, sometimes. A keenness of mind to keep you alive. Perhaps it was simply that I was afraid we'd die out there and I'd never get the chance to put things right. More likely it was because if anything happened to me, Dom and Micah could die.

All the time I was on the roof, I could feel myself getting colder and colder, my hands becoming numb. I'd never known such cold before, but the icy beauty was compelling, distracting. I don't remember falling. I don't remember anything, which, I'm told, is just as well.

Chapter 40

When the boys heard the crash, I was told when I was able to understand, their first thought was, "Oh God, no!" Somehow, Dom got Micah up so he could see out.

"Where's Angel? Is he okay?" demanded Dom.

"Stand still, will yer?" Micah tried not to laugh. "Course he's not okay. Guess he tried to fly. Just... can yer..." With a grunt and a yelp of pain, Micah dragged himself onto the roof and edged himself towards where I lay. His first thought was horror: blood on the snow. His second was almost hysterical – my damned head again. Would it knock some sense into me this time?

"Mikey, is he okay?" Micah heard the fear in Dom's voice.

He felt scared himself but tried to keep his voice even as he replied, "I'm checking him." Gingerly, he turned me over. There was blood on my face and, to his horror, blood coming from my mouth. I groaned as he tried to move me, and bright blood bubbled up. Oh God, Micah thought. Oh fuck, fuck, fuck! Sobbing with frustration – and fear – Micah edged me towards the opening. He didn't want to make things worse, because he already feared I'd punctured a lung. "Dom, we've got a problem."

"Tell me somert I don't know!" he half-sobbed back. "What d'ya need?"

Micah bit back a hysterical giggle – Dom's accent was getting as bad as his. "You're the brains of the outfit – how'd we get him down?" Micah could almost hear his mind working.

"Where's Angel keep his tools?"

"What yer need?"

"A stretcher. If I can get a door off, you can strap him to it and lower him down." Sounded simple, when he put it like that. Yeah. Right!

Micah told him where to try and knelt there shivering.

"C'mon, get yer ass in gear. Grab the fuckin' thing!"

"Language!" Micah responded, but grabbed at the door when it poked out. "What do I do?"

"Strap him on it; what yer think?"

Easier said than done with fingers and mind going numb. I moaned from time to time and Micah's tears turned to ice. He was scared to hell that they'd lose me, that they'd be alone. For all his bravado, Dom wasn't strong, although his mind was.

Micah followed his commands as the rope snaked upwards, wrapping it round himself as he'd seen climbers do to take the weight as he lowered me down.

When Micah joined us, Dom was trying to cut my wet clothing off. My ribs looked angry and my breathing rattled. Then there was the blood...

From time to time they looked at each other.

"Fuck – the radio! Maybe it'll work!" Dom exclaimed suddenly. "You keep him warm. Just keep him warm."

Micah watched him scramble to his feet and snuggled up to me, pulling the cover over us. He tried to cheer himself up by imagining the fun he'd have teasing me about this, but it didn't help much. He listened to my breathing; resting his head lightly on my shoulder and telling himself it was for my benefit and not his. It sounded like I was drowning.

"I got 'em!" Dom burst out exuberantly, almost falling through the door. "Help's on its way."

"He needs help now," Micah whispered, trying not to sob. He wasn't a baby – I needed them... Micah. "Have yer told 'em?"

"Course I have! They're getting' a doc on line. Wait!" He heard the radio crackle and ran to respond. He cursed as he almost pulled the cable out – it was stretched almost to breaking point. "Say again?"

"Is he goin' blue? His lips?" the doctor asked.

"Tell him I can't see for the fuckin' blood!" Micah replied angrily. "He sounds as if he's drownin'."

Dom repeated a somewhat sanitised version.

"What kit you got – over?"

Micah met Dom's eyes with fear in his. "Basic. Tell 'em basic." Dom obeyed.

"Sounds like you're going to have to be very brave, son."

Micah closed his eyes to fight back the tears and struggled to find his voice. "What do I have to do?"

Dom repeated the question.

"Sounds like he's drowning in blood. You need to make a hole – make a drain."

"I can't!"

"You must if you want him to still be alive when we get there," the reassuring voice continued. "Don't worry. I'll talk you through it. Piece of cake."

Yeah, right.

Micah swallowed convulsively. "Tell me what to do."

"You need hot water, antiseptic, a sharp knife, a straw or a piece of narrow tube." He told Micah where to cut, how deep, took him every step of the way before he even started, but God, was his hand shaking!

"You can do it," assured Dom. "It's your chance to save him."

Micah took a deep breath and cut. It was the bit about holding the hole open that almost made him throw up – well, that or the sounds I made – but I seemed to go a better colour.

Together, the boys tried to keep me warm and waited. It seemed forever before they heard the soft hiss of the hatch opening and saw the familiar dark head appear. They were so relieved when Dante lowered his long frame down, flashing a bright smile as he said, "Well, you got your wish, huh?"

Micah blushed red and laughed. "Lot of heavy breathin', not much action."

"Ah well, can't have everything," he sympathised, his face sobering as the second man knelt down beside him.

"I'm getting too old for this shit," the man complained. "Which one o' you was the surgeon?"

"Me." Micah moved gently out of the way so he could get closer.

"You did good, kid. Okay, let's get him out of here. You'll have to get the rig out later," he added to Dante. "You ready, boys?"

They were – more than ready.

As they watched them raise me out, Micah became aware of the expression on Dante's face. "He'll be okay," he assured him.

"Of course he will. More lives than a damned cat, he has." There was a tremor in Dante's voice, though. "Thanks." He gave the boys a quick embrace before hoisting them up through the roof.

Chapter 41

heard Dante before I saw him. The sound of his playing brought me out of my drug-induced haze, but opening my eyes was too much of an effort. I could feel a dull ache low on my ribs and guessed I had a drip in one hand. My mouth felt as if something had curled up and died in it, and my tongue didn't want to work as I tried to speak.

"What's a guy to do to get a drink around here?" I croaked. A crash and a thud brought him to my side and I opened my eyes to see his smile.

"Just ask," he replied, placing the glass close to my lips. "Just a sip."

I wanted to drink it dry and it was hard to pull away. "Hi."

"Hi."

"The boys..."

"Are fine. Saved your life, you dumb prick." He told me what Micah had done lightly, including how the pair of them had kept me warm while help came, but I understood what lay behind the jocular tone. Another close call, he was saying. Laughing hurt. Suddenly, I saw tears in his eyes.

"Dante?" He turned his head away and I caught at his hand with difficulty. "It was an accident," I said softly. "No one's fault."

"If you hadn't come—"

"I'd never have seen snow," I concluded for him. "Where are the boys?"

"Playing in the snow, last I heard," he replied, offering a weak smile. "I'll take you to see the snow caves, soon as you're up. We could go skiing... no... no, that wouldn't be a good idea. Gotta heal properly this time. Six to twelve weeks at least, the doc says. A sled ride. Yeah, that should be safe. I hear they've got an ice hotel that—"

"Dante." I laughed.

"Yeah?"

"Shut up and kiss me, you fool."

He went quiet suddenly and blinked owlishly. "Oh. Sure." He was determined to be gentle, which suited me fine because while the spirit was willing, the flesh was weak.

A cough tore us apart suddenly. "Before this starts to get porno, the doc's on his way," announced Morgan cheerfully from the doorway. "What'd yer think yer was doin', yer stupid prick?"

"I didn't know it was gonna snow!"

"Still, what were yer tryin' ter do?"

"Repair the fuckin' aerial," I snapped. "I was scared the signal wouldn't work 'n' I was scared for the kids, okay?"

He raised his hands in surrender. "Okay, don't crack another rib, but it seems ter me yer owes those two kids yer life."

"He knows. Now, Mr Morgan, if you don't mind?" said the doctor from behind him. Morgan wasn't going to argue with the doc. He made a graceful retreat.

"I'll call by later, Angelus," he said with a wink.

The doctor bent to examine me and asked, "So, how're you feeling? I'm Theo Marks, by the way."

"Pleased ter meet yer, Doc."

"I know who you are, of course. Your Lieutenant here's been keeping the airwaves buzzing to Vesta. Someone called Mo says to 'get on yer feet and you'll soon be back in bed'?" he offered, obviously puzzled. Dante gave a choked laugh and I tried not to. It hurt too much.

"I replied for you," Dante inserted smoothly. "I told him to take charge until you returned and see how easy it was." That wasn't, at a guess, all he'd told him. I could see from Dante's expression that he expected me to bawl him out for promoting himself, but as it was part of the reason I was there, I couldn't, could I? I also guessed that he'd used it as an excuse to stay at my side because he knew some people might not understand.

"So, how soon can I get out of here, Doc?"

He raised his eyes. "Hospital? A few days' observation. Dante here's got a room for you. You won't be able to drive for a while and you need to rest up. I've been looking at your medical history, Angelus. You're lucky to be alive. Next time you might not be so lucky."

"I know."

"Knowing isn't enough, Angelus. Seems to me you need to do some serious healing or your friends will be digging your grave! I'll leave you to rest. Need anything for the pain?"

"No. I'll be okay."

"Sure you will." The bastard stuck a needle in me anyway. "Now you will," I heard him say as sleep took me.

I awoke several hours later to the sight of Dante curled up in the chair next to my bed. His expression was tranquil and I lay simply looking at him, enjoying the sight. He had the guilelessness of a child in sleep, I thought, but if I moved he would be instantly awake and there would be no child in his eyes. I tried not to move: I didn't want to disturb him, but it was fast becoming a necessity.

"Dante," I whispered. His eyes shot open. "I need to take a leak."

"Oh, just a sec. Let me help you."

"No. Thanks." I saw the surprise in his eyes at my rejection and rushed to explain. "If you touch me right now, I won't be responsible."

"Oh!" He thrust the bottle at me and grinned. "You sure?"

"Please," I groaned.

"Touch you?" he offered impishly.

I groaned. "Dante." He took the bottle from me and placed it safely out of harm's way.

"Tell me what you want," he asked very softly.

"Everything," I sighed. "But—"

"I know," he soothed, caressing my jaw with his fingertips. "And you have my word that as soon as you're well I'll give you no more mercy. But until then, dear heart, I promise to be gentle – even if you don't want me to." He smiled. "Do you want me to play for you?"

"I'd rather you played *with* me," I muttered rebelliously.

Dante's earthy chuckle told me he'd heard. "I just bet you would." He gave me a kiss full of promise that had my pulse racing. "Remember, you mustn't exert yourself."

I drowsed for a while and must have fallen asleep, because when I opened my eyes, Dante was gone. I wasn't alone, however. Micah and Dom were sitting in my room.

"Dante's gone to work," announced Micah before I could speak. "He'll be back later. Told us to keep you company."

I grinned. "I bet he did."

Micah's eyes twinkled merrily. "He said you wouldn't be any trouble."

"And that he'd made sure you slept for a while," concluded Dom with a big grin on his face. "We didn't ask."

I closed my eyes and choked back a laugh. Damn them – and bless them! "I hear you had your way with me," I offered by way of revenge.

Micah retaliated with, "As I told Dante, a lot of heavy breathin', not a lot of action."

"Ah well, there you go." I grimaced as my belly rumbled. "I hate to ask, but what's the food like around here? My belly thinks my throat's been cut, and this drip's a pain."

"We'll find out, if you like," smiled Dom, rising to his feet. "Shall I?"

I was hungry, I realised. "Please."

"Okay."

When he left me alone with Micah, I asked, "You okay?"

"Sure. Won't get my surgeon's licence until I've done a couple more ops, though."

"Guess yer can't expect it ter be too easy," I smiled. "How's Dom?"

"He's okay. It was his idea to use the door to get you down. Used ropes 'n' all. I lowered yer and he caught yer. Held my hand, sort of, when I cut yer open." He took a deep breath. "I was real scared, Angel. I didn't want yer to die, and I didn't want Dom to get hurt, and..." His breath caught and I opened my arms to him. I let him sob out his fear, stroking his hair.

"It's okay, Micah. Fear is something I haven't been feeling too much lately. That's why I fell, because I'd forgotten how to be afraid. I've been taking too many risks, and we could've all paid for it. I'm sorry."

"You don't have to—"

"Ssh. I don't apologise often, so let me get it out of my system, huh?" He raised his head and grinned weakly. "Has Dom spoken with his dad?"

"Yeah."

"Is he pissed off with me?"

"He's glad you're alive."

"Probably so's he can kill me himself," I grumbled.

Micah laughed. "No, he really *is* glad you're alive, because he knows that you were trying to get us to safety when you should have probably holed up. Wants you to get well properly this time, and he says that if you come back to work before you get clearance, he'll have your balls for breakfast."

I sighed. If that was all he'd said, I was lucky. Probably waiting to bawl me out face to face, I reasoned.

"Will someone get the door?" Dom called from outside the room. Micah was on his feet, laughing. Dom placed the tray on the bed next to me. "Don't know what it is," he shrugged, "but it was the best they could do at this time of night."

Anything, I thought, was better than the drip. "I'm grateful." It wasn't easy eating with two pairs of eyes watching my every move, but before I realised it, the plate was empty. I sat back, replete, with a sigh of contentment. "So, I hear you've been playing in the snow?"

Dom removed the tray. "We've been playing snowballs. Maybe when you're better you can come out with us."

"I'd like that. Might've melted by then, of course."

"Just a gentle game. We won't hit yer hard."

"You mean you'll be gentle with me?" I asked, amused.

"Bet you've heard that before," he countered.

"Said it once or twice, too," I replied, keeping my face straight.

"Fairly recently, I'll bet," offered Micah, his lips twitching as the door opened and Dante strolled in. "Hasn't he?"

"Hasn't he what?" queried Dante, frowning. Micah told him. Dante rolled his eyes before placing his instrument by the wall and his coat over the chair back. "Say goodnight, boys," he responded. I didn't see his face, although they clearly could.

"Goodnight, boys," they said. "Sleep well."

Dante turned back to me. "Been feeding you, have they?"

"Yeah."

"Might've taken it with 'em."

"I think you scared 'em off." I bit my lip. "You okay, Dante?"

"Fine."

"Bad night?"

He shrugged. "One or two creeps. Nothing I couldn't handle, but—"

"It makes yer want ter get back to our own turf?"

"I guess." He gave a weak smile. "Shall I play for you?"

"As long as it's not to send me to sleep. I've slept enough."

"You heal better when you're asleep."

"I heal better when I'm not in a hospital bed," I replied. "I just want to get out of here."

"I know. Just be patient. A couple of days and we'll have you out of here. I've got a room ready. Oh, and with luck we should have the rig out as soon as the digger can reach it. What would you like to hear?"

"Something cheerful."

"Cheerful? I'll try." He pursed his lips. It wasn't exactly cheerful, but it was a good try. Slowly, his mood eased. I just hoped we hadn't kept anyone else awake, but there was no banging on the walls, so I guessed we were okay.

Chapter 42

Getting out of hospital was a relief. I was surrounded by my friends as I shook the doctor's hand and promised to take it easy. My friends promised that if I didn't, they'd tie me down. I wasn't sure quite how they intended that remark to be taken. My first task was to speak with Mo, my second with Dan Truman. I was a long time talking to Dan. Dante sat at my shoulder, his fingers stroking my neck. It made concentrating hard, but I wasn't about to protest. I was too happy to have him at my side.

Allowing Dante to take care of me wasn't any easier this time than it had been before. I'd been independent for a long time, subject to my own rules alone. This time it was different. Even had I wished to do otherwise, I knew that this time I'd have to listen to advice. Dante wasn't a fool – he knew that I'd be chafing at the bit eventually. He'd tease me, of course, make promises of what we'd do once I was well, but it was hard not to push myself as I always had. I guess I shouldn't have been too surprised when Trinity made contact. I don't know how she knew where I was and I didn't ask, but it was strange talking to her.

"You want me to come?" she asked. "I will, if you want me to."

"I know. I'm well cared for. Wrapped in cotton wool, in fact."

"Yeah?"

"Yeah. If I put a foot outta place, the kids are down on me like a ton o' bricks. How are you? How's Nia?"

"Fine. We're both fine. Is... is Dante with you?"

"Not right now. He's working."

"Oh. Give... give him my love, will yer?"

"I will. Take care, yer hear? I'll be back in Vesta as soon as they'll let me travel."

"Behave yerself, 'kay? Do what the docs tell yer for once. Love yer."

"You, too." So why did I feel as if I were talking to a stranger? Which of us was the liar, I asked myself?

Dante took me out in the sled as he'd promised, soon as he could. Wrapped in fur, I felt pampered. Dante's obvious pleasure in showing me this 'new frontier' was evident. His enthusiasm was something I found hard to empathise with. For me, beautiful as it was, all I could remember was pain. Struggling to breathe. Drowning in my own blood.

Lying on a bed covered with fur, Dante kept me warm. "So, what do you think?" he asked. "Are you warm enough?"

"I'm fine."

"Sure?"

"Quite sure," I laughed. "Look, I'm not shaking any more." Well, not much.

He came into the bedroom, dimming the lights. "Dom and Micah are probably jealous as all hell," he remarked as he began to undress.

"They are?"

"Yeah."

"Er... why?"

He grinned and leaned over to kiss me. "Because there's less heavy breathing and more action?" he suggested.

I laughed softly, grateful that at last, when I pulled him to me, I didn't grit my teeth against the pain. "I don't know what to do about those two."

"There's nothing *to* do," he murmured, settling himself. "They're young, like we were once. They'll find their way."

"Will *we*?"

"I hope so," he replied. "You're not Superman, you know. You're flesh 'n' blood, and you break my heart every time I see you—" He broke off as I kissed him. To silence him? Perhaps. But Dante wasn't to be silenced. "I love you – body and soul. I always will, but I don't know how many times I can watch you die."

I felt my heart lurch. "Is that how you really feel?"

"Yes." The admission didn't come easy, I knew, but I believed what he said.

"I can't make promises," I offered softly, "because I won't make a promise I can't keep. All I can say is that I'll try. I'm only human, Dante."

"I know. I just didn't think *you* did." He chuckled and took my face in his hands, kissing me slowly. "I wouldn't change anything that you are. I love you, and I always will. Just remember that you love me, too, and that any hurt you do to yourself is done to me." That, I think, touched me deeper than anything had before.

It was a long time before I slept. Lying there, listening to his breathing, I did a lot of thinking. I'd loved the open road because I'd had no reason to stay in any one place: no roots. That had changed, as had my feelings for those who shared my life. Although I still loved Trinity, it was Dante to whom I turned, Dante whom I'd followed. I'd have to reckon with that. I knew that Dan wanted me to settle in Vesta and to help him with his dream, and I began to wonder if that might not have its own challenges. Less action, maybe, but there'd be new challenges. I'd been playing up to now, telling myself nothing had changed, that I could still hit the road any time and go back to my old life. The truth was that I couldn't. With luck, that world would die. We could put an end to the shortages, the slavery; it wouldn't be perfect, but we could make it better.

"Have you slept at all?" I turned at the sound of his sleepy voice.

"No," I admitted. "I've been thinking."

He propped himself up on one arm to look at me. "And?"

"I've been a selfish bastard, haven't I?"

"I wouldn't say that exactly. Just inconsiderate."

"Inconsiderate?"

"Inconsiderate," he repeated. "I came out here to give you a chance. Did you take it?"

"I tried. Perhaps not hard enough, but I tried." He waited for me to continue. "All I could think of in the dark was you. She deserves better than that." Still he didn't speak. "It's not that I don't love her – I guess part of me always will – but I don't know what she wants."

"Did you ask her?" he asked finally.

"Perhaps not in the right way. She went away, asked me not to follow her."

"But she wanted you to."

"Did she?"

"I think so."

"Why did she ask me to choose? I thought we were happy."

"Maybe she wanted more," he suggested. "That she deserved more because of your child."

My child, I thought. Whom I hadn't seen in an age, whom I hadn't given more than a passing thought to. What kind of man did that make me? "I'll call her," I promised. "Have a long talk this time."

"Face to face would be better."

"In case you've forgotten, they won't let me travel."

"That's never stopped you before," he returned. I winced. If I waited, it might be too late. Perhaps it already was. "Maybe she could come here. Some of the roads are passable now."

"You'd be okay with that?"

"Angel!" he chided. "Would I suggest it otherwise?"

I wondered. He might if it were what he thought *I* wanted. "Dante, how do you really feel about Trinity?"

Dante lay back, his head cradled on his arms as he stared up at the ceiling. It was a long time before he answered me. "That's not easy to answer. As a woman, I like her, as much as I've ever liked any woman and more than most, in fact. She's a good person. How can I not like her? She's loved you a long time – been with you longer than I have, I guess, physically."

"Have you ever felt jealous of her?" I ventured. I wasn't sure if I'd ever asked him that before. I thought I had, but I wasn't sure.

Dante went very still before exhaling deeply. "Once, I'd have said no, but that's no longer true, is it?" I waited. "Whatever she feels for you now, she loved you enough to carry your child. We both know she could've got rid of it if she'd wanted to. I know it doesn't have to take love to create a child, but there has to be love to carry it inside you for nine months and bring it into the world, doesn't there?" I heard the pain in his voice, but didn't want to move, to break the mood. "It's the one thing, however much I love you, that I can never do. *That's* why I went away. Because I wanted you to have your chance. I didn't want to hate her, you see. Or the baby."

I shouldn't have been surprised at the raw emotion in his voice, but I was. I wanted to say that it didn't matter, that it was all right, but I knew it wasn't and never would be. It hurt. It hurt so badly. And there wasn't a damned thing we could do. "Dante."

"No. Let me finish. Please. I know there are ways. I've heard of ways. People who you can pay. I know it's against the law, artificial... artificial insemination, but…"

I hardly dared look at him, stunned by what I heard in the rushing voice. "I've heard of people you can pay. You know. To carry... maybe... maybe Trinity would—" He fell silent. I believed he'd never ask her, and I wondered if I ever could.

"You know I'd do anything for you," I said softly, raising my eyes to his.

"I know. But there are some steps I won't take." He sat up suddenly. "So, what do you want to do today?"

He was through talking, I realised. As far as he was concerned, the matter was closed. "I guess I should call Trin and I have a check-up later. After that, I'm all yours."

"Then go make your call. I'll work on the 'later'."

"Fair enough."

Chapter 43

spoke a long time with Trinity, in a way I hadn't talked for a long time. I promised again that I'd go to her as soon as I could. I guess I shouldn't have been surprised when she turned up at our door.

Nia had grown a lot, I thought, and Trinity was as lovely as ever, but something had changed. For the first time I felt a distance between us. She had her own life, I realised, and I was a little sad that I wouldn't have a major part in it, but as I suspected, there was a guy in it. I promised myself to be happy for her. If he could give her something I couldn't, I was cool with that and hoped we'd always be friends.

I left her with Dante while I went for a check-up and we all had dinner together before I let her go. Dante was strangely quiet that night and I didn't intrude, simply held him in the darkness and wondered.

We went back to Vesta once the roads were clear and I began to work seriously on formalising the Wayfarers in a way I hadn't done before. Dan gave me the freedom I needed and I travelled a lot during the months that followed, setting up new outposts and doing a hell of a lot of talking. The months simply flew by.

One night I came home to find Dante sitting in darkness. At first, fear hit my belly as I thought his eyes were failing. Oh God, his eyes! He stood up and came to me, putting his hand on mine as I held it poised over the light switch. "Don't," he asked, his voice ragged. "Not yet."

"Your eyes..."

"It's not my eyes." I exhaled with relief. "I want to explain, but I can't. I want to ask you to forgive me, but I don't. I want to ask you to understand..." His voice broke and I struggled to find mine.

"Dante, what have you done?" I croaked.

"I want you to read this first," he replied, placing a letter in my hand. "I'm going into the bedroom. Don't put the light on 'til I'm gone."

I was terrified now, but I did as he asked. Lowering my eyes to the letter, I recognised Trinity's hand. My own shook as I opened it.

> *My dearest Angel,*
>
> *Forgive me for not coming to visit, but there's a reason why. When we last met, we talked like we've not talked in an age. Remember?*
>
> *What you might not know is that when you were gone, I did the same with Dante. He's a good man, Angel, and he loves you in a way I never can. I don't just mean physically, you stupid prick!*

I had to smile.

> *You were right – I have found someone. He's a good man, too. He gives me what I need. He understands me and I think we'll be happy. Be glad for me.*

I was.

> *I have a favour to ask of you. Don't be angry and try to understand. You never really needed me, not in the way you need what Dante can give you. If you hurt him, I'll have your balls, okay?*

Okay, I replied in my head, fondly.

> *Dante asked something of me: a favour. It did not take me long to agree. What you do now is up to you, but remember this: he did it for love of YOU. I hope you love him as he deserves, Michelangelo Raffaello Sabatini, because he's going to need all his strength and yours. I wish you luck, both of you. Remember, part of my heart will always be yours, but ALL of his is.*
>
> *Don't be a stranger – I've a stake in this, too. Go to him, Angel. Take him in your arms and lie through your teeth if you have to when you tell him you understand. If you break his heart, I'll kill you.*
>
> *Your friend,*
> *Trin.*

I lowered the letter and raised my eyes to the bedroom door. I guess part of me knew what I'd find inside, but opening the door was hard because my hand was shaking so much. A braver man might have turned and walked away, or a coward. I wasn't sure which. But I reached out to open the door and face what lay beyond.

Dante was sitting on the edge of the bed, a small, wrapped bundle cradled in his arms. Almost defensively, he drew it closer as I settled myself on the bed next to him and reached out to draw back the material. I wanted to say something, but I couldn't find my voice. I looked from the shock of dark hair into Dante's eyes and wondered which of us was going to break first. We both had tears running down our faces, and I guessed we both felt more than a little stupid. I saw the joy in his eyes as I began to smile. His own response was somewhat shaky, a tentative smile as he freed the struggling limbs.

"Does he have a name?" I asked, my throat dry.

"Not yet," admitted Dante, stroking the downy head. "Do you want to hold him?"

This was some sort of test, I guessed. My acceptance, or not, of Dante and Trinity's son – and, by implication, mine. "Sure." I took the small, wriggling form into my arms without the slightest qualm. "He's beautiful. Got all his parts, I suppose?"

Dante's lips twitched. "So I'm told. And a healthy pair of lungs. Came with a supply of clothes, diapers and formula, too." The smile faltered. "I want to explain."

"You don't need to."

"I think I do." He raised his eyes and I nodded acceptance. "When I met with Trinity, I didn't intend to ask. I really didn't. It just came out. I wanted her advice, who to approach, you know? She told me not to be stupid, that she wasn't about to entrust such a gift to anyone else. People would assume that given our arrangement, it'd been natural, that either I wasn't... that I'd..." I understood. "After all, the hair's a dead giveaway, right? People will talk, but not as much as if they knew the truth. I wanted... I wanted to try but I couldn't." I wanted to soothe his tears, to wipe them away, but I felt that the catharsis was necessary for all our sakes. "I've never tried a woman, but I couldn't. Not even—"

"Ssh. You don't have to."

"I do!" he insisted fiercely. "Because you're gonna have to live with it, too."

Could I live with the lie? Of course I could. We'd have enough problems raising a child without its mother without having the stigma of artificial insemination. Sure I could live with it if he could, if Trinity could. "What did the new guy in her life say about this?"

He shrugged. "Far as I know, all he knows is that she attempted a reconciliation which didn't work out, and that the baby was the result. What he thinks about her giving him up I don't know. Are you angry?"

"I'm not even surprised, not really," I confessed. "But we'll have to get our story right because this ain't gonna remain secret for long."

"Then I guess we'd better have a name," he said. "Any ideas?"

"Let's sleep on it, huh?" I suggested gently, grimacing. "If this little guy lets us. I think he needs changing. You prepare the formula, I'll do the rest."

"Okay."

As he went to comply, I did my bit. He had a healthy pair of lungs all right, and quite a grip. My hair proved too much of a temptation, I guess. I wasn't sure about what we'd say of Trinity's 'abandoning' him. I didn't like the slur on her reputation, but I didn't know what else we could say. Folks would think that with a new man she didn't want a new baby around whether we wanted them to or not. If they wondered why she hadn't 'abandoned' Nia, too, well let them. We'd face that if we had to. I took the bottle from Dante and set about feeding, catching his smile. "You do it," I said impulsively, thrusting both at him. "I need to take a leak." He accepted my excuse, and I was choked to see the softness on his face as I watched him from the bathroom door. It was worth it just for that.

Lying in bed, I wondered just what I was going to tell Dan in the morning. How much of the truth. How much I wouldn't need to. "What about Lucas?" I asked in the darkness. I felt his surprise. "Think I don't know your name after all this time?" I asked him, amused. "What kind of person do you think I am, not to know the name of the father of my son?"